JESSICA SIMS

BETWEEN A VAMP AND A HARD PLACE

Pocket Books

New York   London   Toronto   Sydney   New Delhi

Pocket Books
An Imprint of Simon & Schuster, Inc.
1230 Avenue of the Americas
New York, NY 10020

This book is a work of fiction. Any references to historical events, real people, or real places are used fictitiously. Other names, characters, places, and events are products of the author's imagination, and any resemblance to actual events or places or persons, living or dead, is entirely coincidental.

First Pocket Books paperback edition January 2016

POCKET and colophon are registered trademarks of Simon & Schuster, Inc.

For information about special discounts for bulk purchases, please contact Simon & Schuster Special Sales at 1-866-506-1949 or business@simonandschuster.com.

The Simon & Schuster Speakers Bureau can bring authors to your live event. For more information or to book an event, contact the Simon & Schuster Speakers Bureau at 1-866-248-3049 or visit our website at www.simonspeakers.com.

Interior design by Leydiana Rodríguez

Manufactured in the United States of America

10 9 8 7 6 5 4 3 2 1

ISBN 978-1-4767-5399-7
ISBN 978-1-4767-5402-4 (ebook)

*For Mick and Jen, who always send encouragement,
even when I'm being a whiny beast.*

One

It was a lovely Saturday afternoon . . . and a very un-successful one for Lincoln, Nebraska, estate hunt-ers. I'd hit up four estate sales and come away with a few ginger jars (which always sold at the antique booth), a butter dish shaped like a chicken, an ugly cookie jar that would probably bring in a few hundred online, and a bruise on my arm from being pushed into a wall. People tended to get mean at estate sales.

It was a depressing haul, though, so I immediately went to the grocery store and bought three bags of gummy bears. I ate one on the way home.

The apartment I shared with my BFF Gemma was a mess—packing peanuts were strewn across the carpet, empty boxes were everywhere, the sofa was covered with items in various stages of being shipped, and the photography stand in the corner had a vase sitting on the pedestal. It looked as if a hurricane had rolled through, which didn't help my mood any. I set down the box of useless crap I'd acquired today and headed into the working office of Lindsey's Vintage

Treasures, where I found Gemma typing with two fingers on her keyboard. She looked up at me as I entered, her smile bright. "Hey! How'd it go?"

I grunted at her and sat in my chair, then opened bag number two of gummy bears and began to eat.

"That bad?" Gemma gave me a worried look. "I thought you said there was some Chinese porcelain out there today. I know you love that stuff."

"Fake," I told her between handfuls of gummy bears. "All fake. Made in Taiwan."

"Motherfuckers," Gemma said with a small shake of her head. Her sweet demeanor always seemed at odds with the fact that she could swear a sailor down. "Anything else?"

"A junky cookie jar." I threw another gummy bear into my mouth. "Today was a bust."

"That is some shit-ass luck," Gemma agreed in a sympathetic voice. "We could always sell that ugly-ass bracelet you always wear."

"Har de har har," I said. "You know what that's used for." I touched my ID bracelet, running my fingers over the life-saving lettering. LINDSEY HUGHES. BLOOD TYPE HH. NO BLOOD TRANSFUSIONS. Underneath that was my emergency contact information—Gemma's phone number. It had saved my bacon more than once, because my type of blood was so rare that only sixty people in the world had it. Something about how I didn't make the proper antigens or something. At any rate, a blood transfusion from a normal blood donor would kill me, so I had to wear the bracelet at all times. Sure, it was ugly, but it was useful. I stuck my tongue out at Gemma. "No one would want the damn thing anyhow."

"Not unless they're into hospital chic." She turned in her chair and clapped her hands. "But guess what?"

I gave her a wary look. When Gemma got excited, I got worried. "What?"

"You know Franco? The European guy who always says he can get me a deal on whatever I'm looking for?"

Oh no. "Isn't he the one that wears his shirt unbuttoned down to his navel and a lot of gold chains?"

"That's him," she agreed.

"I thought he was in Europe." Franco only showed up in the States for big-time auctions. That, and occasionally sleeping with Gemma, who had terrible taste in men.

"He is!" Her eyes lit up. "I told him that we've been having a dry run, and he offered to help us out."

I groaned, shoving another handful of gummy bears in my mouth. *Sugar rush, don't fail me now.* "No, Gem. No. Seriously. The last thing we need is Franco's help. There are a bunch of estate sales in the city next weekend, and I'm sure we can rebuild our inventory, and—"

"But that's just it," Gemma said, biting on a nail unhappily. "Franco says that all the good Chinese porcelain is overseas."

"You mean like in China?" I said sarcastically.

"He's trying to be helpful," Gemma said in a small voice.

"I'm sorry," I told her. "My blood sugar's just low and I'm cranky." Ugh. And I hated Franco, who regarded Gemma as a booty call.

"Anyhow, he said he got a great deal on a place that needs to be cleaned out. He paid a lot for it, but he's going on vacation to Grenada, so he offered to let us have it for half price."

I paused, bear midway to my mouth. "Um, what?"

"You know. An estate?"

I choked. "An entire estate? Really?" Most of those went to coordinated businesses that handled everything from top to bottom. Gemma and I just picked through what went up for sale.

"Yes! Well, no, actually." Gemma's pink mouth turned down in a grimace. "It's an apartment that some rich couple owned and vacationed in. They died and left no one in the will, so everything's being sold off. Apparently, the old owners hadn't been there in over twenty years."

I recoiled. "A vacation home?" Visions of seashell decor floated through my head.

"Yeah! Some antique hunters, too. Franco said he was giving us a sweet deal. Only half price, and we have an entire month to clean the place out. Just think of all the good stuff they've got."

I shook my head. "I don't like it. We should probably pass."

She bit her lip. "So, you're going to think I'm a real shit stain, but I already sorta paid him."

I groaned into my bag of gummy bears.

My best friend gave me an apologetic look. "He said we had to jump on it right away and we wouldn't regret it. So I had to wire him the funds."

I nibbled the head off one bear, thinking maybe this wouldn't be so terrible. A vacation home was bound to be sparsely furnished, but what was there might have been selected by an interior decorator, so it wouldn't be so bad. Hopefully we could find something sellable. "That fast, huh?"

"Yeah, the month starts today, so we have a little over four weeks to clean the place out. You want to see the contracts?"

I stared at her. "There were contracts?"

"Of course there were." She looked offended. "It wasn't like I'd hand over ten grand without some sort of contract. I fucking docu-signed the hell out of those bad boys."

"Ten grand?" I shrieked.

She winced. "Too much?"

"Ten freaking grand?" I just stared at her, aghast. That was our entire nest egg. It was the money that was supposed to get us through a dry month or two. It was rent money and shop money and car money and grocery money. And the thought of it all being gone in a flash made me want to tear my hair out. "All ten grand?"

Gemma's lower lip wobbled. "Franco says it's a sweet deal, I promise. He said I'll want to fuck him like a horny stripper once I see the stuff in the house. He wouldn't say that unless it was straight-up legit."

I just stared at her in horror. "Ten grand is everything we have in the business account."

"I know, but we'll have a place to stay for the entire month! The apartment, remember? I'm told it's right on the water."

"So it *is* a beach house?" Maybe a month on the beach would cure me of the recent slump I'd been in. Lately I'd just wanted to do nothing but sleep late and eat more gummy bears. I was so tired of looking for a big break and never finding it. Instead of selling the beautiful Chinese porcelain I adored, we had to resort to selling freaking cookie jars.

Ten grand. Oh my God. That was so many darn cookie jars. I couldn't even process. Gemma and I had been saving our pennies for such a long time. That ten grand was going to change our circumstances. Right now we had to scrape by on small acquisitions and reselling things for a fraction above what we'd paid for them. The truth of the matter was that to make money in antiques, you needed money. And so we'd been saving for a long time, hoping to get to the next level. I had my eye on a cute little storefront on a busy downtown street that would be the perfect place to start a store instead of just renting a booth.

But with all of our savings gone . . . The reality of it hit me, and I felt sick . . . or maybe it was all the sugar. "I can't believe you gave him all our money."

"He says we'll make it back." Her voice was small and unhappy.

"Oh God. I hope so." The thought of losing it all made me want to vomit.

Her lower lip quivered even more. "You have to trust me, Lindsey!"

"I do!"

"No, you say you do, but you don't. You like being in control. I'm just the box-taping lackey. We're supposed to be partners, but all I ever do is ship stuff."

I made a sound of protest, but the truth of the matter was that I was a control freak. I did like handling everything. And I was a crappy friend, because in the "Lindsey and Gemma Antiques" business, all Gemma did was ship things. I didn't let her do much else. "But you're so good at packing things up."

"I can be good at finding antiques too, but you won't let me!" Gemma gave me a sad look. She dashed a hand across her eyes, and I felt guilty. Gemma was the only person in the world I had. We'd grown up at the same state foster home together. She was my family and I was hers. "We can always just forfeit the money and I'll just pack boxes for the rest of my life."

"I'm sorry, Gem. I just get nervous thinking about all that money."

"Which is why you have to trust me." She clasped her hands under her chin and gazed at me. "Please, Linds."

I sighed heavily, because I sensed I was losing this battle. Heck, I'd already lost it. Ten grand down the drain. "All right. I guess we can go check it out."

"Fucking awesome!" Gemma said, and clapped her hands like a little girl. "This is going to be badass. I just know it."

"So where's this beach house at?"

Gemma widened her eyes innocently. "I didn't say it was a beach house. I said it was on the water."

I narrowed my eyes at her. "Where on the water?"

"Venice."

I sputtered.

Two

I pulled the renter's envelope open and found an old, antique key, then held it up to Gemma.

She rubbed her hands together. "Let's do this thing."

"I'm glad one of us is excited," I teased, though I was getting more excited by the minute. Venice was like something out of a fairy tale, and if dreams could come true, why not here? In a six-hundred-year-old apartment building? We stood on the doorstep of our unseen apartment, which could either be filled with untold treasures . . . or copious amounts of junk. I was hoping for the former.

The stairs were narrow and steep, the small hall barely big enough to fit our shoulders. "Jeez, Venetians are some tiny fuckers," Gemma commented, shifting on her feet in the entryway. "How do they get couches upstairs?"

"No clue," I told her, the heavy key clutched in my hand. The door was small, wooden, and unassuming. This was it. This was what ten grand had bought us. "Here we go."

Next to me, Gemma bounced. "I'm so excited!"

And I was so scared. Visions of living out of a cardboard box under a bridge floated through my mind. Uneasy, I put the key in the lock and turned it, then pushed the door open.

A cloud of dust puffed. I coughed, waving my hands in the air. "What the heck?"

"Maybe no one's been up here in a while," Gemma said, then sneezed. "Remember that one apartment in France that no one lived in for sixty years?"

If that was the case, this might not be too bad. I waved my hand in the air, waiting for the dust to clear. The entryway was dark, so I fumbled on the wall for a light switch before stepping inside.

The lights came on with a flicker, and both Gemma and I gasped.

The room was narrow, the ceiling high. And in the dim light, we could see that, floor to ceiling, it was full of boxes. Completely, horrifically full. I could barely step into the place for fear of a teetering tower of boxes crashing down. Piles of newspapers lay on a nearby table, and upholstered chairs were covered with dust and stacks of old frames.

"Oh my God," I coughed.

"Wow," Gemma said. "It's like a hoarder's paradise in here."

"It is," I said, dismayed. "There's so much stuff.

How are we ever going to get through it all?" Everywhere I looked, there were boxes, more boxes, and dust. *Everywhere.*

"Well, we have a month," Gemma said brightly. "Just think of all the money we'll make!" In the packed kitchen, Gemma tried the faucets. While they groaned a protest, they seemed to be in working order. "This place probably hasn't been used in decades. Who the hell owns an apartment in Venice and never uses it?"

"Rich people," I told her.

"Well, if they're rich, then they're bound to have some good shit somewhere. We just have to find it."

She had a point. "The bedrooms might be promising," I told her. We went upstairs and checked them. The closets were full of vintage clothing and crammed with unworn shoes, and one dresser was brimming with costume jewelry. At least I was pretty sure it was costume jewelry, though I'd have to get it inspected just to be sure. I glanced around and then looked at Gemma, whose eyes were big and hopeful as she gazed at me. She desperately, desperately wanted this to be a good thing for us.

I didn't have the heart to burst her bubble, so I smiled and said, "This could work."

Gemma squeezed my arm and gave a happy little squeal. "This is so cool, isn't it? We're in Venice for a month! Digging through someone's old shit! This is the life!"

"It is," I agreed, though with far less enthusiasm. "I guess we should air out the bedding if we're going to stay here for a bit." We couldn't afford a hotel. "We can clean up a bit, clear off a bed, and then maybe head down for dinner before getting to work?"

"Now you're talking," Gemma told me. Then she gasped. "Wait. You don't think this place is haunted, do you? Is that why it's been deserted?"

I snorted. "Please. That stuff is nothing but fairy tales. The only things alive in this place are dust mites."

TWO DAYS LATER

I ran a strip of tape over a box, sealing it, then stood and rubbed the small of my back. I ached everywhere. "Where are we putting the stuff to ship?" I called out to Gemma.

"In the kitchen," she bellowed from upstairs.

I eyed the stack of boxes blocking me and my latest package from getting to the kitchen. "Can't we put them by the door?"

"No," she yelled again. "I have a system. Kitchen!"

Damn it. I shoved a stack of boxes out of the way and hauled my package into the kitchen, staggering as I did so. This was so not my line of work. I was the hunter, the eye for treasure. I went out and scoped out sales and found bargains. Gemma was the one who organized and boxed things. All we'd done for the last two days was pick through old junk, get dirty, and haul more crap off to the local dump.

It was miserable, hard work, and I hated it.

Worse than that, we'd barely scratched the surface of things. We'd cleared enough to open the front door, but we still couldn't access the dining room. The kitchen was an unholy mess, and the tiny walkway we'd made through the living area seemed to fill up with more stuff as quickly as we cleaned it out.

For every box of decent stuff, there were two boxes of junk. Some of it was interesting but didn't warrant being shipped back to the States. I'd contacted the owner of a local curio shop, who would come by in the next day or two to check things out, but I wasn't sure they'd find enough to make a dent in the looming mess.

Three weeks was not going to be enough time to clean this place out. We'd need months. Maybe even a year.

I grew more depressed as I opened another box and found it full of moth-eaten sweaters. More garbage. More stuff we couldn't sell. Gemma and I had stayed up late last night, trying to approximate how much we thought we could make based off what we'd found so far.

The news wasn't good. Sure, there was money to be made, considering that everything in the Venetian apartment was at least thirty years old. But the cost of shipping it home so we could sell it? Expensive. Gemma was so excited about things, though, that I kept my unhappy thoughts to myself and just worked harder.

There had to be something of value in this place. *Had to be.* We just needed to find it.

The doorway to the blocked-off dining room taunted me. I eyed it with new determination and approached. The wood of the door was heavy, and I pushed at it again. Boxes on the other side prevented me from opening it fully, so I gave it another brutal shove, frustrated.

It budged an inch.

Aha. Encouraged, I eyed the crack and wedged my knee in there, then pushed my entire body weight against the door again.

It moved another inch. I kept at it until the door was open enough to wriggle and squirm my way through. By the time I got to the other side, I'd scraped my belly on the door handle and my T-shirt had a tear in it, but I was through. I straightened up, dusted my hands off, and looked around.

More boxes.

With a sigh, I picked my way forward. There was a lovely dining room table and a set of six chairs, all of it thick, heavy wood. That would not be coming back to the States with us. I imagined the shipping costs would be more than the entire fee Gemma had paid for us to come raid this place. I ran a finger over the table's surface and watched a line appear in the thick dust. This was so discouraging. I looked around the room. At the far end was a heavy wooden buffet, with a small, square, ugly painting of a pastoral scene hanging over it. Curious, I peered at the painting. Real oils. Huh. I couldn't make out the name, so I leaned in closer.

The painting fell off the wall and dropped behind the buffet.

"Drat," I muttered, then eyed the buffet. If I'd been able to move that heavy door, surely I could push this aside, right? With a determined shove, I gave it everything I had.

Didn't budge.

I frowned, opening the drawers of the buffet. They were made of a light wood, which was odd, considering how heavy the damn thing was. I opened each drawer; they were filled with tablecloths and a few items for setting the table. Nothing heavy. So why couldn't I push the damn thing aside to get that painting?

Frustrated, I gave the buffet another shove. It didn't move at all. I bent down to the ground and peered at the carved feet.

It was nailed to the floor.

What the heck? I frowned at the dusty marble floor. How exactly did one nail wood to a marble floor? I felt around under the buffet, then snatched my hand back. What if there were mice? I climbed on the buffet again and lay flat along the top of it, my fingers moving against the wall behind it. Maybe if I could snag the edge of the painting's frame, I could pull it back up.

So I reached. And squirmed. And just when I was about to give up, my fingers touched something hard jutting out from behind the buffet. Aha! My painting! I gave a tug with my fingertip.

The entire wall shuddered and moved, spinning around and nearly flinging me off the buffet.

I screamed.

"Lindsey?" Gemma cried out from somewhere upstairs. "Are you all right?"

I had no idea. I stared in shock at my surroundings. Like something out of a Scooby-Doo episode, I'd tripped a secret switch and the entire wall had flipped around, carrying me with it. Now my legs dangled in the dining room while the rest of me peered over the edge of the buffet into darkness.

An echoing darkness.

With a shiver, I sat up, scurried off the furniture, and stumbled backward. Holy cow. A secret door. A secret room! It was all shrouded in darkness, so I couldn't see what was in there. I moved closer, and the room smelled old and dusty, and a bit damp.

"What the fuck, Lindsey! Are you okay?" Gemma pushed her way into the box-filled dining room. Then she stopped in her tracks and stared. "Oh my God, what the hell is that?"

"I think it's a secret room," I told her, panting. My

heart was racing a mile a minute. "Did Franco mention it to you?"

"No!" She moved to my side, her fingers digging into my arm. "Do you think it's haunted?"

I fought the urge to roll my eyes. Gemma thought that because the place was six hundred years old, it was crawling with ghosts. I hadn't believed her, but then again, I hadn't anticipated finding a secret room, either. "Do you have a flashlight? My phone's just about dead."

"What? Why?" She looked shocked. "You're not going in there, are you?"

"I might as well," I told her, warming up to the idea. "I mean, if you were old rich crazy people, where would you hide all your good stuff?"

"In a secret room," she said, her eyes wide. "Fuck-a-doodle, do you think there's treasure? Real treasure?"

"I don't know, but I'm thinking that's the most likely place to hide something," I told her.

"What about ghosts?"

"I can always sell a painting as haunted," I told her dryly. "I bet that'd make it worth more."

Twenty minutes later, we found a pair of flashlights, ran to the corner store for batteries, then braced ourselves to go exploring. Gemma wasn't keen on the idea, but she said that if I was going down there, she was, too.

I shone my flashlight into the dark room, expecting it to be closet sized. To my surprise, it was a tiny room with a turn that led around a corner, and I could see nothing interesting except a few cobwebs. Water dripped from an exposed pipe. That was about it.

"We should see where this goes," I told Gemma.

"You first."

I took the lead, sliding past the buffet into the crawl space. As I turned the corner, I peered around cautiously . . . and gasped.

"Ohmigod, what?" Gemma shrieked behind me. "What do you see?"

"Stairs," I told her. "This goes down." I moved forward and ran a finger over the banister. Instead of dust, here it was all covered with a fine layer of damp. A small, twisting spiral staircase of wrought-iron descended into more darkness.

"Oh fuck," Gemma breathed. "This is some serious Phantom of the Opera shit."

"It's okay," I told her. I gave the stairs a shake, and they didn't budge. "Seems sturdy enough."

"Let's go back."

"Are you kidding? We've barely started exploring," I told her. "We're going down to see what's in there. We paid ten grand for the privilege, remember?"

"I'm starting to regret the purchase."

Yeah, well, that made two of us. Clutching my flashlight, I moved onto the stairs and began to de-

scend. The stairs creaked as Gemma approached behind me, and we shone our beams around us, looking
as best we could. The passage seemed to be heading
straight down, much like a well, and the cool damp
only added to that sensation. The walls were made
of interlocked stone, mortared tightly together. It all
looked so old. I wondered how long it had been here.

Then I wondered what would be waiting at the
bottom.

After what felt like hundreds of steps, my feet
alighted on damp stone flooring. My flashlight beam
showed me I'd landed in a room.

No . . . a treasure trove.

Because what I saw took my breath away. This
wasn't the hoarder's paradise from before. This was
something entirely different. It reminded me of museum storage that I'd seen in a movie once. Wooden
crates spilled their contents onto the cool stone flooring, and everywhere I looked, there were beautiful
things. A beaten copper bowl rested atop a chess-
board. Off to one side, there was a variety of jars
settled in old, musty straw. It was drier here, which
was probably a blessing, or this stuff would have been
covered in mold.

"Jackpot," I announced gleefully to Gemma and
moved forward.

The crates were stacked along one side of the
wall, the contents of a few opened up and picked
through, as if someone had lovingly reviewed old,

familiar friends. I saw a lid slightly askew and moved it, shining my flashlight to see what was inside.

A gleam of white porcelain caught my eye, and my heart hammered. That looked like Chinese porcelain. My favorite. Excited, I pulled the lid off even as Gemma moved past me, exploring.

"I think there's a hanging lantern on the wall," she said, shining her beam. "Too bad they're not wired for electricity down here, but I bet we could find some matches and light it to see a little better."

"Mmmhmm," I said absently, setting my flashlight down and gently setting the lid on the floor. Three perfectly formed jars were nestled amidst what looked like old, musty fabric. I pulled one out gently, admiring it. A ginger jar, I realized happily. The shape was perfect, and the porcelain lid was still attached and looked to be in perfect condition. The only thing that baffled me was the lack of paint on the jar. Most ginger jars were brightly colored. Unless . . .

"Hey, Gemma?" My voice sounded a little shaky. "Can you come here for a sec and shine your flashlight for me?"

"Sure thing," she said, and appeared at my side, her flashlight beam hitting me in the eyes. "Ooo, is that some Chinese shit?"

"A ginger jar," I told her breathlessly. "Can you keep your flashlight shining on it while I examine it?"

She held it aloft, and I gently pulled the lid off and examined it. Most ginger jars didn't have their original tops, or the delicate wood circles were split in half, rendering them worthless. This lid was perfect, the jar with nary a chip. I swallowed hard as a paper rustled inside, and I set the lid down and pulled the paper out, examining it. "This is a receipt of purchase," I told her, shocked. "From 1865."

"Oh-em-gee," she cried. "Provenance, baby!" The flashlight beam wiggled as Gemma did a little dance. We both knew what that meant. Antiques were worth money, of course, but if you could prove how old your stuff was? The value went through the roof. The item I held in my hands was museum quality.

"Keep shining the light," I told her and held the jar up to the beam. The light shone in through the mouth of the jar, and as it did, the plain white turned into the pattern of a dragon.

Gemma gasped.

I might have, too. "Anhua," I breathed.

"What's that?"

"Anhua's a rare form of Chinese pottery," I told her reverently, setting the jar back down and carefully putting the receipt back inside. "It means 'hidden design.' It became popular when Emperor Jiajing decided he didn't like the ornate designs of most porcelain, so it was made a pure, plain white to appease his eyes, and the designs were hidden into the pottery. It's a very difficult art form. I . . . I've always looked for some but never seen any at auction. I don't think I've ever seen anhua in this perfect a state. Not even in a museum." I gingerly turned the jar over and gazed at the markings on the bottom. "Qing period. This has to be from the late eighteenth century."

"Money-wise, what are we looking at?" Gemma asked, excitement in her voice.

I stared at the gorgeous, rare jar. A small, selfish part of me wanted to keep it. To be able to admire its beauty on a daily basis. I felt covetous just looking at it.

I sighed. I had to be smart and sell it. "At least thirty or forty grand, if we can get the right buyers at the auction. Maybe more if we can get investors involved."

"Thirty or forty . . . grand?"

"Maybe more," I agreed, feeling faint at the thought. This was one item. One. I set it gently back into its nest in the crate. Then I looked at Gemma. "Do you think they all have the receipts?"

"They might," she said, and then gave another giddy squeal. "Oh my fucking God. We're going to be rich, aren't we?"

"We just might," I agreed. I grabbed her hand, and we did a happy dance together, amidst the crates in the secret room.

Once the initial excitement was over, Gemma raced back up the stairs to get matches for the lanterns while I pried open the next crate and examined its contents. It was a treasure trove of pottery from time periods I'd only read about. There was a Jiajing drinking vessel in the shape of a chicken that was perfectly intact. There were Ming vases. So many Mings in beautiful shapes. There were meipings and moon-flasks and garlic-neck vases. There were Kraak plates and ginger jars of every size imaginable. There were even art pieces from different geographical regions—Roman busts and a few Greek amphoras.

"It's like these bitches robbed a museum," Gemma breathed next to me. "This is fucking incredible."

"It is," I agreed, scarcely able to believe it myself. "It's almost too good to be true."

"This is our big break!" Gemma did another happy little dance.

"Which means we need to work extra hard down here and carefully pack everything," I said. "Everything. We don't want to get back and have everything broken. We need to make it tip-top shape."

"I'm on it," she said with a jaunty salute. Then she looked around. "Where should we start?"

We grabbed the lantern and looked around the room. It was hard to make out the contents, but in the back, I spied a massive crate. "Wow. What could that be?"

"I don't know," Gemma said, moving to my side. "It's enormous. There's no pottery that big, right?"

"Uh, no." I eyed it, curious myself. We'd found a jackpot of pottery and artifacts, but the crate at the back of the room was bigger than anything else. It was easily three feet tall and six feet long. A few other crates were stacked atop it. I picked one up and moved it, and Gemma held the lantern over me as I cleared off the rest.

"Let's guess," Gemma giggled as I continued to clear it off. "I'm thinking it's . . . a table. A really big ugly table."

"Let's hope not," I told her with a grin. "The cost of shipping something like that back would be ridiculous."

"Who cares?" she said, swinging the lantern around. "We've got a room full of superexpensive jars. I think we can afford a freaking table if we want it. I don't care if it's made of lead!"

I laughed, feeling light and carefree. She was right; we had a fortune here. For the first time in days, I felt happy. Excited about the future. Thrilled about our discovery. And it was all because Gemma had taken a risk. I set the crate down and hugged my friend. "You are the best, you know that?"

"I know," she said, her voice smug but happy. "Now open up that damn table already!"

With a crowbar we'd found upstairs, I pried the heavy lid off as Gemma held up the lantern. Then I gave the lid a mighty heave to the side and we leaned over to see what we'd uncovered.

It was thick, and oblong, and looked to be made of dark stone. For a moment, I didn't realize it wasn't a table. Then, I realized it was a coffin.

Gemma realized it at the same time I did. She gave a tiny scream. I screamed, too, then we both raced up the stairs, frightened out of our minds.

A few hours later, we sat at a well-lit restaurant table, unwilling to go back to the apartment.

"I told you this place was haunted," Gemma wept over her baked ziti and wine. "Why is it when we have a big break, there has to be a coffin downstairs?"

"I don't know," I mused, poking at my linguine. I didn't have much of an appetite . . . except for maybe more gummy bears. I'd packed a few bags in my suitcase, and I'd be breaking them out after dinner. Gemma liked wine when she was bummed. I liked chewy candy.

"Do you think it's safe to stay there tonight, or should we get a hotel?"

My brows drew together. "Of course we'll stay there. Why wouldn't we?"

She gritted her teeth and leaned in so no one could overhear our conversation at the café. "Uh, because there's a dead dude in the cellar?"

"We don't know that anyone's in there," I pointed out. I figured we had a fifty-fifty chance of dead dudes. "And even if there is, he's long dead."

"But . . ." She shivered. "I don't like it. I don't want to go back."

I didn't want to, either. But then I thought of all the beautiful pottery in the secret room. I couldn't just shut the secret door and pretend like we'd never found the stuff. It'd haunt me for the rest of my life if I did.

Clearly Gemma had no such problem. "We should book tickets home tonight. Call the whole thing a wash. I'll phone Franco and tell him that we changed our minds and he doesn't have to know what we found. It'll be our secret."

I gaped at her. "We don't have a choice, Gemma. Dead guy or no dead guy, there's a fortune down there for the taking. It'll get us back on our feet and set us up for a long, long time. We're not leaving it behind."

"It's not so bad being broke."

I just stared at her.

"Well, I'm not going back there," she said stubbornly, then took another big swig of her wine.

Three glasses of wine later, however, I managed to get Gemma back to the apartment. She wept and clung to me drunkenly, saying that the ghosts were going to eat her face. But then again, Gemma was a bad drunk. I put her to bed in the guest room, leaving the lights on, because I knew she'd get scared if she woke up and didn't see me there with her.

Instead of joining her, I grabbed the matches and my flashlight, and left Gemma a note. *Gone downstairs. If I'm not back by morning, there was a dead guy in there after all. Just kidding. Back soon! XO*

Then I took a deep breath and tried to calm my racing heart. I was terrified—Gemma wasn't the only one freaked out by the coffin—but I also had to be practical. Logic told me I was just being silly, the same way it was silly to say a little prayer every time you passed a graveyard.

Even if there was a dead guy in there, he couldn't do anything to me. But all those priceless treasures? They could change our lives. Both Gemma and I had no money, and no family. We had no one to depend on but ourselves. And if those items in that room were legit, it was worth going into a spooky secret room with a dead body.

Or so I told myself.

I could bring them out one at a time, I mused. Maybe bring up one crate at a time so we didn't have to pack things downstairs with the body. Then we could quietly re-close the secret door and never say a peep. Or we could report it to the Venetian authorities. It wasn't as if they could frame us for murder if the dead guy was two hundred (or more) years old, right?

So I put the crowbar, some packing materials, a flashlight, and some extra batteries into a shoulder bag. I added my phone so I could take pictures of any of the items if needed.

Then, taking a deep breath, I shouldered the bag and headed for the secret room.

Three

Upon return, the secret room wasn't so frightening. Once I got past the wet stairs and the sensation of descending into a well, the small room at the bottom was mostly clean and neat if you didn't mind the stacks of crates brimming with priceless things. I certainly didn't.

Soon, though, my suspicions got the better of me, and I immediately checked to see if the pried-off wooden lid had moved from where I'd left it. Nope.

I breathed a sigh of relief and felt a little ridiculous. Of course it hadn't moved. I was just being silly and paranoid from Gemma's freak-out. Gemma was scared of mice, heights, communicable diseases, elevators, and wool blends. Of course she was scared of a coffin. And of course I was freaking out along with her. It *was* a coffin, after all. It wasn't something one would expect to find in a secret room.

Feeling a little better about things, I started to pull the lid back over the coffin, then paused. I stared down at the lid thoughtfully, then lit the lantern and set it atop a nearby crate.

Since I was here, I might as well see what was in the damn thing, right? It was probably nothing, and then Gemma and I would have a good laugh over the fact that we'd freaked out so badly. Then we'd get back to work cataloging the treasures down here, including the anhua jar I was now mentally referring to as My Precious. *We need a two-step plan*, I imagined Gemma saying. *Step one, get shit done. Step two, make all the money.*

But first things first.

I peered at the coffin lid. It was perfectly smooth, made of a solid sort of wood that had a warm cherry color to it and had been polished to a high sheen. It was also completely without design or ornamentation of any kind, so I couldn't tell how old it was. It might have been made two years ago, or two hundred. There was no writing on the surface, and the crate itself was empty of anything except the coffin.

There was no mistaking the shape, though. It was the classic coffin shape—narrower at the feet and broader where the shoulders would be. My heart hammered as I reached out to tentatively touch the wood.

It felt cool under my fingertips, and I relaxed. Of course it did. Now I was the one being a ninny, wasn't I? With a small sigh, I put my fingers to the edge of the lid and pried it off.

As light hit the interior, I gasped.

It wasn't empty.

A man lay inside, a man so stunningly beautiful that he had to be unreal. His mouth was a perfect sculpture of lips, his cheekbones high. His jaw was strong and smooth, his skin pale. Thick, reddish-brown hair tumbled over his brow, and dark brows and thick eyelashes framed his closed eyes. Once I stopped staring at his gorgeous face, I looked at his clothing. It was unfamiliar, a long tunic of a dark shade and equally dark leggings. I did notice that he had one arm at his side, the other over his heart. He gripped a wooden stake.

My jangling nerves suddenly relaxed, and I just shook my head at the sight of that stake. Really? I laughed to myself. This *had* to be a prank. I looked around for hidden cameras. If this wasn't one of those reality TV shticks, I'd be shocked. Of course it made sense that this was a setup. An apartment in Venice that had been untouched for years? A secret room with a vampire? I wasn't born yesterday. I knocked on the edge of the coffin, unamused. "Nice try, buddy, but I don't buy the vampire thing. Get up."

The actor in the coffin didn't move.

Exasperated, I put my hands on my hips. "I'm serious. I don't know who set you up to this, but it isn't funny. I don't believe in ghosts, and I certainly don't believe in vampires. Good effort, though."

He didn't move. Didn't respond. I stared at him

for a long moment to see if his chest rose with breath, but it was hard to tell in the flickering lantern light.

I was quickly getting past amused and heading straight for annoyed. Was all this stuff down here a plant, then? One big prank to get me excited and try to scare me to death? If so, it wasn't working. I was pragmatic at best, and I didn't have time for this stupid stuff.

"Come on," I told the silent actor. "Don't make me call the cops on you. Get up." When he didn't respond again, I lost my patience and grabbed at the stake "in" his chest.

As I grasped it and pulled backward, my fingers brushed against his. I realized, too late, that his fingers were as cold as ice. But then the stake was in my hand and I was stumbling backward, shocked.

No human hand was that cold. No way.

As I stared down at the body in the coffin, the chest expanded, filling with air.

The man's eyes opened.

I gasped.

And he looked right at me.

"Um," I said, clutching the stake in my hand. "Hi?" I held the stake out to him. "This must be yours. A-are you a real vampire, then?" I backed up, then froze when my legs brushed against one of the crates. I was terrified, but I was also not about to break the priceless treasures in here by scrambling backward.

The man sat up slowly, like a man waking up from a nap. He rolled his neck and stretched his shoulders, his movements graceful and sinuous. It would have been a pleasure to watch had I not been holding the stake I'd just pulled from his chest.

He slid his legs over the side and hopped out with an ease that made me nervous. He said something that sounded like a question, and his voice was low and husky.

I shook my head, still clutching the stake. "I didn't catch that."

He tilted his head, watching me, and his eyes narrowed. As I stared at him, his nostrils flared, as if he was scenting the air. Then he said something else in that strange language I couldn't make out. It wasn't exactly Italian. It sure as heck wasn't English.

"I don't understand you," I said as he continued to stalk toward me. I glanced at the stairs, but I was too far away to get to them in time. I was pinned between a gorgeous, mysterious, undead man and crates full of pottery. *Damn it.*

He moved toward me, and I inhaled sharply. He smelled . . . strange. Like exotic spices. It was something I'd never smelled before, but it was pleasant. Except now? Now he was standing so close that I could see the utter perfection of his pale skin and the fact that his eyes were blue under those dark russet lashes.

He touched my cheek, and his hand was ice-cold.

I gasped and stepped backward, but I was still backed against a stack of crates. There was no place for me to go.

The stranger said something else in a low, sooth-ing voice. Then, before I could point out that I still didn't understand him, his lips parted and I watched as fangs emerged from his mouth. With snakelike speed, he hauled me against him and sank his fangs in my throat.

I squealed, choking at the burst of pain. I felt his teeth sink even deeper into my neck, felt his tongue flick against my skin. And even though I was horri-fied, I was also . . . aroused.

He sucked at my throat, and I felt blood trickle against the collar of my shirt. His tongue flicked against my skin again, and he continued to drink, even as I struggled against him. My fingers curled into fists and I beat against his chest, but he grabbed my wrists in his hand and pinned them easily, and then I was helpless to fight.

The world faded, and the last thing I remem-bered was his murmur of soft words against my throat. Oddly enough, it felt as if he was telling me it was going to be all right.

Which was a joke, of course. This was not all right. Not in the slightest.

But then I passed out, and I no longer cared.

"Svegliati!" A cold hand tapped my cheek.

An ache rolled through my body. I felt utterly trampled. My neck felt hot, too. What the . . . ? I opened my eyes, surprised at how heavy my eyelids felt. Something had knocked me on my ass—

A pair of familiar blue eyes met my gaze. Then I remembered. The man in the coffin that I thought was pranking me. His bite. Me passing out.

Vampire!

Oh God! I scrambled backward, shying away.

He continued to crouch on his feet, eyeing me as if I'd been a curious bug. Then he said something to me in Italian. Wait, he was speaking Italian now? I'd have mockingly assumed he was an actor at the sound of that, except the bite had been real and the fact that I was feeling so weak at the moment told me he'd sucked a lot more than he should have.

He spoke to me again, waiting, and his mouth flattened.

That sent a quiver of fear through my body. "I don't speak Italian."

The man cocked his head. He said something else and indicated I should continue speaking.

"Um, I don't know what to say to a vampire," I said slowly, backing up a little more. Damn these crates. I eyed the staircase—so near and yet so far away. "Other than it's a pretty terrible thing to grab a girl and use her as your own personal drinking fountain without asking permission first. And that I'm now regretting opening the coffin. *A lot.*"

He blinked his eyes several times. Then he spoke. "Zzzshou open zzzhe coffin?" His accent was thick, but the words were understandable.

"Yes, that was me." I watched him warily.

"You pull out zzee stahhhke?"

"You speak English?" I stared at him, uncomprehending.

"I am learning," he said slowly. "It is entering my head."

Huh? "What do you mean?"

"The Dragon knows English, thus I learn it," he said.

Yeah, I had *no* idea what that meant. "Well, that's great," I said brightly, getting to my feet. "But I'll be going now—"

"Stay," he commanded.

I gave a muffled peep and dropped back to the floor, my head spinning.

"Where am I?" He gestured at the floor. "This place." His words were becoming clearer, but his accent was still thick, and unlike one I'd ever heard before. "I am not familiar with it. It is . . . a castle? No? Dungeon?"

"It's a secret room. Kind of like a hidden basement." I probably wasn't explaining it very well, but I wasn't totally together.

"A basement . . . that is a room below?" He rubbed his chin, thinking. "Why?"

"Why what?" I said defensively. I shivered from

the cold in the room, and my head was still spinning from loss of blood. "Why there's a room down here? It looks like they stored stuff."

"No. Why . . . me? Why am I down here? In this box?"

"That's a coffin, and I'm the wrong person to ask," I said nervously. "I didn't put you down here." I really, really hoped he believed that, because I'd seen how fast he was. If he decided I was the enemy, he'd have me dismembered before I could even beg for mercy.

"A coffin? Why?"

Really? "Because you're a vampire? That's where vampires sleep."

His mouth curled into a handsome smile, and my heart pounded. "Is that so?"

"You tell me," I said defensively. "You're the vampire."

"I have been *upyri* for two hundred years, and I have never slept in a coffin." He seemed amused.

My eyes widened. "Is that how old you are? Two hundred years old?"

He shrugged. "Once, I was." He looked around the room, rubbing his chin. "But these things here, the walls, the stairs, the roads, the people . . . they are unfamiliar to me."

"What do you mean, roads and people? Did you leave while I was unconscious?" Not that I could have stopped him, but the thought of freeing a vampire to roam the canals of Venice bothered me. It felt irresponsible.

He gave me an impatient look. "I am not a prisoner. What is the year?"

"What year do you think it is?" I asked, curious. Some of my fear was fading out of curiosity for his story. Well, as long as he wasn't biting my neck again.

He studied the room thoughtfully, then me. "When I last slept, the year was 1386. Judging by the changes in the city, I would say it is perhaps . . . 1586? Am I correct?"

I held my fingers up in a pinch. "Wee bit off."

His brows went up. "1650?"

"Keep going."

His expression flattened. "1800. Truly?"

Poor guy. "Um. So what would you say if I told you that the year is actually 2015?"

His lips parted. "Truly?"

"'Fraid so. Hope you weren't late for something. Like the Renaissance."

"The what?"

"Never mind. I'm just talking." I waved a hand in the air. "Carry on."

"Did the Christians ever retake Jerusalem, then? Did they continue to crusade in later years?"

Oh Lord. Talk about ancient history. But I forced a bright smile to my face. "You know, that's a darn good question. I'd have to consult a history book and check. Why don't I just go upstairs and look it up . . ." I trailed off as his expression darkened.

"You will not leave me behind, wench. I can find you by scent."

He could? And wait, what was this "wench" stuff? "Wench? I'm going to let that slide, since you're medieval and all, but I have a name. I'm Lindsey Hughes."

"I am Sir Rand FitzWulf," he told me. "Of the Lionheart's Crusade."

"Oh, um, okay. Nice to meet you. Actually, it's not. You drank from me without asking. Not nice to meet you at all."

The vampire—Rand—looked at me curiously. "You are a peasant, are you not? Why would I ask? You are at my disposal as an overlord."

I pinched the bridge of my nose, because a headache was forming. "I'm not a peasant, and you're not going to make a lot of friends with that kind of attitude."

"I am not interested in friends," he told me coldly, "but vassals. And I have claimed you as my own, so tell me who your lord is so I can tell him I have chosen you."

I stared. He was joking, right? Did he really think he could just own me because he'd decided it? This guy was insane. I had to get away from him. "As your vassal, then, perhaps I should prepare your chambers upstairs before we go any further?"

He appeared to consider this.

But I pounced on the idea as an escape route. "You should let me," I gushed. "I need to make amends. And a lord such as yourself must be befitted in the proper rooms, don't you think? It's tradition now to let a woman—a wench—go upstairs and fix your room for you to welcome you as her lord." I was making up this stuff as I went, but I was desperate—anything to get away from this nut. "Then we'll sit down and have a nice chat over coffee about crusades and the last six hundred years. Sound good?"

Rand's eyes watched me, and I had the strange impression that I was being assessed by a predator. It wasn't a good feeling. "Swear it," he said after a moment. "Swear it on your liege's life."

Since I had no liege, that was a pretty safe thing to swear upon. "I swear it. I swear it on the great Elvis Presley's life."

"Mmm. You were very quick to swear." He regarded me, his gaze moving over my body.

I fought to keep my face neutral. "I'm an enthusiastic girl, what can I say?"

"Yet you had no enthusiasm before now."

"I'm also a delayed-reaction enthusiasm kind of girl."

His brow furrowed, and I knew he had no idea what my words meant. "No," he said. "Stay here with me."

"All righty," I said, keeping my voice light. "Your call."

Rand shifted his weight on his feet, then stood. He moved back toward the coffin, and when his hand brushed against the lid, it slid to the ground, clattering. He jumped backward, his hands going to his waist. He patted his side and glanced back at me. "My sword?"

"In the box behind you," I lied, hoping he'd take the bait. *Just, you know, jump right back in and make yourself cozy.*

He eyed me, clearly not falling for it. "Get it for me."

"Women aren't allowed to carry swords." I kept my face as guileless as possible.

Rand's mouth quirked into what would have been a devastatingly attractive smile if I hadn't known he was a vampire. But I got the impression he was enjoying my tart responses. "Very well," he said, and turned around to dig through crates.

Success! I got up and bolted for the stairs, hoping I could escape before he caught on to what I was doing.

Four

I made it three or four steps up the circular stairs, my feet clanging against the metal loudly. Then a strong, cold arm wrapped around my waist. "You do not leave, wench."

I screamed, flailing my arms against him. "I'm not your captive!"

"You are mine until I am done with you," he told me in that amused, cocky voice. As if what I wanted didn't matter in the slightest. It was infuriating. "And you are not escaping me. Not while I have need of your services."

I could just guess what those services were. Blood, and judging by the way he looked at my heaving breasts as he set me back down on the stairs, other services that had nothing to do with blood and everything to do with submitting. The worst of it all? He wasn't ugly in the slightest, so it wasn't as if it'd be a chore to sleep with the guy.

And that galled the crap out of me.

"Cease fighting," he told me. "You will injure yourself."

I slammed a fist into his arm just to prove that I could. He didn't even bat an eye, though his amused smile widened.

I shouldn't have fought so hard. In the next moment, the room spun, and I felt light-headed. I wobbled and fell against him.

Rand caught me easily, his look one of concern. "Are you well?"

"Of course I'm not well," I snapped at him. "You drank half my blood. I need to sit down." My voice was weak and thready. "Maybe eat something. Maybe . . ."

To my surprise, he picked me up in gentle arms, cradling me against his chest. "I will carry you. Tell me where is the best place we can get you food and ale."

Ale? For some reason, I giggled at that. Here I was pitching around like a drunk on a bender, and he wanted to give me alcohol. "It's way too early in the morning for ale." Actually it was more like late at night, but after midnight, it was morning, right? Right. "But I could use some orange juice and a few cookies." That was what they gave you when you donated blood, and I'd donated quite a bit.

"Tell me where we can get these jews and cookets."

"Juice and cookies," I corrected, and pointed up the stairs. "The kitchen is up there."

"Inside the keep?" he asked, but he began to make his way up the stairs, cradling me against his chest.

It felt a little odd to have my legs dangling over one strong arm, my head pressed against a chest that had no heartbeat, but I was too tired to walk it myself. "It's not really a keep," I told him idly as he climbed the stairs. "And all houses come with a kitchen now. Resale value and all that."

"Mmm."

"What's 'mmm' mean?"

"It means I grasp your words but I do not understand their meaning."

"Yeah, well, I'm still not entirely sure how you suddenly speak English, so we can both be confused."

He chuckled, the sound warm. His chest moved against my ear. "I told you, mistrustful wench. It is because the Dragon knows your language."

"And I told you I have a name," I retorted.

"Ah yes. Lindsey. It is a man's name."

I made a raspberry with my mouth at that, like a child. I was too weak to come up with a coherent comeback, so that would have to do.

He merely chuckled again and continued carrying me up the twisting, narrow stairs. At the top, he pushed aside the secret door as if it weighed nothing, and set me down gently on top of the nailed-down buffet. "Do not move," he instructed me. "You are too weak."

I wanted to protest, but he had a point. I *was* feeling pretty damn weak at the moment, trembling with exhaustion. So I sat there and watched as my vampire captor climbed over the buffet and then pulled me back into his arms again. "Where from here?"

I pointed him out of the dining room and saw that the door had already been pushed open wider than I had been able to move it. Clearly Rand had gone exploring while I'd been passed out. A shiver of fear hit me. I wondered what he'd seen. Gemma, asleep upstairs? Oh no.

Then I wondered why he'd returned.

"The kitchen?" he prompted when we were in the narrow hallway of the Venetian apartment. I wordlessly pointed at another door, and he carried me in. The kitchen was slightly less messy than when we'd discovered it. Gemma had tackled it first, since she'd seen a fair amount of old vintage dishes she knew would bring a fair penny online.

"This is the place?" Rand asked, and when I nodded, he carried me to the counter and set me down gently upon it. "Now, where are the scullery maids? Let me know and I shall wake them. Is it the woman upstairs?"

I stared at him with wide eyes. How had he known Gemma was upstairs? Had he hurt her like he did me? "You—"

He shook his head, as if anticipating my thoughts. "She slumbers. I did not interrupt her. Your blood quenched my thirst for now." He leaned in and sniffed me.

Lucky me. I leaned back, trying to scoot away from him. "There's no scullery," I told him. "It's just me and Gemma here." I pointed at the old, small fridge in the corner. It still worked, and we'd been using it to store food so we didn't have to eat out every day. "There should be some stuff in there."

Rand tilted his head, gazing at me. Then he leaned in and sniffed again.

"Um, what are you doing?"

"I have drunk blood many a time before, but perhaps my senses are . . . overeager. You smell . . ." He inhaled again. " . . . incredible."

"Gee, that's nice." I pointed at the fridge. "Can we eat now?"

He gave me a quizzical look, but at least he wasn't sniffing me anymore. "The trunk carries food?"

"It's not a trunk. It's a refrigerator. Or a fridge. We use it to keep food cold."

I watched his face as he processed this information. His eyes flicked with recognition, as if receiving information. "Ah, a refrigerator. I have this word in my memory." Rand approached the fridge and studied it. "How . . . how does one open it?"

The fridge was an old-fashioned one, like the one Indiana Jones rode in during that last horrible movie.

I pointed at the lever on the side. "Give that a yank."

He did, and the door flew open, swinging backward. Rand nearly stumbled in surprise, and I smothered a laugh. "Not that hard of a yank."

"My apologies," he said, then put his hand inside, tentatively feeling the air. The look on his face was wondrous. "How is it cold? And why does it hum?"

"Electricity," I told him. "There's a current of electricity that goes through the back that tells the coils to stay cold." I was probably botching the whole "how refrigerators work" thing, but I was also pretty sure he didn't need to know the nitty-gritty, just the basics. "The hum is the electricity going to the fridge."

He gave a slow nod. "When I awoke, I heard the hum of many refrigerators. You say these are common?" He gestured at the windows. "The entire city sings with such sounds. It is a cacophony. I miss the crickets and the sighs of horses in their sleep."

I nodded, ignoring the twinge of pity I felt. This had to be weird for the big guy. "No one uses horses anymore. Normally we use cars, but this place runs off of boats."

With that, he curled his lip. "I am not a fan of boats."

"Me, either." I pointed at an orange pitcher in the fridge. "Pass the orange juice?"

"Again, I know these words, but I am not familiar." He handed me the pitcher. "Explain?"

"I guess oranges aren't all that medieval? Hand me two glasses in that cupboard, please," I said, pointing at a cabinet behind his head. "Orange juice comes from a fruit." I didn't want to get into the whole "this actually came from a can of frozen concentrate" thing.

I watched with a raised brow as he pulled out two glass tumblers and stared at them as if they'd been the most valuable things on earth. Reluctantly, he handed me one. I poured a glass of orange juice, then held it out to him.

He took it from me and sniffed it, then a startled look touched his eyes. "I remember this."

"You do?" I poured myself a glass, curious. "Like from the Dragon or whatever that means?"

"No. From the Crusades." Rand sniffed it again, a look of stark longing on his face. "When we took Jerusalem. The infidels had food and drink that they offered us. I remember tasting this. At least, my nose remembers the scent."

"Well, try it and let me know what you think of it." I held my own glass in my hands, curious.

He lifted the glass to his mouth, reverent, and took a small sip. After a moment, he grimaced and spat it on the floor.

"Just so you know, we don't do that sort of thing on the floors here. It's kind of frowned upon."

Rand wiped his mouth, giving me a curious look. "No? Is that why you have no rushes?"

I didn't know what rushes were, but I nodded anyhow. "If you have to spit, you spit in the sink."

"Another word I recognize but do not understand."

I pointed at it. Some other time I'd have to give him the full house tour. Not right now, though. *Actually, scratch that*, I thought to myself. *He can do it on his own*. I grabbed a towel off the counter and handed it to him. "You can clean up your mess."

To my surprise, he did just that, and I watched him carefully mop the marble flooring with the towel as I sipped my orange juice. There were cookies in the cabinet behind my head, so I pulled them out and began to munch on them between sips, feeling a little better as I did. When Rand straightened, I offered him a cookie.

He shook his head and held up a hand. "I suspect it would taste as foul as the juice."

I considered my glass. Sure, it was from concentrate, but I thought it was pretty tasty. "You think it tastes foul?"

"Everything does," he said, a wistful note in his voice that surprised me. He leaned back against the counter and watched me scarf another cookie. "All normal food and drink is like ashes in the mouth of a vampire. I have not tasted pleasant food in the two hundred years since I was turned."

"Oh," I said around a mouthful of cookie. "That has to suck. No pun intended."

Rand gazed at me blankly, then shrugged. "It was not as if I was turned of my own volition. And I suppose it has been more than two hundred years now, has it not?"

"Six hundred," I agreed.

Rand looked around the room, then back at me. "It truly is the year of our Lord two thousand and fifteen?"

"It is," I agreed. The cookies tasted dry in my mouth, and I again felt a stab of unwanted sympathy for the vampire. He looked rather lost despite his big form and easy smiles. "This must be a big change for you."

His look was rueful. "It is not one change. It is everything that has changed," he admitted. "Naught I remember is familiar, and all is strange."

I tried to picture myself waking up six hundred years in the future, and how much things would have changed at that point. Okay, yeah, that would not be fun. "You'll be all right."

"I am utterly adrift," he admitted. "Friendless and alone in a strange place and time. Though one would argue if the men I called my friends from long ago were truly that."

"You think one of them staked you?"

At that, he gave me another rueful, sexy smile. "I know exactly who staked me. It was a blond whore with large tits and bountiful thighs. My last memory is of her riding my cock."

I gave him a look of horror and choked on my cookie. "We need to have a talk about oversharing," I wheezed when I could breathe again.

"Did you not ask?" Rand quirked an eyebrow at me.

For a moment, I wanted to cuss at him like Gemma and her sailor-mouth. "I didn't ask for that level of detail," I told him. "So, a whore staked you? Not a friend? I suppose that's good, right?"

"Nay. Or rather, no." Rand gave a small shake of his head and crossed his arms, leaning back against the counter. His pose was one of such casual sexiness that I wondered if the utter sensuality of every movement he made was part of the vampire package, or if Rand had just been sex on a stick before becoming a vampire. I couldn't ask without embarrassing myself, though. The last thing I wanted was the man to find out that I thought he was attractive. I'd never get away from him, then.

"So you were bouncing around with hookers and you got staked? Did you tick someone off?"

He contemplated this for a moment, and I suspected he was deciphering my words, filtering them through whatever mental ability let him speak the same language as me. "That is the question that repeats in my mind, over and over again. Who have I embraced that was an enemy to me?"

"Maybe start with all the hookers you're so fond of embracing?" I said sweetly. "Maybe you called them 'wench' too often?"

"They were wenches," he said with a roguish smile. "And they served many a man in bed. I do not see what was so different about me that they would lure me to my death. They were not the ones who brought the stake. They had not the strength."

So now all women were wimps as well as wenches?

I must have had a sour look on my face, because Rand grinned at me. "Again, you mistake my words. Do you think it is a simple thing to hold down a man with unnatural strength and drive a blunted length of wood through his chest?"

He had a point. "So you were set up? Is that what you are saying?"

"Perhaps. I knew the women I tupped. They were good, sweet girls with not much between their ears. Certainly not enough to plot a warlord's downfall. They must have been bribed to entice me into their bed."

My eyes widened. "I thought it was just a blonde with big thighs. Now it's more than one? Exactly how many wenches were you bedding at once?"

"Last night? Four."

I sputtered again. "Four?"

"They approached me and offered their services." He gave me another one of those purely masculine grins. "Who am I to refuse the ministrations of four women at once?"

"Gee, and you didn't stop to question this at all?"

"I am a warlord with much wealth at hand, and I have been told I am not unpleasant to the eye. It was not the first time several women offered their services to me. Why should I think anything strange of it?"

"Why indeed," I said dryly. "Next time you get offered a free gang bang, maybe you should think twice about why they're willing."

"Wise words," he agreed. "And now, because I do not know who sought my death, I am alone and unarmed in this strange place and time." For a moment, he looked so sad and lost that my heart gave another unhappy squeeze. "To think that mere hours ago, I was laughing with my soldiers and planning the next day's ride. Now I am here in this strange place, my men are long gone, and I am awash with enemies all around."

"Oh, come on," I muttered. "Not everyone's an enemy."

"Do you mean to tell me that you are not mine?" he said, a small, sad smile on his mouth. "That you would not press that stake back into my breast if you could?"

He had a point. I didn't trust myself to say no, so I said nothing at all.

He nodded at my silence. "You cannot be happy at my appearance here. Indeed, I am not happy with it myself. Until I know more about this place and time, I am afraid you will have to lead me."

"Wait, lead you where?" I had a sneaking suspicion I wouldn't like the answer. "No one said any-thing about helping you."

Rand moved forward, leaning closer to me. I was trapped between him and the cabinet, and I scrunched my body backward as he leaned in. "Let us get to the truth of the matter, Lindsey. You are angry that I suck-led at your neck."

Jeez, when he said it like that, it sounded posi-tively dirty. I clamped my thighs together, hating that parts of me were reacting. I was still outraged, damn it. "Wouldn't anyone be mad about that?"

"Actually, no," he said in a low, soft voice. "I have naught for complaints in the past. Women have re-quested that I bite them during bedsport. I am told it is exceedingly pleasurable."

The way he said that made me want to squirm.

He regarded me with blue-eyed intensity. "So, you tell me that if I asked permission to use your neck and suckle you, you would respond differently to me? That you would be sweet and willing in my arms instead of fighting something that is clearly pleasurable?"

"You're so incredibly arrogant," I whispered, shocked.

"I am," he agreed. "I am used to getting my way. I am a leader of men. I do not ask permission, ever. But if you say I must, I must." He leaned in so close that I could smell his strange, spicy scent. It felt as if he was going to kiss me. Instead, though, he simply leaned in and his lips moved close to mine. "If I ask nicely, Lindsey, may I suckle you?"

A hot bolt of unwanted lust shot through my body. "No," I protested, but my voice sounded weak, even to my own ears.

"No?" That sexy, arrogant little smile touched his mouth again. "You tell me no, but the rest of your body is responding to my nearness. Vampires have heightened senses."

I moaned in embarrassment. So he could smell my arousal? "You jerk. You don't bring that up to a girl," I hissed at him. "And no still means no."

"But I need you," he murmured, that wonderful, beautiful mouth inches from my own. From this angle, he looked like a beautiful, pale man. No fangs were visible. His skin wasn't touching mine, so I couldn't feel how cold he was. Just a pretty man telling me he needed me.

And for a moment, I felt weak. Uncertain. "Need me?"

"To help me navigate this strange time and place." His blue eyes captured mine. "Last I slept, it was six hundred years ago. I know nothing of this place, the people, or its customs."

"I'm not sure I'd be the best guide," I told him. "I'm a stranger here, too."

He looked surprised. "Is this not your home, then?"

"It's not. Gem—uh, a friend and I are cleaning it out for a sale. The owner passed away." I didn't want to tell him Gemma's name. If he'd gone exploring, he'd seen her upstairs, but still. Confessing her name felt suspiciously like betrayal, and that I wouldn't do. "My actual home is a very, very far distance away from this place. Across the ocean."

He gave me another one of those smug smiles and wagged a finger at me. "Lindsey, Lindsey. I am not a peasant. I am a learned man. Even I know that the world is flat."

"You caught me," I agreed, amused. Let him figure it out the hard way. "Regardless, I don't live near here."

Rand accepted that with a nod and pushed away from the counter—and me. He began to pace, hands clasped behind his back. "Then who are the owners of this place? How did my sleeping place come to be in their possession? Why did they not wake me?"

I drummed my fingers on my chin, thinking. I certainly wasn't going to think about how the room seemed less pleasant and exciting now that he wasn't in danger of kissing me anymore. Nope. "The people that lived here before were old and wealthy and collected a lot of stuff. That's why there are so many boxes. But I don't know if they were the ones that bought your coffin. I don't even know if they knew you existed." Quickly, I told him about finding the secret room full of antique treasures from different centuries. "It's possible that a collector from an earlier time purchased your coffin and hid it, and no one's known about you for years. There's no way of us knowing without going through receipts—"

"Receipts?" He touched the side of his nose. "Another word—"

Right, he didn't understand. "Papers that record the sale amount and date," I told him. "I found some of them for the jars, but nothing in your coffin. It doesn't mean that there wasn't something. It just means I haven't found it yet."

"Well," he said agreeably, "you purchased the temporary rights to this place, did you not? And with that, you purchased the rights to all belongings here?"

"That's right," I agreed.

"And did you not find my coffin below?"

I was starting to get a sinking feeling about where this argument was heading. "I did."

His brows went up. "Then would it not stand to reason that you are now my caretaker? Are you not responsible for me?" He pressed his hands to his heart dramatically. "Am I not as a babe in this time and place?"

I snorted. "Rand, you are many things, but helpless, you are not."

"I am certainly glad you think so," the man said, and his voice was practically purring. Gah. It was like he thought I'd complimented him. Double gah. "Regardless, I need you."

"Fine. What is it you want to do?"

The playful look on his face disappeared, all flirtiness erased. "When I was staked, I was in the city of Rome, visiting an old friend. Another one of the Dragon's men. If I am yet living after all this time, it reasons that he is as well."

My eyes widened. "Another vampire? Really?"

"All of us whom the Dragon has claimed are *upyri*. Vampire, as you say in your language. Blood drinkers. Strong. Dangerous. Hunters of men and women. Feasters upon flesh." He gave me another up and down look, as if assessing my flesh. "We are cursed men, though one would argue that it is not always unpleasant."

Yep, he was definitely staring at my boobs. Just when I felt a little sympathy for the guy, he knocked it away again, like we were in some sort of sexual ping-pong match.

"Okay," I said quietly. "I help you find another vampire, and then you're out of my hair, right? No more of this wench crap?"

He gave a nod. "I shall avail myself of a new wench. You have my word." His smile widened. "Though I doubt she will taste as perfect as you."

I rolled my eyes. "I'm sure there are lots of people that taste just like me."

"You'd be surprised. Your flavor is a rather unique one." His eyes were hooded, the look in them sultry.

Was he . . . was he trying to seduce me into volunteering to be his personal blood bank?

I was insulted. "I don't care if I taste like chocolate pudding. If I'm helping you, you don't get to drink from me whenever you like." I waved one of my cookies in the air. "It's clear I'm not good at donating."

"Very well. Then you agree to help me?"

I sighed, thinking of the basement full of treasures that had to be carefully packed, cataloged, photographed, insured, and shipped back home. I wouldn't be able to do that with a vampire hanging around, asking what made the toilet flush. I needed to get rid of Rand. Dropping him off with the nearest vampire sounded like a good idea to me. "How are we going to know where to find a vampire?"

He touched his temple. "It rests in here."

"Like the languages?"

"A little different." Rand touched his breast. "My blood is connected to that of the Dragon. Through him, I have knowledge of your language. It is also through him that I am connected to others. I feel the hum of vampire blood somewhere else nearby. It is faint, but it is here." He rubbed his forehead. "Very faint. I do not know if it is because so much time has passed that my bond has grown weak, or if it's because there are so many other things interfering now. The hum you mentioned—"

"Electricity," I offered.

He nodded. "That, and the scents and sounds of so many other people." For a moment, his eyes looked hollow, tired. "It is so much crowding into my head at once."

"Then we should get you to your vampire friend sooner rather than later, shouldn't we?"

"Indeed. Swear you will not abandon me again?"

Fair enough. It wasn't like I was going to be able to get away. If his senses were so keen that he could smell another vampire, I had no shot of escape. "I swear it."

"Ah, but you are quick to swear. You also swore upon your lord that you would not run, and yet the moment I turned my back, you fled. Your word is not to be trusted."

I licked my lips and hopped down off the counter, brushing off my jeans. How did this get turned around to me being the untrustworthy jerk? You swore one oath on Elvis Presley and people sure got all gripey. "All right then, smarty pants, how did people make oaths in your time?"

He grinned, showing me fangs. "Why, an oath of blood, of course."

"Ix-nay on the blood," I said quickly, taking a step backward. "First of all, I lost too much already. Second, if we share blood, won't that turn me into a vampire?"

"True. You could always swear fealty to me the way a vassal swears fealty to his lord."

"How's that?"

"A kiss."

"I'm starting to think this is all an excuse to make out with me," I grumbled, but I stepped forward anyhow. "So you made out with all your vassals? Tongue included?"

He flashed another smile at me. "No tongue. Just a chaste kiss of fealty on my foot."

"Your foot?" I sputtered. "I'm not kissing your foot!"

"I will allow you to kiss my mouth, then."

Sneaky vampire. But it beat foot-kissing. "I'm not sure I signed on for any of this."

"Then how can I possibly trust you?"

Damn vampire. "Fine. Let's get to it, then." I moved into his arms and tilted my head back.

To my surprise, his arms went around me, one sliding to my waist, the other cupping the back of my neck. If this had been any other man, I'd have thought this was a prelude to an intense make-out session. But this was a vampire. I watched him warily as he leaned in and his lips lightly brushed against mine.

Soft. Sensual. Brief.

Cold.

I shivered.

"Now swear your fealty to me," Rand murmured, and his thumb skimmed over my lower lip thoughtfully.

"I swear I won't abandon you again," I told him.

"Then you are mine—and I am yours."

That sounded so very . . . final.

Five

Upstairs in the bedroom, Gemma was snoring away. I hated to wake her up, but since my world had been upended in the last hour, she needed to know things. We were a team.

I convinced Rand to stay outside the bedroom for a few minutes, trying to assure him that no, I wasn't running away again, and truly, I wasn't trying to betray him. I was just going to break things to Gemma . . . gently. Well, as gently as *Hey we have a vampire* could go. So I tiptoed into the room, sat on the edge of the bed, and nudged her. "Gemma. Wake up."

She came awake with a snort, peered around the room, and groaned, flopping back on the bed. "What time is it?"

I looked at the clock on the wall. "Um, three a.m."

"God, I fucking hate you. Why are you waking me up at this hour?" Gemma whined, pulling a pillow over her face. "Someone better have died."

Oh, the irony. "So I have good news and bad news. Which one do you want to hear first?"

She peered at me from under the pillow. "Uh-oh. Bad news?"

"The coffin wasn't empty."

Gemma gave an earsplitting shriek.

I clapped my hands over her mouth even as Rand slammed into the room, the heavy wooden door banging against the opposite wall. His eyes were wild, his longish hair flying. At the sight of him, all menacing in the doorway, Gemma's shriek died. Then she looked at me, wide-eyed. "That's him?"

"Yeah."

"He's hot."

"I guess that's the good news." If there was any.

"Wow." She stared at him, then at me. Then she leaned over and pinched my arm.

"Ow!" I pinched her back.

"Ow! Okay, I'm definitely not dreaming." Gemma fluttered her lashes, then patted the edge of the bed. "Come sit down. So, what are you, a vampire? Or just incredibly hot and in my room at three in the morning?"

"Why aren't you freaking out a little over this?" I couldn't believe how easily Gemma was accepting the fact that there was a vampire in the bedroom.

"Well, it might be that I'm still half asleep," Gemma said with a yawn. "But you found a hot guy in Venice who's dressed like a guy from the Renaissance faire and you have a big bruise on your neck. And we have a coffin downstairs. So the fact that the dude is hot and not eating our faces? I'm calling this a bonus."

"Give him a few minutes," I muttered.

But Rand came and sat on the edge of the bed. He took Gemma's hand in his and kissed the back of it as if she were a princess instead of a girl in an old ratty T-shirt with her hair standing on end. "It is a pleasure to meet you."

"Oooh," Gemma said. "It must be true about vampires being charming. Do you also turn into a bat?"

Rand gave her his signature sexy grin. "I am afraid that is but a myth."

"Much like the charming part," I countered.

Gemma thwapped my arm and continued beaming at Rand. "Can I see your teeth?"

He smiled widely, pulling back his lips. His fangs shot out, elongating, and both Gemma and I flinched backward. Rand hissed.

"I-I'm good now," Gemma said, her hand clenching my arm. "Thanks for the show." She sidled a little closer to me and gave me a wary look. "So how exactly is it that we went from coffin in basement to vampire in bedroom, pray tell?"

I told her the entire tale. Maybe it would have sounded like a ridiculous story if it hadn't been for the fact that Rand was in the room with us, poking the alarm clock with a wary finger and then moving to the mirror. He didn't show up, but we did, and he kept lifting the edge of it away from the wall to try to see what was "behind" it.

It was clear that Rand had no clue about modern

anything. And that made the whole vampire thing a bit easier to go down, I imagine.

"Soooo, now we have a vampire," Gemma said, watching curiously as Rand picked up a discarded bra from the floor and tried to figure it out. Her lips twitched with amusement, and she looked back to me. "Can we keep him?"

I smacked her arm. "What? No! He's not a puppy!"

"We can't just leave him on his own," Gemma said. "Look at him. He's so sad and confused."

I looked over, and he was trying to open the closet door. Or rather, he didn't know how. His fingers moved along the seam, and he completely ignored the doorknob. Then he tried to peer through the seam and gave up.

"Bless his heart," Gemma said. "He doesn't even know how to use a doorknob. You said he's not a dog, but there are dogs that know more than he does."

He bites like a dog, I thought unhappily. "Well, don't worry about it. I told him I'd take him to the nearest vampire."

"Oh, you don't have to," Gemma said. "I'll take him if you don't want to."

I looked over at her in surprise. "What?"

"We both know you're not good with men. And you're a bit of a control freak." Gemma gave me an apologetic look and a pat on the arm. "And all that stuff in the basement needs to be taken care of, in addition to the rest of this apartment. Like you said, it's going to take all month just to do what we have to for this place. You can't spend your time running around with a stranger."

She had a point. I did like to control things. And with the treasure trove in the basement, there was so, so much that needed to be handled delicately and with the utmost of care.

"And I know you don't trust me with things." Her smile was faint. "So, you know, I can handle the guy. I can do that much at least."

Oh. That felt like reproach. Had I hurt Gemma's feelings with my control-freaky ways? Hurt her self-esteem when it came to helping handle the business? Here I thought we both just focused on the things we did best, but maybe I was wrong. Maybe my need to control everything meant I'd hurt my best friend's feelings somewhere along the way.

I felt like an ass.

"It cannot be thus," Rand said, interrupting my thoughts.

"Hmm?" Both Gemma and I looked over at the vampire in surprise.

"The fair Lindsey has promised to be my blood vassal. She has sworn it with a kiss to her liege."

Gemma's eyes went big as saucers. "Did she, now."

I wanted to kick that smug look off Rand's face. "Yeah, for some reason, he thinks I'm lying when I say the world is round."

"I see," Gemma murmured. "So while I've been sleeping, we've acquired a medieval vampire and you already made out with him."

"He started it."

"Oh, I'm sorry, I must've misunderstood." Gemma patted my arm. "So you have to suck face to survive? Is that it?"

I glared at her.

"Are you two sisters?" Rand asked. His gaze went back and forth, studying us as we argued on the bed.

"We grew up in the same state home," I told him. "Neither of us has family."

"So we're each other's," Gemma said. "Now don't change the subject. I want to know more about this kiss of fealty." She gave a little shiver. "Was it sexy?"

I just kept glaring at her. "I am not answering that."

"Is his mouth cold?"

"Gemma! Let's stay on track, please? I don't want to talk about that. Let's talk about what we're going to do with him."

"I'm right here," Rand said. "I can speak for myself."

Gemma wiggled her eyebrows. "I told you I'd take him."

"Lindsey is my blood vassal," Rand repeated. "It is she who has given her word that she will remain at my side." He moved toward me and put a hand on my shoulder possessively. "I want her and no other."

"Oooo," Gemma said. She made kissy noises. "This is intriguing."

"She simply tastes better than most. It is something in her blood. Like a fine wine. Do you still have wine in this time?"

"Oh yeah," Gemma purred. "So Lindsey here is like a nice merlot? Is that what you're telling me? I wonder if it is because of something in particular? What about my blood?"

He leaned in and sniffed Gemma, then shook his head. "Sour. Metallic."

"Wow, really? I'd almost be hurt if I wasn't so fascinated by the fact that Miss Lindsey here is the tastiest thing on the block."

"Her blood is . . . very fine."

I ignored the heated look he was sending my way. He was driving me crazy as it was. "I'm sure Gemma tastes just dandy," I said out of loyalty to my friend.

"Not like you," Rand said. "Your blood perfumes the very air. I've never tasted anything like it."

Gemma's eyes widened, and she reached over and tapped my ID bracelet. "I bet it's this."

"Shhh," I told her. Let him just think I was tasty. If he found out I was rare, I suspected I'd never get free. "Anyhow—Rand's my burden. I'll take him to his vampire friend. It shouldn't take too long, really. He says he can sense where the guy is, and then I can get back to work." I shrugged. "You'll just have to keep packing without me."

Gemma's hands clasped together. "Really? You trust me to do that?"

Jeez, I wasn't that controlling, was I? "Of course I do."

Her eyes lit up with happiness. "This is so awesome! And you said Venice would suck."

"Suck?" Rand asked, honing in on the word.

I held up a hand. "Don't ask. Just don't ask."

Gemma gave another uncomfortable, inappropriate giggle. "I can't believe we found a vampire."

I wished we hadn't, but with Rand's piercing blue eyes locked onto me, I couldn't exactly say that. I rubbed my forehead instead. "So what now?"

Gemma yawned. "Can we sleep? I'm fucking exhausted."

Sleep sounded incredible, but I looked over at Rand, wary. Somehow going to sleep with him in the room implied a lot more trust than I had at the moment. My neck still throbbed from his earlier bite. My head ached from the blood loss. My body was unsettled with unwanted desire. My lips still remembered that damn vassal kiss.

I was a mess. An exhausted mess. I eyed Rand, who was listening to our hushed conversation intently. "What do we do with him?"

Gemma rubbed a hand through her sleep-tousled hair and yawned. "I dunno, girl. TV? Internet?"

I considered those. It would be the easy way out . . . and we might wake up to an even more insane vampire. "I think that's a bad idea. He probably needs to be eased into the last six hundred years or so. Just a hunch." After all, I'd seen how the man had reacted to the refrigerator. And the door. And, okay, to me. So yeah, the man needed a crash course, and I suspected that the advertisement-and-porn-laden internet would not be the place to do it.

"Books, then?" Gemma asked. "There's a ton of them in the other room. He probably can't read the writing, but I'm sure they have pictures."

I brightened at the thought. "Now that sounds like a plan." I hauled myself off the bed and gestured that Rand should follow me. "Come on."

Reluctant, he trailed behind me as I picked my way through the box-strewn apartment, Gemma padding along behind us. In the living room I found where we'd put several stacks of books. They were all from the '70s or earlier, but there were plenty with lots of pictures and drawings. It could keep him busy long enough for us to sleep, hopefully. I cleared off a winged armchair and indicated that Rand should sit. "Here you go."

He eyed me warily, but he sat down, resting his arms on the chair like a king on his throne. When he gave me a small, jerking nod as if to indicate his approval, my irritation flared. I dumped a stack of books in his lap. "Go nuts. We'll be up in a few hours."

Rand's eyebrows went up and he gazed at me. "And what will you be doing?"

"Sleeping, because if I'm going to escort you around the city, I'm going to need a few hours of shut-eye."

"Mmm." He opened a book. I got the vague impression he wasn't happy, but he said nothing.

"Great, well, have fun. I'll come get you after I wake up." I turned my back and started to head for the stairs.

"Our excursion will have to wait until it is dark," Rand called after me. "I cannot move about during daylight. It is one of the many curses of *upyri*."

Right. Shoot. I'd forgotten what sunlight can do to a vampire. "All right. We can go out at night." That would mean I'd have to get some extra sleep in the daytime if I was going to be up all night. Which meant I wouldn't be able to help as much with packing in the daytime. A vampire was damn inconvenient. "And if that's the case, I really need to head to bed, then. You have fun down here. You know where the fridge is." I waved a hand in the direction of the kitchen, then pointed at the hall. "The bathroom is that way if you need to use it."

His lips twitched with amusement. "Do you truly think a vampire has such human functions?"

"I honestly don't want to know," I told him. But his mention of functions reminded me. "Uh, so . . . when do you need to feed again? Like, how often?"

He was still watching me with that calculating

look. I couldn't tell if it was amused or predatory. Or both. "Do not worry on my behalf. You may see to my needs later, Lindsey."

"Bow chicka bow bow," Gemma called out.

I ignored her and headed for the stairs. "That's my cue to head off to sleep. Later. See you in the morning. Or not."

"Be nice," Gemma murmured sleepily as we went up the narrow stairs.

I heard Rand's subtle laugh in the distance and grew more irritated. Nice? I didn't want to be nice to a bloodsucker that was going to force me to work for him. "Feel free to stake yourself again and save me some trouble," I called out, ignoring Gemma's thwap to my arm. "Nighty night!"

I was feeling pretty smug with my taunts and crawled under the covers, flicking off the light. I didn't even care that I was fully clothed. I just wanted some sleep, I wanted to forget about today.

Immediately, something heavy thumped below.

I sat bolt upright in the bed. "What was that?"

Gemma groaned and rolled over, hugging her pillow. "Probably the vampire. Go to sleep."

The heavy thump happened again, and again, over and over. With an irritated snarl, I leapt back out of bed and headed for the door to the bedroom.

As soon as I opened it, I saw Rand standing there with the chair in his arms. A stack of books was in the seat, and as I watched, one of the books slid off the chair and thumped to the floor, making the same noise that had been driving me nuts.

"What are you doing?" I asked him.

"I am coming to be with you." He pushed past me, and I had no choice but to step aside as he brought the large chair into the room, spilling books as he did so. "I do not trust you not to flee once more."

I sputtered. "You can't come in here and just sit while we're sleeping."

"Why not?"

I looked over at Gemma for help, but she stuffed a pillow over her face and turned her back to me, not getting out of bed. Traitor. I turned back to Rand. "Because we're trying to sleep!"

"I will be silent. I will look at pictures in your books." He set the chair down near the door. I crossed my arms over my chest and watched as he returned to the stairs and began to pick up the books he'd dropped along the way. When he returned a few moments later, he set his chair against the door, sat down in it, and pulled the stack of books into his lap as if to say, *See? Harmless vampire.*

As Gemma would say, bull-fucking-shit he was harmless. I wanted to argue, but I was exhausted, and I suspected I wouldn't win this one. I wanted to protest that he could trust me, but he was probably right. Who was to say I wouldn't wake up, freak out a bit more, and run for the hills? "You suck."

"I do," he told me, a puzzled look on his face. "Why do you ask?"

"No reason," I said, feeling smug that he couldn't understand my insult. I crawled back into bed and hauled the covers over my body, now happy that I hadn't undressed after all. I closed my eyes and tried to sleep

The soft *swish* of a page turning grated on my nerves. I pursed my lips and ignored it.

Swish.

Swish.

Swish.

Then, no swish.

My eyes flicked open. I looked over. Rand was looking at me thoughtfully. In the darkness, his eyes seemed bluer than ever, and a little shiver moved through me. *A shiver of fear,* I tried to tell myself. *Not desire. That's just because he's a vampire and vampires are supposed to be sexy predators. That's how they find it so easy to kill.*

Gemma's soft snore told me she'd had no trouble falling asleep. I sighed and closed my eyes again, determined to ignore Rand staring at me.

That worked for about all of two minutes. I could feel his gaze on me. It made my nipples prick and my skin tingle with awareness. Stupid vampire. I squinted an eye open again. Still staring at me. The look on his face wasn't predatory, though.

It was sad. Lost.

My heart squeezed despite myself. "You going to be okay while we sleep?" I whispered.

His mouth tugged in a reluctant half smile. "My entire world has been turned whilst I slept. I am not sure if I will ever be 'okay' again." Again, he looked sad in the darkness. I watched his fingers touch a picture on one of the pages. "Everything is unfamiliar. Strange. I know nothing and I find I dislike it, but I have no choice. Two days ago, I had no surprises in the world. Today, I know nothing of the world itself." He shrugged his shoulders. "I will adjust. It will just take time."

"I hate that I feel sorry for you."

His smile was rueful. "I imagine you do."

Six

I woke up at some point to the sun streaming in through the blinds. I sat up in bed and rubbed my eyes, glancing at the clock. Almost one in the afternoon. Gemma had disappeared; the bed beside me was empty. I looked at the door.

No Rand. His chair had been pushed to the side, and the stacks of books on the floor lay in neat piles.

My heart stirred with a thump of panic. "Rand?" I swung my legs over the edge of the bed—and noticed the corner of a blanket sticking out from under it.

Heart thumping, I dropped to the floor and crouched on my knees, looking.

There was a man-sized body covered in a blanket. It didn't move, but then again, Rand didn't breathe. I slid a hand under the blanket and felt cool fingers under mine.

It was him. I gave his hand a squeeze of relief, and I didn't even mind that he didn't respond. He was just hibernating, or whatever it was that vampires did in the daytime.

Still alive. Thank goodness. I didn't want him to be my problem, but he was a living, breathing human with feelings.

Okay, so he wasn't exactly living and he wasn't exactly breathing . . . but he did have feelings, and he'd been courteous to Gemma. And to me, once he'd recovered his bearings. I needed to get over myself and just help the guy.

I headed downstairs and made myself a quick sandwich. On reflection, I ate a second one and pulled out one of my "emergency" bags of gummy bears. If I was going to be feeding a vampire—and all signs pointed to yes—then I'd need to keep my strength up. I was polishing off the last of my gummies when Gemma returned with a bag of groceries.

"Hey, sleepyhead," she sang out at the sight of me. "How's our guest?"

"Asleep under the bed." I hesitated. "Do you think I should wake him?"

"Nah. Let him be. We can work." Gemma beamed at me, as if we found a vampire in a secret basement every day and it was no big deal. "You sleep good?"

I rubbed my face. "I guess. Gemma, what are we going to do?"

"Work?"

"I meant with the vampire."

She shrugged, sauntering past me with the groceries. "I mean, as vampires go, he's not the worst. Like we said last night, we can find his buddy, give him a nice pat on the back, and send him on his way."

She made it sound so easy. Me, I was worried. I was the control freak, and I had zero control in this situation. I followed her as she moved around the kitchen, putting things away. "What if something goes wrong? What if his friend is a . . . I don't know, a bad guy?"

"A monster? You mean, like a vampire?"

"Not funny. You know what I mean." I crossed my arms and thought about Rand upstairs. "He's kind of helpless, you know?"

"Yeah, I noticed. Dude tore a doorknob off last night. We really need to show him how to work those things. Who would have thought they'd be so hard to figure out?" She shrugged. "Look, if you're feeling a little wiggy about the whole thing, just prepare."

"Prepare?"

"Yup. I got you a few things while I went out." She pulled a tiny bag out of her pocket and handed it to me. "It might be a good idea to keep this secret from a certain someone, but I want you to be ready for action."

I examined the bag. It was hot pink plastic with a zipper, small enough to fit in my pocket. "This looks like a makeup case."

"Precisely. Open it."

I unzipped it and pulled out a tiny bottle with a cross on the front. "Holy water?"

"Yup. There's also a tiny vial of minced garlic, a few toothpicks that I'm hoping can act as mini stakes, and dirt from a grave."

My eyes widened. "Dirt from a grave?"

"Some old nun down in the city told me to get it. Something about how it'll make a vampire stop in its tracks. I don't know if it'll work, but I figured it's worth a shot. I don't want you running around unarmed."

"Wow. You've been busy." I was impressed. Here I'd been flailing and wondering what to do, and she'd been quietly getting things done. More and more, my flighty friend made me think I wasn't giving her enough credit. Impulsively, I hugged her. "Thank you. I feel better having this."

"Of course," she said, hugging me back. "Just because we're not used to dealing with this sort of thing doesn't mean we have to go in blind. Just keep your wits about you, and if he wants to lead, let him lead. Oh, and take this," she said, handing me a small packet of cookies. "In case he needs to drink again, you have to keep your blood sugar up."

I blushed but took the packet and put it and my new vampire kit in my handbag. "I think he's going to be out until sundown. We can work on packing the porcelain away for a bit."

"Correction," Gemma said, folding the grocery bag and putting it away for use again later. "I can get to work on the porcelain. You need to find some clothes for that vampire that won't attract too much attention. There's bound to be something around here he can wear."

"Bossy," I teased, but I liked it. Gemma's assertiveness was making my own fears melt away.

Much later in the afternoon, I had a small pile of clothing for Rand to try on once he awoke, and Gemma and I had packed up the most valuable of the anhua jars. We continued working in the secret basement, cataloging the treasures while Rand slept.

It turned out there were three of the precious "hidden design" jars, and I'd held my breath each time we'd touched one. They were utter perfection, so lovely it made my teeth ache, and so priceless that I lived in terror of a single chip or hairline crack. It wouldn't destroy the value entirely, but as they were now, they were beyond compare. Each one looked as if it had come straight out of the kiln. The quality of the workmanship and the tiny paper invoices tucked into each jar told the story of their true age. They were so perfectly preserved, and with the proof that gave them provenance? They were incredibly valuable.

The only thing that made me relax was to see how lovingly Gemma packed them. The care she took with each photo for insurance records, the detailed notes she kept before packing each item away, made me realize that while Gemma was a partner, I didn't think of her as one and didn't treat her like my equal. I'd been overlooking her all this time. I was a bad friend, and I felt awful about it.

A thump upstairs told me that our vampire was awake. Was it sunset already? I suppressed the groan rising in my throat and steeled myself. "I should go and say hello."

"I'll be up in a minute," Gemma said, running a line of packing tape across a lid. "Just in case you guys need a few moments of privacy."

It was on the tip of my tongue to protest that I was not about to do anything of the sort with Rand, but the truth was, I didn't know how Rand would react upon waking up. When I'd removed the stake, he'd been wild, almost feral. He'd said that had been with hunger, but I didn't know how to predict how he'd react this evening now that he'd awoken again. I had to assume the worst.

But I'd promised to help the guy. Rand had been impossible and annoying at times, but he hadn't been cruel or abusive, and I knew that his strength was inhuman. He could have easily hurt Gemma while she'd slept. Heck, he could have killed me instead of stopping.

So I deserved to give him the benefit of the doubt. Right?

I trudged toward the stairs. "If I don't come back in fifteen minutes," I warned Gemma, "lock the doors and wait for dawn."

"That's not funny," she told me with a frown.

I wasn't trying to be funny.

I put a hand on the railing and headed upstairs, determined. I pinned a smile to my face, trying to make it seem like I went to greet a strange vampire every day. No big deal, right? By the time I made it past the secret door, I almost had myself fooled. Almost.

I found Rand upstairs, perched on the edge of the bed. His head hung, and his hands were braced on his knees. He looked exhausted. I gave a soft knock on the open door to get his attention. "You okay?"

"I had hoped it was all a bad dream." His voice was soft. "That I would awaken from my slumber to find things had not changed, and that I am yet who I thought I was."

Damn it, there were those sympathy pangs again. "I'm sorry."

He looked up at me, that faint smile of amusement on his face. "It is not your fault. You are not the one who put me there. You are not the one who should fear my retaliation."

A shiver moved down my spine. "Retaliation?"

"Indeed," he said, standing up and stretching to his full height. He rolled his shoulders and strode toward me. "When I find who has done this to me, they and their family will burn."

For a moment, he looked completely, utterly inhuman. I took a step backward, away from him.

"You have nothing to fear from me, blood vassal," he said, voice soft. I watched his eyes move over my face, his focus going to my neck. I could practically hear him drooling. "In fact, you are the only thing I find pleasant about this time and place."

"*Me?*" My voice squeaked, and even though I hated myself for it, I felt a rush of pleasure at his words.

"You are kind to me despite the situation," he agreed, moving closer. He sauntered like a predator. A big, sexy predator. I stared at him, my mouth open just a little. He oozed sensuality, and I couldn't stop watching him. Couldn't stop gazing at the way he moved, the curve of his lips, the elegance of his brow. He was beautiful, and I was helpless before him. "You could have attempted to destroy me, but you have welcomed me into your home. For that, I thank you, Lindsey."

"O-of course," I stammered, surprised at my immediate reaction to him. I could feel myself growing wet between my legs, my nipples hard. Just the sight of him was making me insane with lust.

And that wasn't natural.

"Are you," I breathed, not entirely sure how to phrase my question, "influencing me?"

"It is the hunger," Rand admitted, even as he continued to approach me. "When a vampire thirsts for blood, he becomes that much more attractive to his prey."

"Oh." I should have been upset at that. Horrified. Freaked out at the very least. Instead, I wanted him to keep coming closer to me. "That's probably going to piss me off later, huh?"

"Probably," Rand murmured. He was standing close enough to me that he could touch me, and his fingers brushed the short sleeve of my T-shirt.

I shivered in response to that small, innocent touch. "Do you . . . do you want to feed?"

"I do," he murmured. "I must. But the question must be asked. Do you wish to feed me?"

I stared at his mouth. His pretty, pretty mouth. Despite the fact that he had no blood flow, it was flushed a soft pink. It looked inviting. Kissable. Heck, the entire man looked like he needed to be tongued, and my loins were volunteering for the job. "I agreed to be your blood vassal," I said faintly. "But not your dinner. There's a difference, right?"

He gave me a crooked smile. "I care how my blood vassal feels when I am done with her."

"Let's go with blood vassal, then."

His fingers traced down my arm as he gave me the slow, sleepy gaze of a man hot with need, and I had to bite back a moan. "I will not drink as much as last time, if that is your biggest fear."

It wasn't my biggest fear, actually. My biggest one was that I'd come to my senses only after I was naked under him and screaming his name. Or that he'd lose his senses and drain me entirely. Yeah, those were much bigger fears. Despite that, though, I didn't pull away. I couldn't. I was trapped, his gaze hypnotic, his scent enticing. I felt like a cobra caught in the grip of a snake charmer.

Except cobras were dangerous things on their own, weren't they? And I was just a helpless woman leaning far too close to a sexy predator.

"Just . . . be gentle, all right? And don't take too much."

"I won't," he murmured, moving ever so subtly closer. Now he held me in the embrace of a lover, my aching breasts pressed to his chest, my stomach against his, my hands moving over his shoulders. "I shall take great care with you, Lindsey," he said in a soft voice. "Now that I know how incredibly sweet you taste and how fragile your form is. The last thing I wish is to be prevented from drinking again."

And he smiled at me. Long white fangs distended, and I watched in entranced fascination as he leaned in. At first I thought he was going to kiss me. My arms went around his neck, but he bypassed my mouth and went for my neck instead.

Rand bit my throat, and I gasped in surprise at the sensation. Not because it hurt—it definitely did—but because I felt the jolt of pleasure it gave me straight through to my core. I couldn't swallow the moan, and as he pressed his tongue against my vein and sucked at my throat, I rubbed my hips against his and tangled my hands in his hair, holding him against me.

"My God," he murmured. "You taste sweeter than anything I've ever had. I thought my memory from before was skewed, but it is you that is impossibly delicious. Why is this so?"

I could only moan in response, shivering as his tongue lapped the blood from my throat.

It seemed he'd barely begun when he reluctantly pulled away, and I stifled a whimper of protest. That was it? That was all I got? Rand's hot gaze devoured me, and I looked up at him, breathless, so full of need. So full of hunger for his body. His lips were soft and wet, and I impulsively pushed my mouth against his.

"Ah, sweet," Rand whispered. His hand clenched my bottom, dragging me against him, then he pulled my thigh around his. "Come to bed with me, wench. I have other needs that must be sated, too."

That broke the spell real damn fast. I struggled to pull away from him. "Wait, what? Let go of me!"

He looked surprised at my resistance. "You kissed me."

"That doesn't mean I want to have sex with you! And you really need to stop throwing around that 'wench' word, damn it!"

"God give me strength," he muttered, but he released me.

I straightened my clothing, trying to look as indignant as I felt. Now if only my wobbly knees and alert nipples would play along. "I agreed to feed you.

That was it. And I'm not entirely sure why I did that, either."

"It is because a vampire is irresistible to his prey," Rand said, straightening his own clothing. His tunic-thing was belted low at his waist, but I could make out a discernible bulge from his erection . . . which was pretty impressive, given the fact that the guy had no pulse. I wondered how that worked with blood flow and all, but I didn't ask. Bad enough that I encouraged the man by kissing him and letting him drink from me.

I swiped a hand at my neck. "I hope you got enough to drink, because the water fountain is closed."

"It is sufficient for now. I will require more later."

Over my dead body. My cheeks were hot with humiliation, and I thought of his words. *Come, wench. I have other needs.* What was saddest? I'd wanted to go with him. And here it was all because vampires were sexy to their prey. He didn't want me. He wanted a snack. It was humiliating.

There wouldn't be a later, that was for sure. I was suddenly looking forward to dropping him off at his vampire buddy's and washing my hands of him. "Come on. Let's get you dressed."

"Dressed?" He eyed my jeans and T-shirt. "In something like that?"

"Not exactly." I produced the small stack of clothing we'd managed to find that wasn't moth-eaten or entirely too small. It was a Christmas sweater and a pair of warm-up pants, but it'd be better than him walking around in a medieval getup.

Not that a Christmas sweater was going to be much help, but maybe we could get by with "eccentric" instead of "freakish."

I retrieved Gemma from downstairs, and we talked Rand through how to put the clothing on. Ten minutes later, though, Gemma was giggling and I was blushing.

The pants we'd found for Rand were too short and too tight. From my spot next to Gemma, I could see a clear outline of his, ahem, equipment.

"Looks like he's a shower and not a grower," she whispered to me. "And not circumcised. Damn. I'm sad I'm the brussels sprouts to your steak."

I hushed her, cheeks burning, as Rand turned, thoughtful. "Are you sure these are correct?" he asked, tugging at one leg cuff that only went to mid-calf. "They seem different from yours."

"They're track pants," Gemma said helpfully. "They're supposed to be different."

"Maybe we'd be better off with him in his regular clothing," I said. "He's less, um . . ." I tried not to stare at his package. "Obvious."

"Good point," Gemma said, a purr in her voice. "Maybe you guys can hit up a clothing store on your way out. Something with a little more room in the crotch."

I batted her arm, hiding a laugh.

We left the room and Rand changed back. When we returned, he was adjusting his belt, all conspicuous parts covered.

"Shall we go?" I asked him. I was antsy and ready to get moving. I'd choked down a few cookies while he'd changed and I wasn't weak like before, which told me he hadn't taken nearly as much blood. I also hadn't told Gemma, because I didn't want to hear the teasing. "This other vampire's in Rome, right? We'll take a train and I'll be back before you know it."

"It's five hours from here," Gemma pointed out. "You guys take a train, then get a hotel room just in case things take longer than anticipated." She pushed a wad of cash into my hand. "Take your time. I'll hold the fort down here. Just keep your phone on."

"Are you sure?" I asked her. It was going to be a big deal for both of us. If I went off with the vampire, she'd be the only one left to tackle the mess in the apartment, and it was a daunting job for two people.

"I'm sure," she told me with a smile and a quick hug. "Get him to his new home, and when our hands are free, we'll get a lot more done. I'll be fine."

"All right," I agreed, then turned to Rand. "Ready to go, then?"

He frowned at me imperiously. "Weapons?"

"What do you mean, 'weapons'?"

"I need weapons if I am to venture out into the

city." He shook his head. "No warrior in his right mind would go about unarmed."

"Uh, things have changed. You can't carry a weapon out into public. That's a sure sign of attracting attention."

"I care not if we attract attention." Rand crossed his arms over his chest. "I refuse to go out defenseless."

I groaned. "This is clearly going to be an uphill battle—"

"If there is a battle, I am most definitely not going out unarmed!"

"Oh boy," Gemma said. "He's lucky he's so hot. No guy is worth this much trouble."

But Rand's concern also had me a little concerned, and as I watched him, I had an idea. "Hey, Rand? There are some great knives in the kitchen that might make decent swords. Why don't you check them out?"

He looked up and nodded, then left the room, heading for the kitchen.

The moment he disappeared, I turned to Gemma. "While we're gone, I need you to do me a favor."

"What?" Her eyes were big.

"Find out anything you can about vampires. Look up old books if you have to. I need to know more about them—any weaknesses, any strengths, anything to avoid." I crossed my arms and then drummed my fingers, thinking. "It might help if we found out why someone bought that coffin, too. Check it for a ledger of purchase of some kind?"

She saluted me. "Daphne is on the prowl for clues to the mystery, Velma."

Great, I got to be Velma in the Scooby-Doo gang. Lucky me. "Just don't say anything to Rand, okay?" I glanced toward the kitchen, where I could hear him rattling about, opening drawers.

If at some point I had to take the guy out, it would be best to have the element of surprise.

Seven

At my side, Rand pushed his face against the glass window of the train, watching the nighttime scenery whizz past.

"Almost there," I told him.

"Miraculous," he murmured, keeping his voice low so the other passengers wouldn't pay attention. Not that he wasn't already drawing a ton of attention. But Italians seemed to keep their distance despite the fact that Rand was dressed like a medieval re-enactor and gasped at everything.

He'd gasped as the train had rolled into the station. Gasped at the escalator. Nearly lost his mind at the sight of a TV rolling commercials in the background. He'd jumped at some kid's remote control car. He'd been awed by a popcorn machine. He didn't seem to grasp the concept of cell phones, much less why everyone stared at the screen so much. I didn't let him play with mine, for fear I'd miss a text from Gemma. That, and I was afraid he'd drop it the first time it made a noise.

It was amusing and heartbreaking at the same time to watch Rand. I could tell by the expression on his face that he'd be delighted by a new discovery in one moment and incredibly sad the next, no doubt imagining how much time had passed. He ogled women in short dresses and eyed my cleavage as I sat on the train next to him. He sniffed everything I ate but would touch none of it.

And for the most part, he was silent as everyone around us chattered in Italian. Instead, he just sat and stared out the window as scenery zoomed past, though it was entirely too dark to make anything out.

I had no idea what he was thinking. I tried to imagine how I'd cope in his place, and failed miserably. Six hundred years from now, where would the world be? Would I even want to be around for it?

Did Rand?

My phone buzzed with a text. Gemma had been pinging me all night long with information. I glanced down at the screen and saw a lot of text and an image. While Rand couldn't read the words—at least, I didn't think so—I didn't want to incriminate myself with any pictures on my phone. "Hey, I'm going to go to the restroom. Be right back."

He pressed his nose to the glass, ignoring me.

Right. I got up and headed down the aisle of the train car, giving an awkward smile here and there to people as I moved past. When I made it to the bathroom, I locked the door, sat down on the seat, and pulled my phone out again.

So far, Gemma had been texting me with various tidbits gleaned from the internet. Unfortunately, most of it we already knew.

Vampires avoided sunlight.

Vampires hated garlic.

Vampires didn't like holy water or crosses.

Vampires couldn't cross running water.

Vampires couldn't enter a home without being invited.

Really, it wasn't all that interesting. As I glanced at her text this time, I wondered what image she'd sent that could possibly be of interest.

Hey bb, found this in ur coffin, along with a bill of lading. I think our peeps were into antiques and that's how ol' Rand got purchased.

The picture was of one of the receipts, and then what looked like an illuminated manuscript page of some kind. The writing was loopy and indecipherable. I squinted at it for a few minutes and then texted her back. What does it say?

I think it's In old English or something. I typed it into Google Translate and it spit something out at me about freedom being found at the heart of darkness and then something about a burrito.

A burrito?? I sent back. That has to be a mistranslation.

I know. I tried a different website and got something more along the lines of The heart of the darkness must be destroyed to have freedom. Only the Dragon can give you death's release.

Got it. Thanks, Gem.

I'll ping ya if I find any more goodies! XOXO

The train began to slow, and a voice came over the intercom, smoothly reciting stops in Italian. I pocketed my phone and dashed back to my seat just as the train headed toward the station. "Almost there," I told Rand again. "Once the train has stopped, we can get out and see about getting a hotel for the night. It might take some time to locate your friend, so it's best to be prepared in case we strike out before dawn."

"Mmm." He ran a finger down the glass window, watching the smear he left behind with fascination.

Only the Dragon can give you death's release. I considered that, gazing at Rand's shaggy, handsome head. Dragons weren't real, but then again, I hadn't thought vampires were either. God, I *hoped* dragons weren't real and it was just a clever euphemism for the Black Plague or something cheery like that. "So what's this friend's name?" I asked Rand. "Is he medieval like yourself? Or older?" It felt impolite to ask, but the thought of being around someone that was as old as Rand and hadn't been asleep for the last six hundred years disturbed me. What would he be like? I'd seen how ruthless Rand could get when he was hungry, how I'd reacted when he'd turned his charm on me. What would that be like around a truly old vampire? I shuddered to think. "And how do you know this friend will be happy to see you?"

"I imagine much has changed in six hundred

years, but I know William and Frederic will remain the same," he said. "Even Guy."

I looked at him in surprise. "Three vampires? We're looking for three?"

He shrugged. "There were four of us, originally. The Dragon's Claws, we were called."

I froze at the mention of "dragon." "Dragon's . . . claws?"

"Aye. Myself, William, Frederic, and Guy. We were four young knights, plucked from the ranks of obscurity to fight alongside the Dragon. He made us *upyri*, trained us as warriors, and turned us into his personal assassins. And while we might have resented the Dragon for controlling our lives, we bonded together, my brothers and I. If one yet lives, he will be happy to see me."

Ah. Okay, so Dragon was just a clever name for someone. I breathed a little easier. Only the Dragon could give Rand death's release. That made sense and went along with the vampire lore that Gemma had found.

Rand gazed around us, distant. "I do not feel Guy in this city. I feel William and Frederic, though they are both faint." He closed his eyes and became utterly still, as if searching inwardly for some sort of sign. After a long moment, he opened his eyes again. "Two brothers here in the city. But my connection to them is extremely slight. I do not know if it is because time has passed or if it is due to something else."

"Which begs another question," I pointed out. "If you can feel them, and they can feel you . . ."

"Why did no one come to save me? Why did they let me molder in a coffin for six hundred years?" He nodded, gazing out the window again. "I have asked the same question, over and over again, and I can come to no pleasing solution."

"You must have had enemies," I protested. "Someone you pissed off?"

His jaw clamped. "Enough to murder?"

I shrugged. "You tell me."

He shook his head, as if unwilling to believe it. I had no suggestions either, so we fell into silence.

The train stopped, and I put my fingers on Rand's arm to keep him in place as people surged to their feet around us. If someone brushed up against his cold skin, they might react badly. Best to keep our distance. When the train was nearly emptied of passengers, we got to our feet and exited. I slung my purse over my shoulder and looked around the station, still busy despite the late hour. "Which way does your spidey sense tell you we should go?"

"My what?"

Gah. Every conversation with the guy was a dead end. "Never mind. Your blood sense or whatever. The thing that lets you tell where the other vampires are. What is it telling you?"

He closed his eyes and turned slowly, then pointed

off in one direction. "There. They're both coming from there."

"Okay, great," I told him, pulling out my phone. "I'll look up a nearby hotel and we can get set up, and then we can head off . . ." I trailed off. I'd looked up, and Rand was gone. "Um, Rand?"

People milled around me, happily chatting. No one was a weird medieval guy dressed in a skirted tunic and leggings.

"Rand?" Oh crap, had I lost a medieval vampire at a train station?

A hand grabbed my arm.

I shrieked, only to turn and slap at Rand's arm when I realized it was him. "Don't freaking grab me!" God, I was going to have a heart attack before this was over.

He gave me a dismissive look. "Come, Lindsey. We must waste no time." His expression was serious. Gone was the laughing flirt from before, or even the awed man filled with wonder at a popcorn machine. This was the hunter, the warlord. "Follow me."

I wanted to protest. To take my time to get to know the city. To prep myself and my vampire kit. Instead, I followed him wordlessly, letting him drag me through the train station.

It was as if I was with a different person. Rand tore through the streets like a man possessed. It was all I could do to keep up with him, my feet racing as we sped down one street after another, leaping over medians and bushes, darting through alleyways and around parked bikes. "Wait," I called after him. "Let's take a taxi, all right?" When he ignored me, I tried again. "We'll get there even faster with a taxi."

That made him pause and he nodded, a wild look in his eyes as he scanned the streets. "Get this 'taxi,' then, and let us be on our way."

I watched Rand warily as I flagged down a taxi, then tried to explain to the driver in my limited Italian that we needed to go where Rand pointed.

"You race, yes?" the taxi cab driver asked me. "TV race?"

Were we on a game show? "Sure, whatever," I said. Whatever got the man moving. I handed him a wad of euros and gestured for Rand to get in next to me. I shut his door and buckled him in, and for the next ten minutes, we pointed at streets and tried to follow Rand's directions . . .

. . . Which led us to a graveyard. The Protestant Cemetery of Rome.

"No, no, no," I whispered under my breath. I did not want to go into a damn graveyard looking for vampires. I gazed at the thick stone wall, the decorative crenellations at least ten feet above my head. There was a massive door, and guards patrolled the way in front.

"Is closed," our cab driver pointed out. "You wait until morning?"

I looked over at Rand, but he was already pushing at the door of the cab, trying to figure a way out. I reached over and popped the handle on his door. "We'll get out here." I paid the driver a few more euros, thanked him, and hopped out after Rand.

"So what are we doing?" I asked as he strolled toward the wall. One of the guards was standing a few feet away, but he hadn't noticed us yet. When he did, I suspected things would get ugly.

Rand touched the door. "I sense both of them in there." He pushed on the door, and it made a creaking, groaning noise.

"Stop," I said, swatting his hands. "We can't go in there right now." A plaque on the wall said visiting hours were 9:00 a.m. to 5:00 p.m. At this rate, we'd never get inside, considering that vampires couldn't come out in sunlight.

He ignored me. Instead, he took a few steps back and studied the wall. It was shorter the farther away one got from the door, and he began to pace down the length of it. "We're getting in."

"What about the guard?"

As if attuned to my voice, the guard began jogging toward us. "*Scuzi*," he called out.

Faster than I could blink, Rand had the man by his neck. He sank his fangs deep, and as I stared in shock, he began to drink. The guard's eyes went wide and then he shuddered, his body stiffening in an expression of what could only be pure ecstasy.

"Rand!" I hissed. "You can't do that!" Oh my God. I glanced around the empty street to see if anyone had noticed. We were totally going to jail now. What was I going to do if I ended up in an Italian jail? What would Rand do once daylight hit?

But the vampire ignored me. He continued to drink from the twitching guard, who wasn't fighting him in the slightest. A moment later, the guard's eyes rolled back and he fell limply to the ground.

Rand released him, setting him down gently. Then he licked red-tinged lips and looked up at me. "Shall we go?"

I just stared at him. "I cannot believe you did that! Did you just kill that man?"

He gave a small shake of his head. "Only drank enough to make him lose consciousness. Come. We haven't much time before he awakens and wonders what happened." He strode toward the doors again and gave them another shake.

"Oh jeez," I murmured to myself. I stepped over the guard, then, as Rand tugged at the door again, I leaned down and unclipped the key ring from the guard's belt. "Here, let me do it. If I'm going to be an accomplice, I suppose I'd better go all in." I pushed past Rand and began to try keys. A moment later, I had the door unlocked and I swung it open, gesturing Rand should lead.

His hand clasped mine and he tugged me forward.

As he did, I noticed his fingers weren't ice-cold underneath mine. "How come your skin is warm?"

"Borrowed heat," he said softly, scanning the crowded-looking cemetery. "The guard's blood will warm me for a short time."

"Oh." I should have found that disturbing, but instead, I couldn't help but cling to his hand. There was something comforting about the feel of his warm skin under mine. It made him a little less distant, a little more real.

"Come," Rand said. "This way." He led me forward into the night.

The cemetery wasn't wired for lighting. Actually, I was surprised the cemetery was still open for business . . . or whatever it was that cemeteries did. Trees and foliage seemed to cover almost every inch of ground, and gravestones were dotted and clustered in claustrophobic fashion. As graveyards went, this one was creepier than most, simply because of the sheer amount of people squeezed into the small space.

Rand unerringly headed toward the back of the place, tugging on my hand. There was no point in asking where we were going—it was obvious the moment my eyes adjusted to the moonlight. A large marble mausoleum sat at the far end of the property, looming over the tumble of graves. Once we made it there, Rand stopped.

He looked at me. "I can go no further. You must go on from here."

"Me?" My voice squeaked. "What?"

"They are beyond this door," Rand said. He placed a hand on the iron door of the mausoleum, and immediately I heard the soft sizzle of something burning. He pulled away and showed me his palm, dark and blistered from a burn. "Hallowed ground."

I groaned. "You're kidding, right? Please tell me you're kidding."

"I do not lie." His face was unusually pale, his expression somber. "Please, Lindsey. Do this for me."

I think that was the first time I'd ever heard Rand say "please." It threw me off. I stared at the doorway. Bad enough that I was in a graveyard with a vampire after dark. Now he wanted me to go raid a mausoleum by myself? "Can I ask a stupid question? If you can't get through that door because it's hallowed, how can they possibly—"

"I know," he said, and his voice was rough with emotion. "But I must know for certain. All I can tell you is that with the bond I share with the Dragon's Claws, I can sense their blood. And I sense the blood of both William and Frederic behind that door. I cannot leave this place until I find out their fate for certain."

Oh. I stared at him.

This wasn't a "meet up with buddies" mission any longer. This was a search for answers. Rand suspected they were dead, and he needed to know the truth.

And I was the only one who could give him that truth. My stomach knotted unhappily, but I nodded and turned to the door. "All right. I'll check it out."

I closed my eyes and put my hand on the doorknob, hoping vainly for a brief moment that it would be locked. Unfortunately, it swung open, and I had no choice but to step inside.

The interior of the mausoleum was small in comparison to the exterior. The interior was a small room with a bench along one wall, facing an alcove of decorative urns that had name plaques under each one. Oh no. I turned to look at Rand through the open door, hating that this was happening. "Do you still feel them here?"

"Tell me what you see." His pale face was expressionless. "Is it them?"

I bent and read each plaque, my fingers brushing over the engraved lettering. The two oldest names were the ones I sought. Frederic Arnault, died January 8, 1763. William de Beauchamp, died January 8, 1763. There were no other Frederics or Williams. I swallowed hard. "I'm sorry, Rand. It looks like they died two hundred fifty years ago. Same day." I looked at the small urns. "These must be their ashes."

"That . . ." His voice cracked, and then he cleared his throat. "That must be why they felt so faint. It doesn't feel the same as when they were alive. More like an echo or a memory." His fists clenched and he turned away, his head bent.

I bit my lip, hurting for him. I'd started tonight hoping we'd find a vampire, and now we had two dead ones. There was no happy friend to drop Rand off with. No pleasant reunion for him. His friends were gone. Long gone. And he was the only one that remained. Tears pricked my eyes. "Maybe . . . maybe there's a secret door or something, like where I found you. Maybe they're just hiding."

"They're dead," he said harshly. "I knew it, but did not want to believe." He glanced over his shoulder. "Come. We shall leave this place."

"But what about your other friend?" I struggled to think of the name. "Guy? Do you feel him? You said you could feel all three of them, right?"

"I feel Guy," he said as I stepped out of the mausoleum and shut the door quietly behind me. "I feel him, and I do not know what to think. He is faint, but his echo moves back and forth, unlike the others. They were static. So he is alive. I get pulses of emotion from him."

"That's good, right? We can find him and you can go visit him?"

Rand's hollow gaze turned to me. "And if he was the one that staked me? The one that destroyed William and Frederic? What then?"

My eyes widened. "Do you think he did that? I thought you were like brothers."

"I thought so, too, but yet here I am." He spread his arms. "Betrayed. And William and Frederic were destroyed together. The same year. The same date. If it was Guy that did it, should I run to him and embrace him like a brother?"

"What are you going to do?"

"I am going to find out who did this," Rand said, voice even. He took my hand in his and escorted me down the steps of the mausoleum. "We are going to find Guy, and we are going to get answers. And if it was Guy that betrayed Frederic and William and trapped me, then I will pull his heart from his chest and feed it to him." His hand fell to my shoulder, possessive. "And I will need your help to do so, Lindsey. You must remain my blood vassal and my guide in this quest."

Yep. Somehow, I'd known he was going to say that. "Rand, I don't know," I stammered. "I need to get back and help Gemma with the apartment. There's so much work to be done, and all of our finances are riding on things—"

"But you must help me, Lindsey." Rand brought my hand to his lips—still warm from his stolen blood—and kissed the back of it. "For you are the only person I have left."

Aw, jeez. How could I say no to that?

Eight

Okay," I said, trying to keep calm. "We'll get this figured out. First things first. We'll get a hotel, call Gemma, regroup, and decide what our next steps are to get you settled." I pulled out my cell phone. "This is just a setback. We—"

I swallowed the rest of my words because he grabbed my hand and began to drag me through the graveyard. "Um, Rand?" I stumbled behind him, narrowly missing tripping over a headstone. "Where are we going?"

"We are going to find weapons. I will not go around this city without protection."

"We can't carry weapons!"

His hand tightened on mine, and his fingers felt less warm than before. "My friends are dead," he said, voice bitter and clipped with anger. "I have enemies all around. I refuse to walk about without protection. I do not care what the laws of this time and place are. I have never cared what the laws are. A sword makes the law."

"But—"

He turned so quickly that I nearly ran into him. His hand went to my chin, and he forced me to look into his eyes. "Lindsey," he said, the tone of his voice strange. I noticed an odd flare of color in his eyes, like a flash of green in the deep blue.

And then I couldn't look away. It was like I was hypnotized. I stared, entranced.

"Find me a weapons broker," he said, voice low and thrumming. "That is what I wish right now. Weapons."

Even though my mind knew it was a bad idea, I was helpless to disobey. "We should look for a rare dealer," I told him. "Let me check my phone."

"Do so quickly," he said, that strange flash in his eyes.

I fumbled with my phone, typing as fast as I could. Sure enough, there was a rare arms dealer a few streets over. I mapped the instructions, and then we set off, Rand dragging me along by my hand. As we exited the cemetery, Rand released my hand. "Wait here."

I couldn't have moved if I'd wanted to.

He stepped forward and crouched near the fallen guard. As I watched, he leaned over and tapped the man's cheek. The guard blinked awake, then his gaze was caught by Rand's.

Rand said something in Italian. The guard nodded, that blank look on his face. He got up, straightened his uniform, and began to walk away in the other direction, as if we weren't there. I watched his unnatural movement and set his keys down on the pavement, just in case he decided to come looking for them.

Something about this was very wrong, but it was like one level of my brain had shut off. I wanted to protest all of this but couldn't. It was like I was a puppet and Rand was pulling the strings.

"Let us go," Rand said to me, taking my hand again. "I wish to get weapons before it gets too late in the evening."

"What did you say to him?" I asked as Rand began to drag me behind him again.

"I told him to forget what he'd seen here." Rand surged forward, hauling me over a median.

I sputtered at that. He could just tell someone to forget and they would? This was mind control. I suspected he was using mind control on me, too, because the more I tried to pry my hand from his and protest where we were going, the more my mind shut down and refused to obey. So I trotted behind Rand like a good little soldier as I called out directions to the weapons shop, all the while mentally seething that I couldn't disobey. He was using mind control on me? That utter shit. How dare he? Did he think I didn't have feelings? That I wouldn't help him?

Because that ship sure had sailed the moment he'd decided to take the decision away from me.

We arrived at the weapons shop to see the store closed. It was one of those buildings where the living quarters were nestled over the shop, and I guessed someone was home even if the lights were out. Still, I didn't want to force our way in if we didn't have to. "We should come back later," I told Rand. "They're not open right now. You can tell me what you want, and I can come buy it in the morning."

"No," Rand said. "We are purchasing our things now. I refuse to leave without weapons."

"But it's not like you're defenseless," I protested, even as he let go of my hand. The man had super-strength and fangs and hypnotic eyes. Of course he wasn't defenseless. It was all in his mind, this obsession with finding a stinking sword or two. "Just let it go for now, Rand."

"No. Wait here."

A command? Ugh. I crossed my arms and glared at him as he studied the front door to the place. It was a small mom-and-pop shop with a heavy glass door nestled between two big windows that displayed old war collectables. In one window was an old cavalry saber and a helmet from World War II. I watched as Rand tested the doorknob and shook the door.

He turned to me, clearly impatient. "Can you open this?"

"It's locked."

"How can we get in?"

That felt compulsively like a command, and I found myself answering, "You'd have to break in."

"Then that is what we shall do." He pulled back one fist, and before I could protest, he slammed it through the glass.

It shattered into a thousand pieces and I flinched backward.

He looked at me expectantly.

"What?" I hissed at him, crouching so no one would see me.

"Invite me in." He gestured at the door.

"Invite you in? Why?" I stared at him like he was crazy. Maybe he was. "It's not my house! Why would I invite you in?"

This time, Rand rolled his eyes at me. "Vampires cannot enter a dwelling unless they are invited."

"Oh, great. Just frickin' great," I muttered. "Any other vampire trivia you want to impart to me while we're at it?"

"We cannot cross running water," he said, ticking off each fact on a finger. "We cannot walk on hallowed ground. We cannot see the daylight. Stakes—"

"Okay, okay," I told him. "We don't have all night." I reached through the broken glass and fumbled on the other side of the door, then flipped the lock. I opened the door, stepped through, and gave him a mocking bow. "Please come in, Lord Vampire."

If Rand noticed my snark, he didn't show it. Or

he just didn't care. He pushed past me, entering the shop and looking around as if he'd owned the place. I stared around us in horror, waiting for the local police to suddenly swarm, but no one showed up. Jesus. This was like a nightmare come to life. I watched as Rand took a few more steps in, and I took another step backward, exiting out into the street. No way was I following him. No freaking way.

"Come, Lindsey," Rand said.

Damn it. Damn it damn it damn it. I stepped inside.

The store was small, full of war memorabilia from different time periods. Most of it didn't catch my eye, but I watched as Rand headed unerringly toward a glass case in the back full of swords.

"Please, can we just go?" I asked, shivering in fear. He might be able to get out of a breaking and entering plea with his vampire powers, but I wouldn't be able to. "We shouldn't be here."

"I will get my weapons and then we will be on our way," Rand said, ignoring me. He pressed his hands to the glass case and eyed the contents. "How do you suppose we get into this? Should I just smash it?"

"I imagine there's a key somewhere," I began, then fell silent at the sound of a pair of feet thumping down the stairs.

In the corner of the shop, a woman appeared, slightly older than me, her figure thicker. Her hair was wild, and she wore a bathrobe, and it was clear we'd woken her from her sleep. She said something in Italian and looked at me, then at Rand. Her words took on a higher-pitched tone, and I heard the word *polizia*.

Oh God. "Rand, we have to go *now*."

"We're not leaving," he told me. Instead, he pointed at the case and spoke to the lady in Italian. Her voice went up a hysterical note again. Rand flung himself away from the case and began to stalk toward her.

Oh no, no, no. I watched in horror as Rand grabbed her and, as if things were moving in slow motion, pulled her against him to drink from her throat. This was like a bad movie. Her limbs twitched, then she gave a soft, breathless moan that made my body respond despite myself. I hugged my arms to my body, watching in horror as he drank from her. When she went limp, he set her gently to the ground.

This was all wrong. So, so wrong. I couldn't do this.

He straightened and wiped his mouth with one sleeve. He glanced back at me and flicked his eyebrows, as if pleased with how things were going. "Come and open this case for me, Lindsey."

Just like that? As if I was nothing to him but another tool? Another person to be used? Resentment and fear bubbled inside me. Because I was helpless to disobey Rand's commands, I moved to the shopkeeper, searched her pockets for keys, and opened the case. The glass doors swung to the side and Rand stepped in, admiring the selection before him.

I automatically moved to the entrance of the shop, leaving the keys on the counter. I couldn't stop shivering. I looked over at Rand, but he was touching the hilt of one sword, brows drawn in a thoughtful expression.

It would be so easy to get away, if only he'd let me. Tentatively, I took a step outside to see if I could.

I could.

I looked back at Rand, heart hammering. He remained with his back turned to me, studying the swords intently. I realized his last command to me had been for me to unlock the case. Now that that was done, he was no longer controlling me. I took a few more quiet steps out the door, checked to see if he was paying attention, and bolted.

I ran, my lungs hammering, as if the hounds of hell were at my feet. I didn't know where I was running, the only thing I knew was *away*. Away from Rand. Away from the vampire who used and controlled and scared me. I didn't want to be a puppet. I flung myself down one side street and then another, trying to make my path as hard to follow as possible. As I ran, I looked for a taxi. All I needed was one to stop and I could get away. Then I'd be free once more. Rand couldn't bother me again because I'd go back to Venice right away, and Rand wouldn't be able to enter the apartment without my permission. I just needed one smooth getaway. Right into someone's home, maybe, because I could enter and Rand could not. I spotted a hotel down the street and sprinted, my purse slamming against my hip. That was almost like a home, right? That would work, and I wouldn't invite Rand in, because—

A hard arm grabbed me by the waist and spun me around, knocking me off my feet.

I screamed.

A cool hand clamped over my mouth, and I felt the scrape of fangs against my throat. "Shhh, Lindsey," Rand said, even as he pulled me into the shadows of a nearby building. "Not so loud. I thought you did not wish to attract attention?"

Yeah, but that was before the vampire went all crazy on me. Now I just wanted to get away from him. My heart pounded like a frightened rabbit's, and I didn't respond. Instead, I struggled in his iron grip, trying futilely to get away.

"Why are you running from me?" Rand asked. He was plainly puzzled by my behavior. "What is wrong?"

I shoved against his grip again, hating how strong he was. "You! You're what's wrong!"

"What did I do?"

"How can you not know?" I pushed at his chest, hating how he felt like stone against me. He wouldn't let go of me; he just held tighter. "You're on a rampage," I hissed at him. "First the guard at the cemetery, now the lady at the store? Who next? Are you going to drain half the city of blood and leave a path of destruction in your wake?"

"Does it matter?" he asked coldly.

"It matters to me," I said, slamming a hand against his chest. To my horror, I felt angry, frustrated tears coming to my eyes. "It matters to me because I'm frightened and you won't listen to reason. Because you're breaking the law and using people like they're nothing to you. You're using *me*. I'm not a meal. I'm not a tool. I'm supposed to be your fucking friend!" And damn it, I'd just cussed at the man, but he deserved it. I hammered a fist on his chest again, knowing it wouldn't get him to release me, knowing it wouldn't hurt, but not caring. "We're supposed to be a team, and you're running around trying to get us both killed."

Rand stared at me, those incredibly blue eyes blazing with a mixture of emotions.

A sob caught in my throat. "I know you don't want to be in this world, but I freaking care what happens to me and you, you know. You can't keep doing this. I'm not someone to be used and discarded like trash."

The steely arm around my waist softened. "You're frightened."

"Of course I'm frightened," I said, a hiccup in my throat. "You're controlling me just like you're controlling everyone else. Why wouldn't I be terrified of you? It's clear I'm nothing to you but another . . . thing . . . you can just use to get your way."

Was this how Gemma felt when I got all controlling on her? Guilt shot through me. I really needed to be a better friend, didn't I?

"That is not true, Lindsey. You are *not* nothing to me," Rand said in a soft voice. His hand cupped my chin.

I pulled away violently, averting my gaze. "No! I don't want you to hypnotize me again!"

"Shhh," he soothed. "I won't. I promise. You have my vow as one of the Dragon's Claws." When I still wouldn't turn to look at him, he added, "I swear on the bones of my brothers William and Frederic."

I paused. That didn't seem like something he would throw out there unless he meant it, given the events of tonight. Reluctantly, I looked up at him, meeting his gaze.

"I am sorry, Lindsey," Rand said, voice soft. His fingers caressed my cheek. "I have made you afraid of me, and that wasn't my intent. This is . . . difficult for me. I have been 'using people,' as you say, for over two hundred years. It will be hard for me to change."

"Well, try," I said, hurt. "I've upended my entire life to help you out, and all I'm getting out of this is scared." And probably my face tacked on to a Most Wanted poster.

Rand's expression became sad. "I'm scared, too. Nothing is as I thought it would be. I cannot even look back on my past fondly, because now I see enemies in every corner. All I know is that I must somehow fix things."

"This isn't the way to do it," I said softly. "This is just going to make things worse in the long run. I promise that."

"Then help me, Lindsey, please. I need you. You are the only person I can trust."

I stared up at him, uncertain. "You have to promise to never do the mind control thing again. You can't use me if we're going to be partners. Because I should be with Gemma, helping her clean out the apartment. I should be working. I should be making money, not here in Rome, breaking and entering."

"I know," he said softly. "All these things, I know. And yet you are here with me. I am grateful, even if I don't show it properly."

"If we're going to do this, we're going to be equals," I told him. "Equals in *everything*. If one of us doesn't like a decision, we get a say in things. Understand? No more of this running off and doing what you want despite what I say. If we disagree, we talk it out."

"Equals," he agreed, then tilted his head, assessing me. "This will be a big change for me. I have never considered a woman an equal before."

I patted his chest. "We're both going to ignore that you said that."

He laughed. "I like it! It is a refreshing change." He took my hand in his and released me from his embrace. "If ever there was a woman to equal a man, it is you, Lindsey."

I wasn't sure if that was a compliment or not, but I'd take it. "Women have been men's equals for a while now, so get used to it."

"I shall."

I gestured at myself. "I'm serious. Equal in everything. You and me." I pointed at him. "Swear it."

He cocked a brow at me. "Shall I give you the kiss of fealty?"

"I think your lips have been enough places tonight," I said primly.

Rand laughed. "I see you blush, Lindsey. If it is but a simple kiss between equals, why does it embarrass you?"

Was he goading me? Jerk. What was worse was the fact that I was going to fall for it. I thought about offering a handshake, but if it didn't mean anything to him, what was the point? "Fine, then, a kiss of fealty and we'll regroup and figure out a new plan. Deal?"

"Very well," Rand said. He pulled me against him once more. "I am sorry I have frightened you, Lindsey. It was not my intent. I have not been myself tonight. Forgive me?"

"For now," I said softly. "But we can't let it happen again."

"I will be more careful," he told me. "I will think before I act, and I will consult you. You are my guide in this strange land, and I should trust you."

"You should," I agreed.

"Shall we kiss to seal our bargain?"

"It feels like I just agreed to kiss the devil," I muttered, but I tilted my head back.

The look Rand gave me was surprisingly intense just before he brushed his lips against mine. And the kiss? It was anything but chaste. His mouth was warm against mine, which should have been a danger signal, but it was drowned out by the fact that his lips caressed my own, and his tongue flicked against mine in a quiet invitation. It was supposed to be a short, quick, businesslike kiss, but as his mouth moved over mine and I melted against him, I realized there was nothing fealty-like in this at all.

And God help me, I wasn't sure I cared.

Nine

Rand and I sat at a dark booth in a small restaurant. There were drunks at the bar, but it was late at night and our choices for dining weren't plentiful. I spun my fork into my pasta noodles, stifling a yawn. "So let's go over our plan of attack one more time, okay?" After a moment, I added, "And when I say plan of attack, I mean it in the most figurative sense of the word."

Rand just stared at me over his coffee. "I understand nothing of what you just said."

"It's because I'm tired," I told him. "I'm not choosing my words carefully." If I had been, I sure wouldn't have picked *attack* around a vampire with control issues.

But it was extra late, heading toward dawn. My entire body was dragging with the need for sleep. Rand was super-antsy, so after we'd checked into a hotel room, I'd suggested heading down to the bar-slash-restaurant to get some late-night food. It kept me from thinking about the fact that I was going to have to share a room with him. My credit card wasn't unlimited, and I hadn't planned on this being a multiple-night thing, which it now was.

Nor had I planned on Rand going on a blood-sucking rampage through Rome at the deaths of his friends and making me afraid of him. These sorts of things tended to make a girl think twice.

So here we were, Rand drinking coffee he couldn't stand, and me eating noodles I didn't want, all because neither of us wished to retire just yet.

Rand wasn't in a talkative mood, though. I supposed that was understandable, given all we'd gone through tonight. He toyed with the ceramic mug, not drinking.

So I did my best to keep conversation flowing. "Tomorrow," I told him, "will be a better day. We'll get our feet underneath us. First things first, though. We need to get you some normal clothes. Some good shoes, some underwear, maybe a nice jacket or some-thing. We'll get stuff that will hide your weapons, since you insist on carrying them around."

Rand and I had argued again once we'd gotten to the hotel. He'd wanted to keep a sword strapped to his side at all times, and I'd tried to point out various laws that wouldn't allow something like that. We'd eventually compromised, and Rand was now wear-ing matching daggers under his tunic and one slipped into a boot. While he didn't stand out as much as he had with a sword, I'd still be happier if he was dressed like a normal guy so he wouldn't call as much attention to himself.

"Once we get some clothing, we should probably return to Venice and regroup with Gemma. We can get you settled in the apartment while we figure out the next course of action. I mean, it's not the most spacious place, but I'm sure we can set up a room for you."

He looked at me thoughtfully over his coffee. "I'm not returning to Venice."

I frowned as I chewed my fettuccine. What had happened to the "let's work on a plan together" part of being partners? Once I swallowed, I asked, "So where do you want to go, then?"

He closed his eyes and turned his head, as if sensing something. Then he looked back to me. "I still feel Guy. He is alive somewhere. North, perhaps. Austria? Brittany? Perhaps Prussia. I must find him. I must find out the truth of what has happened. Of why I was targeted, and why both Frederic and William were killed on the same day. Why he is the only one of the Claws that survives. Only then can I settle in and claim a new life for myself. And if Guy does not have answers, I must find the Dragon himself."

"Why not head straight to the source?" I asked. I suppressed a shiver, remembering the warning scroll Gemma had read. The Dragon was the big vampire hub, it seemed. "The Dragon is the one with all the answers. Maybe we should just go after him." At the cold look Rand gave me, I added, "What? Is that bad?"

Why were so many unpleasant things pointing back to the Dragon? None of this could be coincidence.

"The Dragon is not a man one wishes to know." He shook his head. "I would avoid bringing you to him. Your blood is a sweet taste, and if he decided he wanted you, there would be nothing I could do to keep you safe."

I pushed the food around on my plate, not hungry anymore. Great. Now I was in danger simply because I tasted yummy. I needed details. "So . . . why don't you tell me about this Dragon guy? How did you meet him? Did you ask to be a vampire?"

He looked at me as if I were insane. "Ask to be *upyri*? One might as well ask to be damned to hell."

I blinked. "That seems harsh."

"It is not the life one would choose. And no, I did not choose it." His mouth curled a bit at the edges, as if amused by the thought. "Do you see anything admirable in my form, then, Lindsey? Something that one would admire and wish to become?"

"Well." I hesitated. "You're strong. You can charm people with a look. And apparently you're immortal. Some people would really like those powers."

"Some would," he agreed, looking thoughtful. "Some would also point out that I am bound by more laws than ever before. I cannot enter a place without being invited. I cannot see the sunlight ever again. I cannot cross hallowed ground. I cannot pass running water. I can be taken out by a tiny stick of wood in the heart."

"Hey now," I said, pointing my fork at him. "I'd like to point out that I can also be taken out by a stick of wood in the heart. That's not exclusive to vampires."

He chuckled. "I think you like to put me in my place."

Maybe I did. "All I'm saying is that there are some bum raps out there, and while yours isn't the best, you have to agree that it does have some perks."

Rand was silent for a long moment, staring at his cup of coffee for so long that I wondered if I'd somehow angered him again. I began to poke at my food, when he finally spoke once more. "I was born a bastard, you know. My mother was the daughter of a blacksmith and my father was a marcher lord. She died in childbirth, and I was left with a grandfather who did not want to claim me and a father who was amused by me but wanted nothing to do with me. He had three other legitimate sons, you see. A bastard is only useful to shine their boots and feed the horses. In other words, I was just like any other servant to him." He shrugged. "I think the other servants did not get kicked nearly as often as I did. The lady of the castle did not like me much."

I put down my fork, feeling uncomfortable again. Just when I thought Rand's story couldn't get any sadder, he put a new spin on things for me.

"When I got older, I grew tired of it. I didn't like being treated as if I didn't matter. As if I were filth because my mother had been a blacksmith's daughter instead of a highborn lady. One of my brothers, you see, looked just like me, except he had bad teeth. I think his mother hated me especially because I had good teeth and Sigmund did not." He grinned, giving me a flash of those pearly white fangs. "The older I got, the worse things became, until one day I was caught speaking with a maid that one of my brothers had his eye on. They cracked three of my ribs and blackened both of my eyes and I could not fight back, because they were the lord's legitimate sons."

"That's horrible."

"Mmm." Rand traced a finger around the lip of his coffee cup. "They were not kind men, my brothers. The local priest patched me up and said last rites on me in case I should die of a pierced lung during the night. It was a good thing that he did, because as I lay in his care, I met a traveling knight."

"The Dragon?"

He shook his head. "The Dragon comes much later in this tale. This knight was leaving to join the Lionheart's Crusade, you see. It was a quest to retake the Holy Land from the infidels that had infested it. A mission from God. And I was so desperate for a new life and a chance to be seen as anything other than a bastard boy that I immediately volunteered my services. I left without telling a soul, even though I should have sought my lord's permission first. No one truly cared what a bastard did, after all." His lip curled slightly. "No one came after me."

My heart twinged with sadness, picturing a younger Rand, all skinny legs and bright blue eyes. I pictured him tanned by the sun, his hair a few shades lighter than the dark brown color it was now.

"We joined the Archbishop of Canterbury, who was encouraging men across England to take up arms for a holy army of God. I believe the year was either 1187 or 1188." He shrugged. "I did not feel particularly holy or driven to serve God, but it sounded like a grand adventure to a boy like myself. By the time we finally reached Jerusalem, though, it had been many years and many battles later. I was no longer a young, idealistic boy, and I no longer thought God was blessing one side over the other. It was one terrible battle after another, with both sides committing atrocities. At this time, I was the squire of an elderly gentleman who had seen my tireless fighting in the field, and although I was not noble, he made me his new squire when his died of pleurisy. His name was Frederic."

"The Frederic from before?"

Rand nodded, and for a long moment he was quiet. "He was a good man. Very kind. Scholarly. I think he believed we were truly doing God's work in Jerusalem . . . for a time. Then came Ayyadieh."

"Ayyadieh?"

"It was a hill outside the city of Acre." The look

on Rand's face was far away. "We had just captured Acre after a long siege. The garrison there was more than two thousand men, women, and children. Maybe three thousand. King Saladin of Jerusalem wanted his prisoners back. The Lionheart wanted his English prisoners back, but they could not agree as to which ones should be exchanged. King Richard grew tired of waiting, and he had all of the Musulmen prisoners executed. All of them. All men. All women. All children. He had them beheaded where the infidel troops could see them." Rand looked down at his coffee cup, toying with it. "Some of the men on the enemy side were so upset that they charged at us and tried to save them, only to be slaughtered themselves. It was not a good day. War is an ugly thing." He rubbed his jaw and looked sick at the memory. "I still think of them."

My heart ached. "That sounds awful. So awful."

"It was. I can still hear the screams in my head sometimes. I have seen many terrible things wrought in the name of God and glory, but that, I think, will forever haunt me."

I shook my head, stunned. "I can't even imagine." The horrors he was relating in such a casual voice were unthinkable. Yet I knew from the miserable look on his face that they were all true.

He nodded. "Frederic lost heart at that. A day or two later, we found out that Saladin retaliated and killed all Christian prisoners he held. It was a terrible time on both sides, but I do not think King Richard cared. All he was interested in was waging more war. So even though we were tired, dispirited, and questioning ourselves, he drove us onward, seeking his next victory. Frederic and I never made it, though. We were captured in a skirmish and brought to Saladin's army, along with a few other soldiers. One of the captured men was a knight called Guy de Verdun, and another was William de Beauchamp. We were dragged through the desert behind Saladin's men, who were still angry at how their people had been massacred in Acre. Rightfully so, I might add. And we were brought near Jaffa to await our fate. We knew what it would be."

"Death," I guessed.

He gave a small nod of his head, still studying his mug of coffee intently. "The infidels were still furious over the deaths of the people of Acre. They thought us heartless and cruel. They thought us the infidels trying to steal their land. Interesting, is it not? Yet we were convinced God had sent us to murder the enemy and their children." He shook his head. "We knew death awaited us. The moment Saladin arrived, we would be beheaded in front of him and his men. We accepted our fates, inasmuch as anyone can."

"What did you do?"

"We prayed, of course. But everything changed when a new man arrived. He came after dark, escorted by his own contingent of troops. And he was called Al Tineen by the enemy. I learned later that it means 'the dragon.'"

My eyes widened. "He saved you?"

Rand's smile grew thin-lipped. "Saved me? I do not know if it was that he saved me inasmuch as he indentured me into a new kind of servitude. But yes, he rode into camp. And we were very shocked when he slaughtered all of the men around us save for a few that he deemed worthy. When he rounded up all of the survivors, there were six prisoners and six Musulmen. He gave us a choice. We could swear fealty to him and fight, or we could die. His men fought like dervishes. Like nothing I had ever seen before." Rand gave a small shake of his head. "I was fascinated despite myself, and I wanted to live. So I agreed. And because I did, Frederic agreed as well. Those of us that chose to live were eight in number, and that was too many for the Dragon, so he had us fight each other. The four of us that remained were declared 'special.' Al Tineen took us into his ranks, and once we were fed, clothed, and back to our full strength, he turned us into *upyri* so we could better serve him. And I served him for the next two hundred years."

Two hundred years. Wow. I couldn't fathom. "What . . . what kind of stuff did you do for him?"

"War." He shrugged. "Despicable, terrible things. I was a warlord under him. I went from squire to commander. Under the Dragon, all fell under my command.

I spoke on his behalf, and warriors answered. In return, I gave the Dragon my fealty."

That explained the bossiness and the people-using. "And the Dragon . . . what was he like?"

"He was not an infidel, if that is what you ask." Rand looked thoughtful. "He was old when I met him. Centuries old. No one knows exactly how old. Like a snake, he changes skins over and over again so people are at ease. A man who comes to the land a stranger is more trustworthy than a man who never ages and roosts atop a pile of bones. The Dragon learned that long ago, so he would always travel, always seek new places. I learned that much from him. Under his banner, we took up many names and many identities, discarding them when they were no longer of use to us."

I shook my head. "And so you don't want to find this Dragon?"

His smile was rueful. "Why should I? The last two days are the first bit of true freedom I have had in the last two hundred years. I am only regretful it came at such a high cost. I am not yet certain it was worth it. Nor am I certain it will last."

"What do you mean?"

He gave his coffee a nudge in my direction. I noticed it had not been drunk, not a single drop. He'd simply played with the mug the entire time. "Because once the Dragon figures out I have returned, he will either come to retrieve me, or he will come to finish the job."

Only the Dragon can give you death's release. "So what will you do?"

"I will do what any soldier would do in my position," Rand said, studying me. "I will attack first. I will find Guy and I will determine if he is with the Dragon or with me. And when I do, I will either destroy my old friend, or we will unite to take down the Dragon. One thing is for certain—I cannot go back to the way things were. *Ever again.*"

Ten

There was something utterly delicious about waking up in a hotel bed, buried underneath a mountain of covers, a plush pillow under your head and a big, warm male body pressed up against yours . . .

I blinked awake. "Um?"

A hand stroked through my hair. "Your hair is very soft and clean, Lindsey. I have decided that I like the bathing habits of women in this time. You do not seem to be afraid of catching the plague."

"No plague," I told him sleepily. I really should have pulled away. Any moment now, I would.

Any. Moment. Now.

His fingers tugged through my long brown hair, fanning it over my shoulders. "You smell as wonderful as you taste. I like that. But then, there are a great many things I like about you."

"My smell and my taste. Great."

He chuckled, and I hated to admit that it made me quiver. Just a little. "Not just your smell and your taste. Your bravery. Your cleverness. Your concern for others. All of it is admirable."

That wasn't so bad, then. I yawned, trying not to notice that his fingers brushed my jawline as he played with my hair, and that it made my body respond. "How come you're warm?" I asked.

"The sun went down some time ago." His thumb brushed my lower lip. "I fed."

I stiffened in his arms, pulling away and sitting up in bed. All delicious sleepiness was gone. "Wait, what? You fed? From me?"

While I was *asleep*?

"Not from you," he said, gazing at me thoughtfully. There was a sleepy look of desire in his eyes that was making me tingle despite myself. Damn it. Wasn't I supposed to only want to jump his bones when he was hungry? Stupid body. Stupid hormones.

"Then who?"

He shrugged. "Another woman I found in the street. She did not smell nearly as pleasant as you." His sensual gaze swept over my body. "Or taste as succulent."

I blinked, then shook my head to clear it. Underneath all the compliments was an unpleasant little nugget. "You just snatched someone off the street and used them as your personal Slurpee?"

Rand studied me, and I could practically see the wheels turning in his head as he tried to digest my outrage. "I do not know this word, *Slurpee*. Nor did I snatch someone. A woman approached me and asked if I wished for a good time. I did." He shrugged. "I did indeed have a good time, though I have also had better with you."

Ohmigod. He drank from a hooker and then cuddled with me? I gave an outraged squeal. "Please tell me you showered before climbing into bed with me?"

He looked surprised. "Why are you offended? I thought you would be more upset if I drank from you without permission. You know you are my blood vassal of choice."

I pointed at the shower. "In there. *Now.* Do it. You do not cuddle with one woman while reeking of another."

A smile touched his lips. "Are you jealous you did not receive my full attentions?" He took my hand in his, and even though I tried to snatch it away, he caught it again and began to play with my fingers. "I was trying to spare you, Lindsey. I know you are fragile and soft and cannot be drunk from constantly, though I admit I would enjoy it muchly."

"Flattery will get you nowhere," I told him and pointed at the shower again.

He wiggled his eyebrows. "You are certain I won't catch the plague if I bathe?"

"You're a vampire," I told him. "Nice try with the medieval beliefs, though. Now, go shower."

His chuckle of laughter echoed even after he got up and sauntered to the restroom. I rubbed a hand

over my face, trying to wake up. Okay. Rand had already fed. I wondered why it irritated me. I wasn't
jealous. I wasn't. In reality, it was probably a good
thing, because I'd have my full strength, and we had
a big day—or night—ahead of us. First step, contact
Gemma and let her know that things weren't exactly
going to plan. Then we'd have to find some late-night
shops, get Rand outfitted like a normal guy. Then,
maybe a car rental—

"Lindsey?" Rand's voice came from the other side
of the bathroom door.

"I don't hear water running," I pointed out.
"Freaking shower already!"

"I do not know how to operate these things."

Oh, right. The man was just now figuring out
doorknobs. Okay, fine. "I'll come in. Are you decent?"

"Of course."

I entered the small bathroom and was confronted
by fully frontal medieval vampire. I stared, blinking
at the sight of him. Definitely not circumcised. Definitely a *show*er and not a *grow*er. I kept staring, even
though I knew I wasn't supposed to. It was like gazing at a perfect marble statue . . . with one very big
exception. Rand was far more built than anything that
had come out of the Renaissance. Dumbly, I stared
at his cock for a moment longer, then forced myself
to make eye contact with the smugly grinning man.
"I . . . I thought you said you were decent."

"Is this not?" He rubbed a hand on his belly, and

so naturally my gaze went there. "I like to think it is all very decent."

That ass. What was worse was that he was right. It was all extremely more than decent, and I hated that I was now going to think about it for the next several days. I forced myself to look up, and when I did, I noticed several scars on his pale chest. Old war wounds, perhaps? There was a history there, and I was interested, but I wasn't going to ask about it while he was naked and fresh from his latest blood vassal. So, blushing, I pushed past him and showed him how to turn on the shower. "Here. Go clean yourself. Have fun."

"In my time, a woman would scrub the back of a lord—"

"In my time, I'd shove your face into the tile for suggesting it," I retorted before he could even finish the sentence.

Rand burst out laughing. "Your spirit is one of the things I like best about you, Lindsey."

"Just shower already," I said, cheeks hot as I escaped the bathroom.

It was easy to tell when Rand had actually used the shower. A sharp cry, followed by "This is miraculous!" came from the bathroom. Then I got a play-by-play. "This water is hot! How is it so? Where is it coming from? Why is this soap so soft?"

I ignored all of it and tidied myself as best I could. I didn't have fresh clothes to change into, but my purse at least had a bit of makeup and a hairbrush, so I did what I could and put my shoes on, then pulled out my phone to text Gemma a bit while Rand discovered the magic of terry-cloth towels.

You there? I sent.

OMG yes! came the immediate reply. Did you deliver the package? Were you sad to see him off? Did you give him one last suck before sending him on his way? And by suck I mean taste, not that you couldn't suck the rest of him, you know. But I didn't mean it as dirty as it sounded. Well, actually, I might have.

Sometimes I was amazed at how fast Gemma could text. Change of plans, I sent. His friend? Dead. Actually 2 friends dead.

WHAT?

Don't worry—they died in 1760 or something. Rand was sensing their ashes or something.

Oh no. Poor baby. Did you give him a pity fuck to distract him?

No!

Aw. But you guys would make a cute couple. I've been totally shipping it ever since you two left. That and I'm bored here by myself. No one to talk to. At least you're with a hottie vampire who wants to bone you.

I saw him naked btw. I couldn't resist texting that back to her. Tried to show him how to shower. He's definitely a SHOWer.

OMG DETAILS.

That was it! That, and he has scars on his chest. And he's rather proud of his equipment. And not circumcised.

Fanning myself over here. Fanning! Did you just want to get down on your knees and take him in your mouth?

NO! Gemma!

Did I mention I'm really bored?

You're killing me.

So for real, tell me what's going on.

Rand says he has another vampire friend and he has to find out if the guy is his enemy or not. He wants to go find him. I'm going to see what we can find out locally and get Rand some clothes before we head out. How you doing back there?

I'm ok. Working hard. I dropped the anhua vase btw.

My heart dropped. YOU WHAT?

Hahah jk. I wouldn't do that.

I hate you.

You <3 me. And in all seriousness, I met with a dealer earlier today. He is going to come dig through some of this stuff and give us a bulk price and take it off our hands. So we can sell him the heavy stuff and ship the rest home to auction later.

Good thinking.

Thank you! I'm pretty pleased with myself. He's going to come by tomorrow. Says he's super interested in what wo've found. Told him I wouldn't accept bids less than 20k and he was fine with that.

Wow really?

Yup! Wheeling and dealing on this end!

You rock, I sent back, super-pleased. Gemma was kicking ass while I was farting around Rome with a vampire. Is it going to bother you if I stick with Rand for a few more days to get him settled?

Not at all! Poor guy's like a puppy in this time period. A big, randy puppy with fangs. He needs a friend.

She had a point. Rand did need someone looking

out for him. I'd seen all the trouble he'd gotten into, so I couldn't imagine what he'd be like on his own. I might have to run up the credit card a bit.

No worries. We're going to make bank on this place. And I won't touch the anhua until you get back, I promise. I know how you are about the porcelain!

You're the best.

Keep me posted on deets. Remember, I am shipping you two. SHIPPING. YOU.

Nothing is happening on that front, no matter how much Rand might wish it.

I wish it too! You guys would make a cute couple.

Stop it, Gemma! He's a vampire.

So? My last boyfriend was married and didn't tell me. Vampire is better.

There was no arguing with her.

Ooo, there's someone at the door. Maybe it's the dealer. I'll keep you posted!

Just in time. I ended the conversation with a quick XOXO and pocketed my phone. Time to retrieve my vampire, I supposed.

I tried not to think about Gemma's hints that Rand and I should hook up. Gemma liked sex more than the average girl, and she didn't understand my long periods of celibacy. I didn't date much, and when I did, it usually turned out poorly. My control issues and my childhood abandonment issues didn't exactly make me a winner in long-term relationships. As a result, I hadn't gotten laid in the last year, and it had been even longer since I'd dated someone seriously.

I thought of Rand again. Naked. Warm against me in bed. Telling me how good I tasted.

Nope. Nope nope nope.

That was a path I didn't need to head down. Not only would that mess things up between us but he was also a wild card. He was dangerous. He was . . . lonely. Like me.

Nope. Bad idea, Lindsey. He was also a people user and a man who didn't know how to ask permission. He had no clue how to behave in a relationship.

But it wouldn't be a relationship, I reminded myself. Rand said he had needs and that was all they were. Did I have needs, too? Could I think like a medieval vampire and have casual sex?

I squeezed my eyes shut, ignoring the thought. Nope. Sex was the last thing that should have been on my mind at the moment. I was ashamed I was even thinking about it. A lot. I was thinking about it a lot. But still a bad idea.

"Hurry up, Rand," I called through the door. "We'll go shopping and I'll introduce you to the magic of underwear."

Eleven

Rand gazed down at the clothing on his body. "Are you sure this is tailored correctly?" He ran his hands down his chest, as if testing the material. "It fits tighter in some areas than I am used to. And there are so many layers."

"Oh, I'm sure," the saleswoman breathed in accented English. Her gaze moved over him repeatedly. "You look wonderful. Stunning. But if it's tight somewhere, maybe I should feel—"

"You look fine," I snapped. "We'll take it." I handed her my card before she could "feel" Rand's fit again. She'd already felt it twice. That was plenty, darn it.

Rand looked more than fine, actually. I hated to admit it, but he was downright gorgeous in modern clothing. We'd headed to a department store for undergarments, then hit the road, since I couldn't afford much of anything else at the pricey store. Instead, we'd found a resale boutique that was open late. Luckily for us, Rand happened to be a fairly common size, and his body made everything look incredible. The jeans on his hips hung slightly low, which we'd solved with a belt and lots of salivating from the saleswoman. Now Rand wore underwear and an undershirt, a pair of jeans, a leather belt, socks, leather shoes, a button-up shirt, and a casual blazer. I'd grabbed three other shirts and another pair of jeans for him, along with a T-shirt or two to complete his wardrobe for now.

It wasn't Rand's fault he was like a walking pheromone, right? I shouldn't get mad that the salesclerk was practically groping him in her excitement to dress him. And I shouldn't be jealous.

But "shouldn't" and "were" ended up being two very different things. I didn't like seeing Rand flirt with the salesclerk. She was young and pretty and giggled at all his words, and I wondered how her blood smelled to him. Did she taste half as good as me?

And why did I even care? I didn't have enough blood to keep a vampire fully fed. It was clear that I sucked at donating, no pun intended. Maybe if he wasn't flirting back, it wouldn't matter.

Maybe maybe maybe.

Maybe I needed to stop being so proprietary with the man. He was going to be out of my life the moment we figured out the situation with Guy and the Dragon. Part of me hoped that it would turn out to be nothing but a big misunderstanding. That nothing dire had happened to his friends and they'd died in a freak accident. A boat crash. *Something*. Then Rand would give me a friendly little hug and waltz right back out of my life.

And I'd go back to playing with antiques. Go back to Nebraska and save my pennies for a few more years in the hopes of opening up a store . . . and . . .

I frowned to myself, following the salesclerk as she headed to the counter with my card. Why did my life sound so bland and . . . terrible? I'd worked hard to get to where I was, being my own boss and working with my best friend. I didn't date much, and I normally didn't have a lot of money in the bank, but it worked for me, didn't it? I mean, I had Gemma, but beyond her I had a hard time trusting people. And she dated so much and fell in love so quickly that she often ended up disappearing for days or weeks on end, caught up in the romance of her newest relationship. And that left me with a lot of time to catch up on my TiVo, I supposed.

"Honeymoon?" the clerk asked as she scanned the tags she'd pulled from Rand's clothing.

"Hmm?" I looked up at her, distracted.

"It is, how do you say, elope?" She smiled at me. "Your man is very handsome. We get couples in sometimes. They buy clothes because they elope."

I felt a hot blush on my cheeks. Was it worth trying to explain? "Yes, sure," I said instead of correcting her.

"Aha," she said, beaming at me, and I felt guilty that I'd been glaring at the back of her head not five minutes earlier. She raised a finger in the air. "I have something for you. No charge." She winked and pulled something out from under the counter. Plastic crinkled as she pushed it toward me.

Panties. Luridly pink *crotchless* panties sealed in plastic.

I stared.

She winked at me again and dropped them in the bag, along with the rest of the clothing we were purchasing. "It is on the house."

That's what I got for not explaining. I stammered a thank-you as Rand moved throughout the store, poking at things. "So did you bring gold?" Rand asked me.

"Gold? No, we pay with plastic now."

"Plastic." He mulled the word. "I do not have a grasp of what this plastic is."

"It's something new," I told him. "My money is on the card."

The salesclerk handed the card back and Rand picked it up, then flipped it over.

"'On the card' being a figure of speech," I pointed out. "It's actually in a bank. This little piece of plastic tells my bank what I want to purchase, and they pull the money from my account to pay for it."

"Hmm." Rand studied the card, then handed it back to me. "Is it safe to carry it with you?"

"As safe as anything, I suppose. Sometimes people steal credit cards, but I'm lucky so far."

"I kept my treasure in a locked box buried in my courtyard."

I tried not to stare at that. Instead, I watched as he picked up a brochure for women's clothing and began to flip through it, as if fascinated by the pictures.

"Treasure?" I asked when he didn't clarify.

"Near a wall," he agreed. "Back at my castle in Lancashire. I buried it so it would remain safe whilst I was gone." He looked thoughtful. "I do wonder if it's still there."

"I suppose we could always check," I told him. I was always in the mood for a treasure hunt. I smiled at the thought. Imagine finding items from the fourteenth century.

The saleslady caught my smile, gave me another horrifying wink, and slid a small tube into the bag. "Is also on the house."

Dear God, that looked like lube. My face hurt from blushing so much. "Thank you," I murmured, praying that Rand wouldn't ask about it. This woman needed to stop being so nice already, or I was going to die of embarrassment.

"Boots," Rand declared.

"Hmm?" I backed away from the counter as he came to stand next to me, his hand moving to where the panties had been a scant moment ago. My face felt red-hot.

"I should like some boots," Rand said. "Where do we find them?"

The saleslady lit up. "We have boots," she said, gesturing at the back of the store. "What kind are you looking for?"

"I need to hide a blade—" Rand began.

"Cowboy boots," I blurted. "Can you add it to his tab?"

"In Italy?" The saleswoman frowned. "Cowboys?"

"Okay then, whatever leather boots you have. Riding boots? Fox hunting boots? I don't know. Just something tall." I pinned an overly bright smile to my face and slapped the card down on the counter. "I'm going to run next door and get a coffee. I'm super-thirsty. In the meantime, you two can look at boots."

And I could hide until I stopped blushing. Crotch-less panties. Jesus, Mary, and Joseph.

The café was actually down the street, so I slipped through the door of the boutique and sprinted down to the place. If I'd stayed in the boutique much longer, the woman might have started pulling sex toys out from under the counter, and then wouldn't *that* have been an explanation to Rand. Oy. I headed into the small café and ordered a cappuccino to go. By the time my coffee was ready, my cheeks had cooled down and I could manage the thought of facing the salesclerk without a goofy, awkward smile on my face. With my drink in hand, I turned back up the street toward the boutique.

The streets were shadowy due to the late hour, but there were charming lampposts along the way, so it wasn't unpleasant. There were a few people on the street, a pair of men talking and sharing a cigarette under one of the lampposts. I held my coffee close and took a sip, but it was scalding hot. I headed toward the shop and paused to fix the lid on my coffee, since it seemed to be leaking ultrahot cappuccino on my fingers.

As I did, I noticed that the streets had gotten very quiet. It was a bit unusual for a bustling city like Rome, but we weren't in one of the busier areas. I glanced over my shoulder and saw that the men who had been under the streetlight were now a good deal closer but were turned away from me.

My hackles went up.

They'd moved. They were trying to make it look like they weren't following me, but it was obvious they were. Fear rushed through me. Okay, I needed to think. I was being followed by two guys. There could be a few reasons behind that, none of them good. They could have been pickpockets wanting my wallet. Actually, that would be the best scenario, because then I'd only be broke.

The other two scenarios were much scarier: rapists looking for easy prey . . .

. . . or vampires, looking for Rand.

I pretended to fiddle with my coffee cup for a moment longer, loosening the lid. If someone tried to touch me, they were going to get a faceful of boiling hot cappuccino. I glanced up. The boutique was just a few shops away, but there was no sign of Rand. Was he still inside flirting with the clerk? Damn it. Would I even be able to make it there?

I had to think. I took a few steps forward, then decided to fix my shoelace. I knelt down on the sidewalk and set my coffee down, and as I did, I saw a pair of legs approaching.

That did it.

I turned and screamed bloody murder, and as I did, I flung my coffee into the man's face.

The coffee splattered on his cheeks, steam rising, and he gave a horrible cry. For a horrible moment, I thought I'd made a mistake. Did I just hurt a civilian?

But then his cry turned into a teeth-bearing hiss, and long fangs shot out.

Oh hell, I'd been right after all. "Rand!" I bellowed as I ducked to one side. A vampire grabbed my arm and swiped his sleeve over his brow. One vamp had snuck up on me while I'd attacked the other. I gave a small scream even as the vampire clenched an arm around my shoulders, pinning me against him.

He inhaled deeply, then said something in another language to his friend. His long, sharp fingernail traced the veins in my throat. I could just guess what he was saying. *Yummy yummy in my tummy.*

The coffee-wearing vampire spit out an epithet and gestured at me as I struggled in his friend's arms. I could guess what he was saying, too. *Kill her.*

I opened my mouth to yell, when the coffee-wearing vampire's head suddenly flew off his shoulders. Standing behind him was Rand, his sword off to one side, freshly used. Blood rained down on the sidewalks. The look on Rand's face was that of a cold-blooded killer, his eyes narrow with concentration.

He said something to the other vampire. Something in a dark, deadly language. *Something something Al Tineen.*

I knew what that word was. The Dragon.

The vampire clutching me grabbed me hard, and I gasped just as hot, hard teeth sank into my neck, taking a bite out of me. Blood gushed and I screamed weakly. Why was someone trying to tear my throat out just because of who I was with? I was an innocent bystander.

As Rand surged forward with his sword in hand, an ugly snarl on his face, the world around me faded to black. *Too much blood*, I thought idly. Too much blood lost too fast. He must have ripped my jugular.

As I faded into darkness, I thought this wouldn't have happened if I'd had some nice garlic food beforehand. Amused by my own thoughts, I let them carry me under.

My entire body felt like it had been run over, but my neck hurt the worst, like a raw sunburn to the tenth degree. I winced as I came to. I wanted to put a hand to my neck, but I was too exhausted. I licked dry lips and settled for an "Ow."

Cool fingers brushed my cheek. "Lindsey."

I opened my eyes and gazed up at Rand's looming face. Worry creased his handsome features. "What happened?"

"Blood vassals. They are gone now."

I frowned up at him as he helped me sit up. It seemed that I was lying on the sidewalk in an alley. Lovely. "Um, I'm still not clear on everything. Give me a moment."

I leaned on him, surprised at how weak I was. And good gravy, my throat hurt. Even though it felt like a sandbag was attached to my hand, I lifted it and touched my neck . . . and was surprised to feel two gouges there. "What . . ."

Rand's fingers brushed over mine. "Don't touch it. The wound is still healing. I licked it to seal the wounds, but I'm afraid you still lost quite a bit of blood." His hand caressed my jaw. "Are you hurting anywhere else? I nearly lost my mind when he bit you."

"You worried because I'm your blood vassal?"

"Because he tried to tear your throat out," Rand corrected. "Luckily I was able to dispatch him easily." He gave a derisive snort. "The men of this time are pathetic warriors."

A vision of the sword flashing through the air

tore through my fuzzy mind. The blood spraying. The man's head just sort of flopping off to one side as Rand's sword cut through. Dear God. I would have been sick to my stomach if I'd had the energy for it. Instead, all I could do was swallow hard and lean against Rand's strong shoulder. "Are you hurt?" I asked him.

"No. He was not fast enough. He knew he would die, so he attacked me where I was vulnerable—you."

"They were vampires, Rand."

"Yes, I know."

My fingers dug into his arm. "I thought you said they were blood vassals."

"There are many kinds of blood vassals, Lindsey." His fingers rubbed at my cheek, and I realized he was probably wiping away blood. Ugh. "I am a blood vassal to the Dragon. I serve him and am bound to his will. You are a blood vassal to me because you have pledged yourself. Those men were vampires, and all vampires are blood vassals to another. I did not sense them coming, or I would not have left you alone."

"I thought you had a vampire homing beacon in that head of yours? That it lets you learn languages and you can tell where other vampires are?"

"I am the Dragon's vassal. That means I am tied to him. I can feel his other vassals. I can learn the languages he knows because of my blood bond. And I did not feel these men, so they were not vassals to the Dragon."

"Then . . . who are they vassals to? I thought you said all vassals are tied to the Dragon."

His return smile was thin. "They are not my vassals. Frederic and William are dead. Who is left?"

"Guy?"

"That can be the only assumption I can make. There are other vampires in the world, I imagine, but they would have no interest in me or my blood vassal." His fingers rubbed my cheek again. "I am sorry you were drawn into this."

"Me, too." I winced as I sat up a little straighter.

"This does prove my point, however," Rand added.

"Your point?"

"I told you weapons would come in handy." He couldn't resist adding a teasing note in his voice.

I snorted. "Just help me stand up."

"Not yet." Rand produced a few Saran Wrap–covered cookies and a scone from a bag at his side. "Eat these."

I took one, puzzled. "Where did you get this?"

"I knew you would need this to keep up your strength. I gave the saleswoman your plastic and told her to purchase them."

My eyes widened. "Please tell me you got my card back from her."

"Did you still need it? I was surprised that she kept trying to hand it back to me." He shrugged and dug into the paper bag, then produced my Visa card.

I breathed a sigh of relief. We were not completely screwed.

"This is good, yes?" He handed it to me.

"Yes," I said, pocketing it and taking a bite of cookie. "Are you okay? Did anyone else see the fight? What happened to their bodies?"

Rand gave me an amused look. "So many questions. Can you not relax and recover your strength, Lindsey?"

"I'm relaxing," I said, stuffing cookie into my mouth. My energy was slowly returning, though I still felt utterly exhausted. I could not keep "donating" blood like this. "Keep talking."

"They turn to ash once beheaded."

I swallowed hard around a chunk of cookie. "The bodies?"

"Yes. It takes about a minute for the mental memory to cut off. Then everything turns to dust." He made a flicking gesture with his hand. "Dust and carried away by the breeze. A fitting end for two cowards."

"What if you didn't behead them?" I asked, morbidly curious.

He shrugged. "If they were staked, they would have remained where they were, in limbo . . . until the sun rose, at least."

Ah. The sun, the great vampire incinerator. "And the saleslady?" I asked between bites of cookie. "Did she freak out at the sight of the beheadings and stuff?"

"I calmed her into going back into her store. She will remember none of this." His eyes had a familiar gleam in them.

"You totally hypnotized her, didn't you?"

"It suited our needs."

Ugh. Yeah, suited our needs as we manipulated and killed our way through Rome. Good Lord. "I guess it's a good thing you had those weapons," I told him. I finished my cookie and got to my feet. "We need to go back to our hotel room, Rand. Do you think it's safe?"

"As safe as anywhere," he said. "I cannot hide from either Guy or the Dragon. It will be obvious to Guy that his men failed soon enough."

"Great," I said weakly. "Maybe we should keep moving, then."

"No," said Rand, and he looped an arm around my waist. "We are going to take you home and you are going to rest. Remember that they cannot enter our domicile without being invited in."

Oh, right. That was good. "So we just need to avoid the streets and we'll be fine."

"Something like that."

"Okay, cool," I said, and then I passed out again.

Twelve

Some time later, I woke up to find myself back in the hotel bed. There was a bare, warm chest pressed against my cheek, and I tried to process that for a moment before alerting Rand that I was awake.

I'd been out for some time, so he must've fed recently on some other hapless woman. I couldn't be jealous, because I'd been totally passed out due to someone else attacking me like the last bag of popcorn at a movie theater, but I still didn't like it. The faint scent of soap touched my nostrils, and I guessed that he'd bathed himself again after feeding, since he knew I didn't like it.

For some reason, that touched me.

So I let myself drowse on his chest for a moment longer, enjoying the feel of his body warm against mine. This was what it would be like if Rand were human, and we were in a relationship. I'd curl up against him at night, and he'd . . . well, he wouldn't be a vampire.

I sighed to myself. Too far away from reality. What a shame.

A hand toyed with my hair. "You should bathe, Lindsey. There's blood in your hair."

Ick. Way to bring a girl out of a mood. "Gee, thanks, Rand."

"Do you feel better? How are you?" His hand slid down my arm, stroking it. "It nears dawn."

"I've been asleep for a while, then." I yawned and stretched, getting up. I winced at the way certain muscles pulled as I did. My neck felt hot and tight, and it hurt like the dickens. I touched the wound and hissed at the stab of pain. Maybe it'd feel better after a few aspirin.

I crawled out of bed and into the shower, then took a few pills. My own clothing was filthy, so I hand-washed my T-shirt and jeans in the sink, scrubbing them with the hotel soap to try to get the blood out. When I'd done the best I could, I put on one of Rand's new T-shirts, since there wasn't much else to wear.

Then, because it was near dawn and I was still exhausted, I crawled right back into bed next to Rand and flopped down on a pillow. When he pulled me against him, I didn't even protest. Even though his body was rock hard and now a bit cooler to the touch, I still liked cuddling him.

Cuddling with a vampire. That was probably high up on the list of things one shouldn't cuddle with, next to scorpion and porcupine. But I couldn't help myself. So I settled my cheek against the crook of his shoulder and relaxed. "Guess we're staying in for the rest of the evening, hmm?"

"I must," Rand agreed. "And I ask that you not leave while I am asleep due to the daylight. I do not like this newest revelation of strange vampires I cannot sense."

I didn't care for it much myself. "If there's still cookies, I'll eat those," I said. I closed my eyes and pulled the blankets up around my chin, feeling relaxed and dazed. Or maybe that was the blood loss. "Or I can raid the minibar. No big."

"Let me see your neck," he said, just as I was drifting back off to sleep. I groaned at him, but when he continued to nudge me, I rolled onto my back so he could examine it. His fingers brushed my collarbone. "The wound has come open again in the shower."

His skimming fingers were doing naughty things to my body. My nipples had reacted immediately, perking at the touch. My entire body tingled with awareness of his against my own, and I felt my pulse speed up.

"I need to lick you to assist with the healing, Lindsey," Rand said, hands moving along my jaw and throat. "Tilt your head back for me."

I need to lick you. Oh sweet heavens. "Rand, I—"

"Do it, Lindsey."

And because I wanted to do it despite myself, I

tilted my head back and waited, feeling a little awkward and a lot tense and turned on all at once.

I started as Rand's head bent to my neck and his nose brushed against my throat. His hair tickled my chin, and I had the most insane urge to twine my fingers in those long, thick locks and hold him against me, as if we'd been lovers in a make-out session.

We weren't, of course. This was healing. Nothing more. I had a boo-boo and he was going to make it all better . . . with his tongue.

Oh, who was I kidding? I was totally getting turned on by this. I squirmed underneath him as I felt his weight settle on top of me. This was . . . okay, this felt like sex. It wasn't, I kept telling myself. Totally wasn't.

Then his tongue touched my neck and he gave it a long, sultry lick.

A moan escaped me.

I clapped a hand over my mouth, shocked.

Rand groaned against my throat, and the sound went straight to my sex. "God have mercy upon me. Do not sound so delicious, Lindsey. The last thing you need is more blood taken from you, and you tempt me sorely."

"Sorry," I breathed. I wasn't, though. I liked hearing that I was tempting him. He was sexy and dangerous and gorgeous, so of course I liked the thought of making him half as wild as he made me. But this was about healing the gouge in my throat, so

I bit down on my lip and tried to think nice, sweet, chaste thoughts.

Like teddy bears.

Candy hearts.

Nice warm hugs and—

Oh God, was he stroking his tongue against the hollow of my throat?

A whimper escaped, and this time I gave in to the temptation of burying my fingers in his hair. I clung to him, full of need, and moaned again when he licked my skin. I forgot all about my wound or how I'd received it. The only thought in my head was Rand, and Rand's tongue, and the weight of Rand's body over mine.

"Lindsey," he rasped, and his mouth moved up the column of my neck, pressing light kisses to my skin. Then his mouth was on mine and he was kissing me. At first, he was soft, tender, almost hesitant. As if testing if I really wanted this or not.

And oh boy, did I *ever*. I slicked my tongue against his, moaning my need. His fangs pricked me, and the taste of my blood tinged the kiss. This time, Rand moaned, and his fingers dug into my hair, and then we were both kissing with abandon, a mesh of tongues, lips, and teeth. Every time his tongue stroked mine, I felt it between my legs, and my hips rose in response. His body had somehow settled between my legs, and I wrapped one around his thigh, pushing him against me. The hard press of his cock against my sex told me

I wasn't the only one full of need, and I thrust against him, wanting him deep inside me.

"Please, Rand," I whispered, taking his hand and pulling it to my breast. My nipples ached, desperate to be touched. "Put your hands on me." I wasn't wearing panties, and I was acutely aware of how little clothing separated us. "I need you."

Rand's mouth pulled away from mine and he pressed his forehead against me. "We shouldn't."

"I know we shouldn't, but I don't care at the moment," I protested, covering his hand before he could remove it from my breast. "Just give it one little squeeze to let it know you care—"

"We can't," he said again, and lifted his head to stare into my confused eyes. He leaned in and gave me a chaste kiss on the tip of my nose. "You are not strong enough at the moment for my attentions. What you need now is rest."

"I promise not to move around too much," I protested, smoothing my hands over his shoulders. "You can do all the work. Really. I'll just lie back and think of England."

He gave me a puzzled look, then shook his head. "I cannot, Lindsey. Much as I want to, I would drink from you when we tupped. I wouldn't be able to stop myself. And you are too weak as it is."

He was right, I supposed. I was getting tired of the word *weak*, though. I sat up, disgruntled. Was it me? Was he not attracted to me? "All you want is my blood. Just say it. You're not going to hurt my feelings."

Just like that, I was pushed back onto the bed again, his big body covering mine. His face inches from my own. "Do you know why you like it when I lick your throat, Lindsey?" His eyes were dangerous blue slits.

Silently I shook my head.

"Because I have had two hundred years to perfect my licking. I know just where and how to put my tongue to a woman." Those beautiful lashes flicked, and I was trapped in his gaze. "I know just how to lick her cunny so that she's screaming with pleasure. And if you think I don't want to lick yours? You are mad."

I stared at him, utterly breathless.

"I want nothing more, Lindsey," he whispered. "But I will wait. I am a patient man."

My mouth was dry. "O-okay."

"Now sleep," he murmured, rolling to his side. He pulled me against him once more, nestling me in the crook of his arm as if we hadn't just had a make-out session that made me want to jump his bones. "You need your rest."

Rest was the last thing I was thinking of. "I'll try," I said with a yawn.

His hand moved against my wet hair, fanning it over my shoulders. "You will succeed," he murmured, and indeed, I began to feel sleepier as I snuggled against him and he toyed with my hair. Was he using mind control to make me rest? Did I care?

It wasn't until I'd nearly nodded back off to sleep that my brain focused on the thing that was bothering me.

I gasped and bolted out of bed, pushing aside the covers. I looked at the time. Five a.m. Shit. I scrambled for my phone. "Gemma," I said.

She'd been quiet for far too long. Gemma was a serial texter, and the fact that she hadn't said a peep in the last twenty-four hours? I was worried. I picked up my phone and flicked the screen on. No new text messages. My stomach clenching with fear, I scrolled back through the texts we'd sent earlier, rereading them.

Her last message was Ooo, there's someone at the door. Maybe it's the dealer. I'll keep you posted!

Someone at the door?

I thought of the vampires that had ambushed me in the streets, and my body went cold. It hadn't been a casual overtaking. They'd been following us. Expecting us. "I think they might have Gemma," I told him, utterly sick at the thought. If she'd thought they were antiques dealers, she'd have invited them in, no questions asked. And once you invited a vampire inside . . . "We have to go back to Venice."

"We can't now," he murmured. "Dawn is almost here. If I leave this room, it will be a death sentence for me."

I looked at the window, where we'd tossed a blanket over the curtains and used a few hair scrunchies to secure it to the curtain rod. No light came in, but I knew he was right. It was extremely late—or early, depending on how you looked at it. Gemma's text had been sent hours and hours ago, before I'd known there were other vampires hunting for Rand.

At the time, I'd thought nothing of it.

Now, however, my hands trembled as I sent her a message. Hey, Gemma—wakey wakey. Question for you.

No answer. Of course there was no answer, I told myself, trying to be reasonable. It was five in the morning. She was asleep. Gemma tried not to wake up before the crack of noon unless I made her.

I could leave and go after her. Five or six hours and I'd be in Venice . . .

And Rand would be all alone.

And Gemma might be fine.

Or she might be dead already.

I had no way of knowing. Rand could take care of himself when it came to combat, but he was helpless when it came to simple things. The man had just now figured out doorknobs.

I needed to stay. Even as I told myself that, I felt horrible guilt.

Please be okay, Gemma. Please.

Thirteen

I didn't sleep a wink the entire time Rand was out. In vain, I texted Gemma over and over again.

No response. Not a one. It wasn't like Gemma to not check her phone. I knew something had happened to her. I knew it, and I hated myself for not abandoning Rand. How could I abandon my friend when she needed me? But at the same time, how could I abandon Rand if Gemma was already dead?

Tormented, I paced back and forth in the small hotel room. I kept the packet that she'd given me at hand. The toothpicks were a cute gesture but not super useful considering their size. I could try the holy water, I supposed. Instead, I drank half the bottle and downed (okay, gagged down) the vial of garlic, then brushed my teeth and rinsed with mouthwash over and over again until it no longer smelled on my breath. If everyone was so fired up about drinking from me, well, I'd give them a surprise, wouldn't I?

I'd just have to warn Rand that my blood was currently off-limits.

It wasn't such a bad idea to make myself verboten to him. I'd been grinding against him while Gemma had been confronting murderous vampires. It wasn't my best moment, and I was ashamed that I hadn't thought of her until bedtime. How had I not thought about my best friend? I hoped it was the blood loss and not me just being careless and led by my lust for Rand.

I hoped.

As I waited, I booked train tickets and scanned our bank account, hoping that I was just overthinking things and that charges from the local corner store in Venice would show up on our shared card.

Nothing. No purchases since the night before, when I'd purchased my coffee at the café. The clothing we'd bought for Rand. The hotel room.

That was it. Gemma's presence in the world was a big blank, and it was scaring me.

By the time Rand woke, I was a twitchy, nervous mess. He sat and swung his legs over the edge of the bed, and the delicious spicy scent that accompanied him was thicker than ever, signalizing his hunger. He moved closer and kissed my neck. "You smell . . . different."

"I ate a bunch of garlic," I admitted to him. "You don't want any of my blood right now."

He chuckled, shaking his head. "I should be offended, but I am impressed by your ingenuity. Garlic?"

"Doesn't that work against vampires?"

"As a soporific, yes. You will only make them drowsy."

"Oh. And I might have done a shot of holy water."

"I suppose I should be thankful you didn't test it out on me while I was sleeping."

"The thought did cross my mind," I admitted. "But I didn't want to hurt you." I clenched my hands and unclenched them. "Rand, I'm so scared for Gemma. I don't know what to do. I—" I broke off, swallowing hard. I was fighting back tears. Every moment that I wasn't at Gemma's side felt like a brand-new betrayal.

"If they have gone after her, she will be safe." He reached over and squeezed my hand. "There is no benefit to them killing her."

"Do you really think so?" I clung to the hope.

"I do," he said, his fingers lacing through mine. I didn't even mind the chill of his skin, because I desperately needed the comfort of his touch. "If they keep her alive, she produces blood. And they know if they keep her alive, we will come after her. They get nothing out of killing her, other than petty revenge." He shook his head. "If they are looking to bring me forward, they will use her as bait, but they will not kill her."

I didn't point out that a vampire had nearly chewed a hole in my throat a day or so ago.

Rand knew Guy. If he said he wouldn't kill Gemma, I had to believe him. Had to. "We should leave," I told Rand. "I have train tickets back to Venice. I can't stand not knowing what happened to Gemma. I'm sure it's a trap, but I don't care." My fingers tightened against his. "So I hope you understand when I say I have to go, and I'll understand if you want to part ways here."

He gazed at me for so long that I began to think he'd take me up on it. Which made me feel even worse. I didn't want him to leave, but I felt like I had to offer it. After all, sticking with me had gotten Gemma where, exactly? In trouble. But Rand gave his head a small shake, and his grip tightened on mine. "I am with you."

I exhaled in relief. "Thank you."

"Venice is along the way to Guy." He shrugged.

"I . . . oh. Okay." So it was just convenient for him? I didn't know what to think of that. Then again, it didn't matter. "Let's get going, then."

As Rand dressed, I thought about all the logistics. Rand would have to feed from someone before we got on the train. Or while on the train, I supposed, though that might make things messy. I'd have to grant him permission to cross water, since it left him writhing in pain otherwise. I'd need to invite him in if I crossed a threshold.

I needed more holy water and garlic.

Traveling with a vampire? Damned inconvenient.

I must have been more exhausted than I thought, because I dozed fitfully on the train. When I awoke, we were nearing Venice, and Rand was warm and flushed with someone else's blood. I didn't ask questions. My mind was on Gemma.

I texted her again, frantic. Please, please, Gemma. Answer me! 911! 911! I'm about to show up on your doorstep!

No response. There hadn't been a single one, no matter how many times I'd texted her. It made my stomach sink a little more every time, until I felt as if I were dragging it around my feet, along with my hopes that Gemma would be fine and her phone was just dead.

Gemma was many things, but she never forgot her phone. She was hooked to it like a smoker to their lighter.

There could be no explanation other than the other vampires had found her and taken her.

Still, I refused to stubbornly give up hope. I wouldn't believe Gemma was hurt / in danger / dead unless I saw her body myself. She was alive and she was fine. Gemma was sweet and charming and pretty, and she could talk her way out of most things. Everyone who met her adored her. Even if she was captive, she was likely charming them with her wit and her inventive cusswords.

I tried not to think about her having sour-tasting blood.

I trembled as we rode a water taxi back through the canals of Venice. We got off at our "street," and

I rushed to the door of the apartment building. I stepped across the portal, then looked at Rand, who was patiently waiting in the alleyway.

"I invite you to join me inside this doorway," I told him.

As if an invisible barrier had dropped, Rand entered. We'd gone through this scenario over and over again, to the point that I wondered how anyone was possibly afraid of a vampire, when all they had to do was shut a door in their face. But as I headed back to the second door, the one to the overcrowded, box-filled apartment that belonged to Gemma and me for three more weeks, I thought of Rand's glowing eyes, his hypnotic commands. His imperious expectation of being obeyed.

The way that one vampire had carelessly tried to tear my throat out.

Oh, Gemma.

Stop it, Lindsey, I told myself. My fingers shook hard as I put the big iron key in the lock and turned it. The door pushed open slowly, creaking. The apartment was dark.

I swallowed hard, not yet stepping across the entryway. "Gemma?"

No response. It was just after midnight; maybe she was asleep. I fumbled for the light switch and flicked it on.

The apartment was trashed.

I sucked in a breath as I surveyed the damage.

Torn boxes were scattered along the marble tiles, and shattered dishes covered the floor. One red bowl I remembered Gemma lovingly packing now sparkled in a hundred pieces at my feet.

My stomach gave a sick lurch. "Gemma," I bellowed, pushing forward. "Gemma, are you here?"

"Lindsey," Rand hissed behind me. "Don't go in alone! Call me in to enter! I cannot follow unless invited!"

"Right! Whatever! Come in already!" I cried, even as I rushed down the narrow hall in search of my missing friend. "Gemma! Answer me!"

A heavier body grabbed me from behind and threw me against one of the plaster walls. It was Rand, his eyes flashing that eerie green instead of the normal blue. "Lindsey," he whispered. "If there is someone still here, you must let me go first so I can protect you."

"But—" I began.

His gaze on mine, he reached for his belt and brandished a knife a moment later.

"Can I have one?" I said at the sight of it.

"Take this one," he told me. "I have another. And stay behind me."

I nodded, grasping the hilt. My heart pounded. I prayed I wouldn't have to use it, but at least I had some sort of weapon.

And garlic blood, I reminded myself. If anyone took a bite out of me again, they were going to get a surprise. It might mean I would die, too, but at least I'd go down swinging.

Hopefully.

Rand stalked forward into the crowded apartment, pulling his other blade from his belt. He stopped and scented the air. "Two strangers and Gemma."

"Still here?" I asked, feeling a little panicky.

He gave a soft shake of his head. "Scents are old, but they could be false."

It was on the tip of my tongue to ask how one made a scent false, when Rand disappeared into one of the rooms. I peeked in behind him. Equally trashed, days of hard work down the drain. Whoever had come in looking for Gemma—*or me, or Rand*, my brain whispered—had wanted to make a statement.

"No one in this room," Rand said, then shut the door behind him. "We'll eliminate all possibilities first, just in case someone is hiding."

I swallowed hard and stuck close to his back. "You could tell by scenting the room?"

"No scents, no sounds, no taste."

"Taste?" I asked.

"Vampires leave a taste of old blood on the mouth, like a trail," he explained, heading for the next door. "It's like a stain of their last victim soaking the air. I can feel it on my tongue."

Wow, that sounded . . . gross. I supposed it was handy if it helped him find other vampires, though.

Room by room we went through the apartment,

checking the bedrooms next. Everything looked in order, right down to the messy bedsheets. Gemma never made the bed. The sight of them gave me a terrible pang of grief. *Be safe, Gemma. Please be safe.*

Last was the dining room. I swallowed hard, wondering if we'd see the secret door sealed and intact. Maybe Gemma had hid herself . . .

My hopes were dashed the moment we went in. The dining room was destroyed, two feet of debris covering the floor. The secret door hung open. "How is this even possible?" I asked as Rand approached the secret door. "How can someone destroy so much? This must have taken them hours. And for what?"

"To send a message to us," Rand said, leading the way to the stairwell. At the top of the stairs, he sniffed the air again and turned back to me. "I taste none of her blood on the air, only the vampires. They came here, but they did not hurt Gemma. She went with them, and when she left, she was alive."

I sagged with relief. "Oh, thank God." Gemma was all right for now. Whatever else happened, I could still save her.

Then I looked at the destroyed room around me. A horrible thought crossed my mind. "Oh . . . oh no." I pushed past Rand, heading down the spiral stairs.

"She is not down there, Lindsey," Rand called after me, a few steps behind. "I do not scent her—"

"The anhua!" I interrupted. "The pottery!"

By the time I got to the bottom of the stairs, I was

frantic. I fumbled on the end of the railing, looking for the flashlight we'd kept attached to a cord there. I clicked on the light.

Shards of pottery were everywhere. All those priceless treasures, lovingly packed away and hidden for centuries . . . destroyed. One triangle was near my shoe, and I reached down to pick it up. Plain white. I shone the light against the other side and saw the fine etching of a bird shine through.

It was a piece of an anhua jar. Or rather, what was left of an anhua jar. The priceless jars should've been in a museum. More than that, they were going to have saved me and Gemma from being broke.

I burst into tears. Everything I touched was ruined. The shattered anhua broke my heart. It had been perfect for decades, preserved to a degree I'd barely seen before. And now, because I hadn't been able to keep myself from sticking my nose into a coffin to see what was inside it, it was destroyed. It was more than just the money it would have brought in for me and Gemma.

It was everything.

And now I didn't even have my best friend at my side. She was in danger, and it was all because of me.

I sobbed, clutching the pottery fragment, and let the flashlight drop. What did it matter if I saw the rest of the room? I knew. They would've left nothing in one piece. Everything would be broken, shattered, decimated, obliterated because they wanted to scare us. To bring us down. To make us afraid.

Well, mission accomplished. I was completely and utterly demoralized.

The warm, spicy scent of vampire touched my nose a moment before I felt Rand's hand on my shoulder. "We'll get her back, Lindsey. Do not worry. Guy has no reason to harm her. And in all the years I knew him, I never found him to be indiscriminately cruel."

Yeah, but six hundred years have passed, I wanted to tell him. I just sniffed and stared at the piece of pottery in my hand. "I'm ruining everything," I told him softly. "Gemma trusted me to take care of things, and now her life is in danger."

"We'll find her," he told me, brushing his fingers over my cheek. "This I promise you."

"I should have known when she didn't text me," I said, pulling out my phone. I stared at my quiet screen, wishing my phone would vibrate with an incoming message from Gemma. Something. Anything. I clicked on Call, half expecting it to start ringing upstairs, or down here. They wouldn't have let her take her phone, would they?

To my surprise, someone picked up on the other line. "I was wondering when you would say hello." The voice was unfamiliar, masculine. A light accent. "I don't respond to text messages. All that typing. It's annoying."

"You . . ." I was so startled that I couldn't think. "Who is this?"

The man made an annoyed sound. "Who do you think this is?"

"You . . . You took Gemma. Where is she? Let me talk to her!"

"She's fine, for now," the man on the other end said. "Do me a favor and put Rand on."

"First I want to talk to Gemma."

"No, you're going to do what I say and put Rand on the phone, because I'm the one controlling things here." The voice was utterly pleasant, but there was a layer of steel underneath that warned me not to push him.

Wordless, I handed the phone to Rand.

He stared down at it, frowning at me. Then, gingerly, he raised it to his ear, waiting.

Guy must have said something. Rand started, surprised, and my phone went crashing to the ground.

I gasped, scrambling to pick it up. The screen was cracked, but the phone didn't show that the call had been dropped. Nervous, I put the phone back to my ear. "Hello? Hello? Are you still there?"

"I'm here," he snarled. "Perhaps you explain how to use a phone before you hand it over?"

"Right. I'm doing that now," I said frantically. I held the phone out to Rand. "You hold this to your ear and he's going to talk to you."

"Guy," he said, startled. "He has put his mind into this thing?"

"No, it's just his voice from a distance." Hadn't he seen me use my phone before now? What did he think I was doing with it all this time? I hadn't called anyone, but I'd texted . . . Maybe he didn't correlate texting with actual communication. "Look, just take it, okay? He's going to talk to you—"

Rand was aghast. "His spirit?"

"No, him," I said. "I promise it's him. He's not here, but his voice is."

Rand frowned at me, clearly suspicious, but he took the phone when I urged him to again. This time, when the stranger spoke, I was ready to grab the phone if Rand dropped it. Instead, he held it awkwardly, giving it an occasional startled look. He stared into space, as if clearly unable to believe what he was hearing. Then he looked back at me. "I wish to tell him something."

"Just speak," I said impatiently. "He'll hear you."

"I wish to tell you something," Rand yelled.

I winced. "Speak normally."

"Give us back Gemma," he said into the phone. "She is not part of whatever vendetta you have created, Guy."

I waited on pins and needles, listening. So it was Guy on the phone with the soft accent. There was silence for a long moment, then Rand shook his head.

"He can't hear that," I whispered.

Rand looked over at me. Then he stared into space again, Guy clearly talking on the other end of the phone. After a moment Rand said, "Then we shall exchange."

Exchange who? I wanted to nudge Rand, but he wasn't good at multitasking.

"Yes."

I bit my lip.

"Yes. But the agreement is null if you harm the girl." Pause. "Yes." Pause. "I care naught for it." Pause again. "Very well. We await your message."

He looked over at me, phone still at his ear. "He is making curious horn noises now."

Horn noises? I took the phone from him, and the disconnect signal blared in my ear. I clicked off the call. "What did he say?" I asked eagerly. "Is Gemma all right?"

"She is his guest," Rand told me. "She is fine. And he will contact us again in one week to do a prisoner exchange."

"A prisoner exchange?" I sputtered.

"Me for Gemma." Rand's face was full of shadow in the dim light of my cell phone.

"*What?* We can't do that. And a week? Why are we waiting a week?"

"Likely we are waiting so he can lay his trap."

"We can't—"

"We can and we will," Rand interrupted me, eyes gleaming with menace. "But we're not going to wait a week. We're going to find him and destroy him ourselves."

Fourteen

Once I calmed down, we headed out to a restaurant for a bite to eat. With all the mess in the house, it was near impossible to get to the kitchen, but Rand had insisted that I eat to keep up my strength. I wasn't big on the idea—just the thought of Gemma in the hands of the enemy made my stomach shrivel, and I hadn't been able to even think of eating.

Gelato helped, though. Especially Italian gelato. Now, with a cone in hand, I sat across from Rand at a tiny all-night café and licked my cone while sipping a coffee that was placed in front of Rand so we'd look "normal." Even though I'd protested getting food, I found that I was ravenous, and every lick of the gelato was heaven itself.

"Tell me again how this is going to work?" I leaned in to catch a drip on the side of my cone.

Rand stared at me.

"Quit watching me."

"I cannot help it. Every time your tongue darts out, I think impure thoughts."

Well . . . that made a girl want to put down her gelato. Almost. "Can we focus please?"

"I'm trying. Watching you eat is very distracting. Perhaps you should have eaten bread instead."

"Just tell me what you're thinking about the plans already."

He gave his head a little shake to clear it, then glanced out the window. "My plan is simple. Guy said he has Gemma and she is a guest in his home. He says he will send instructions in a week so we can meet them at a location that is conducive to both parties. However, he forgets one thing."

"That you can track him by his blood, right?"

He nodded, still not watching me as I ate my gelato. Was it bothering him that much? Did vampires have a mouth fetish? Probably. I resolved to try to eat it as unsexily as possible so we could continue our conversation. "That is correct," he said. "We can approach with the element of surprise."

"Um, correct me if I'm wrong"—I felt the need to point it out—"but if you can track him, he can track you, right? So how does that give us an advantage if he's going to know we're coming?"

"We are not going together."

I paused. "We . . . what?"

"You'll need to go in alone to rescue Gemma."

I stared at him, aghast. "This is a terrible plan. Me? Go in alone?"

"I do not like it, either," Rand agreed, "but we do not have many options."

"I can think of one big one—you know, waiting for Guy to invite us and we meet him."

Rand's mouth quirked. "You would turn me over to him?"

Shoot. No, I wouldn't. "I don't suppose we could overpower them at the meet and greet?"

"We do not know he would go there alone," Rand said. "What if he has made a hundred vampires at this point and they will all be waiting for us?"

Ugh. I didn't want to consider it. "Do you think that's possible?"

"*Anything* is possible. It has been six hundred years, Lindsey. He has had time to build himself an army if he wished."

"So what are we going to do?"

Rand closed his eyes, turning his head as if sensing something. "I can feel him through our shared connection. He has moved back and forth some, but remains in the same location over and over again. North of here. I think we will find he has a dwelling and it is there he has likely taken Gemma."

"And I'm going to go in there alone?" I shook my head, not liking this idea. "How is this going to work?"

"We will travel with each other until we get close. Then we will separate. I will go in one direction and draw his men away. While I do this, you will sneak into his keep and find Gemma and rescue her. My presence will draw away any guards he has, and you will go about unmolested."

"But what if he thinks we're going after him and then decides to hurt Gemma?"

Rand shook his head. "As I have said before, he gains no advantage in hurting her. The moment she dies, he loses all leverage."

"And what if you die?"

His smile was wintry. "Then that solves all of our problems, does it not?"

"No, it does not," I snapped. "Don't even suggest it."

He shrugged.

Feeling a little desperate, I took one last lick of my cone, but it tasted like ashes. "I'm not a big fan of this plan, but if it's all we've got, we'll make it work."

"Mmm."

"What's that mean?"

I must have sounded annoyed, because Rand flashed me an apologetic grin. "It means this is all very strange. Why Guy interests himself with me, I am not certain." Rand rubbed his jaw thoughtfully. "Guy has always been more of a soldier than a leader. This turn of events makes no sense to me, but then again, nothing has made sense since my staking. Unless I miss my guess, someone else is commanding and Guy is simply following orders."

"So someone else wants you dead," I pointed out.

"Is there anyone that wants you alive? Anyone at all?"

The look on his face was weary, sad. "It would be easier for everyone if I was dead, would it not?"

"Don't say that," I told him. The look of intense loneliness on his face made me hurt for him. I tossed the rest of my gelato in the coffee cup and took his fingers in mine, not even caring that they were cold to the touch. "*I* care about you. *I* want you alive." I gave his hand a reassuring squeeze. "We're going to figure this out, and we're going to save Gemma. Figure out who's after you—solve that problem, and then we can return to our normal lives."

But . . . what *would* happen with Rand once we "solved" the problem of the other vampires? It was clear he had no allies except me. Dropping him off with a buddy was no longer an option. Nor was simply abandoning him to figure stuff out on his own.

Rand was now mine, whether I liked it or not.

And oddly enough, I kind of liked it. I rolled around the idea of him returning home with me and Gemma. It'd be rough getting him into the States, but we could work an amnesia angle if we had to. Or since he didn't have to breathe, we could maybe ship him back home. Whatever. We'd figure something out. Regardless, he was coming with me.

He was mine. I gave his hand another squeeze. "Have I ever told you about my home? Nebraska? I think you'd like it. It's very flat, and in the summer it's superhot, and in the winter it's incredibly cold, but it's nice and the people are friendly. There's lots of cows and corn and, um, sunshine. Plenty of room to stretch out and buy some land, if that's what you're into."

"And this is the place on the far side of the world?" Rand chuckled. "Again with your stories."

I just grinned and held his hand, rubbing his fingers with mine. Like we were a couple. "Just trust me."

"You're the only one I do trust."

I swallowed hard. Other than Gemma, Rand was the only person I had. "I won't let you down. I promise." I gave his hand another squeeze. "But this means I'm probably going to need to load up on garlic for a while."

Rand's expression of distaste mirrored mine. Garlic, ugh. Why couldn't vampires hate chocolate?

I tossed and turned in bed that day, unable to sleep. I was trying to switch my schedule to nights to sync with Rand's, but between Gemma's kidnapping, the destruction in the apartment, and a head full of worries, I didn't sleep a wink. The fact that the old bed sagged on one side and had been slashed to ribbons on the other didn't help matters. Those stupid jerks had destroyed everything.

When I finally dragged myself from the rickety bed at sundown, I dressed in jeans and a T-shirt and headed down the trash-strewn stairs. There I met a bright-eyed and hungry vampire.

He frowned at the sight of me, without makeup and my hair unbrushed. "You do not look well, Lindsey."

I stared at him. "How am I supposed to feel when my best friend has been taken by vampires?" I gestured at the walls of the wrecked apartment. "You'll forgive me if I didn't dress up to clean house."

"Clean?" He gave me an imperious look. "Have your servants do it."

"What servants?" I gestured at my chest. "Who do you think was hired to clean this place up?"

His eyebrows went up. "You are a servant?" His gaze scanned up and down my form, and a hint of a smile curved his mouth. "I must say that if you are, I have rarely met a servant that smelled as good as you do. Your blood is positively succulent, fair Lindsey."

Oy. "You know what? Let's just table this conversation, okay?" I rubbed my forehead, staring at the wreckage around me. Where to even start? I moved down the stairs toward a torn box, picking it up half-heartedly.

Cool hands gripped my shoulders, and I could feel Rand's big form press up against me from behind. "Let the chores wait another night, Lindsey," he murmured against my ear.

"But I need to," I began helplessly.

"It will not bring Gemma back any faster."

Tears pricked my eyes. Was I that obvious? "But it'll give me something to do. You don't know me, Rand. I like control. I have to have things in order. That's who I am."

"Then tonight, you have no control," he said, steering me toward the door of the apartment.

"I . . . what?" I sniffed. "What are you talking about?"

"We shall not begin our hunt for Guy just yet. Tonight, you will take your time and recoup your energy." He brushed his fingers over my cheek, then moved toward the door. "We shall go out and explore Venice, yes? And I shall be your guide."

"I . . . I don't know." I looked around the apartment helplessly. "Gemma—"

"Will be fine," he said in a soft voice. His cool fingers touched my cheek again. "You can do nothing for her as of yet. You are heartsick and exhausted, and we will confront Guy when the time is right."

"Why don't we confront him now?"

"Because he will either expect us to charge directly to him or to wait for his instructions. For us to take our time? That he will not suspect." And he gave me a smug look.

"Are you sure?"

"You must trust me, Lindsey. Do you trust anyone?"

"I trust Gemma."

"And what has she done to earn that trust?"

I jerked out of his grip. "Are you kidding me? We've grown up together. We're closer than sisters. I'd trust her with my life."

"So you are friends—"

"More than friends," I corrected. "We shared bunks in the home. We went to school together as kids and we graduated together. Gemma flunked a grade so she could stay with me. When I had no one else, I had Gemma." My stupid tears were threatening again. "When we got booted out of the home at eighteen, Gemma and I got an apartment together. It's always been us against the world."

He nodded. "She sounds like a wonderful friend."

"She is." My throat ached with tears.

"Would she not want you to make the best plan to save her?"

"Well, yes—"

"And would she wish for you to drive yourself mad with worry?"

I frowned. Gemma was very much a a "seize the day" kind of girl. "That's not who I am, though—"

Rand gave me a seductive smile and looped his arm around my shoulders again, guiding me toward the door once more. "Then we shall go out and you will learn to trust me, and you will tell me more about Gemma." He tapped my cheek with cold fingers. "And bring your plastic money."

Despite my protests, we went out after all. Rand wanted me to go blindfolded so he could surprise me, but I absolutely put my foot down at the thought. Hadn't we just been ambushed in Rome? Instead, I wore a bandanna as a scarf to cover my gigantic, still-healing bite, and closed my eyes when he asked me to. He held my hand and led the way, though sometimes we took a water taxi to cross a canal. Each time we did, I murmured my "invite" to Rand to allow him to cross with me, and I noticed his face grew pale with strain each time. Running water, indeed.

He led me through the dark streets of Venice, talking about a battle he'd once fought. And he encouraged me to talk about Gemma—about how when we were kids, Gemma was dropped off at the state home by her prison-bound mother, and I, who was already at the home, welcomed her by sticking Play-Doh in her bright yellow pigtails. We'd been inseperable ever since, and I shared story after story of my bestie with him. Of the time that I didn't get a date to prom and Gemma ditched her guy to be my date. Of the time we were caught egging the local church and Gemma took the fall for me because I couldn't afford to miss school. Over and over, I thought of the ways Gemma had always been there for me.

Even now. And I resolved to be a better friend.

Rand was surprisingly good company, other than the one time he disappeared down an empty street and returned flushed with blood. I didn't ask questions. But after that, he was easygoing and cheerful, encouraging me to tell funny Gemma stories and pointing out some of the buildings in Venice. He knew the area much better than I did.

"Now close your eyes once more, Lindsey," he told me as we walked again. "If the building is yet here, it will be a pleasant surprise."

Obediently, I closed my eyes and let him lead me forward. "Is it food?" We'd been stuffing ourselves with food from small cafés as we'd walked, and I was full.

"Not food," he said, and gave my hand a squeeze. "Do you not trust me?"

"All right, all right," I grumbled. And I squeezed his hand back.

"Ah," Rand said after a long moment. "Here we are."

I opened my eyes, expecting to see another pastry shop . . . and gasped. We stood at the entrance of an enormous plaza, lined with lit buildings that seemed to go on forever in an orderly line. Tourists wandered the area despite the late hour, taking pictures and chatting merrily. At the far end of the massive plaza sat a lit up building next to a tower. The entire place looked like something out of a tourist guidebook. "What is this place?" I asked with wonder as Rand led me forward through the crowd.

"This is the Piazza San Marco," he told me, giving me a boyish look of sincere happiness. "And it is still here. I am pleased." His hand squeezed mine again. "This place was old even when I came through Venice last."

"Really?" I breathed, surprised. Sometimes Rand didn't seem old to me as much as just out of place. I wondered at how strange all of this must be to him—the electric lights, the motor-driven water taxis . . . I wondered what he'd think of my hometown in Nebraska, full of cars, highways, and cornfields.

"Come," Rand said, tugging me forward when my steps slowed. "They will have finished the basilica by now!"

Basilica? I perked up, and the eager history nerd inside me raced after him. When his footsteps sped up, I kept pace. We were running through the piazza like two drunk idiots, but I didn't care. It was Venice by night, and it was gorgeous, and I was here with a mysterious, handsome man who wanted nothing more than to make me smile for an evening.

He'd accomplished that, for sure.

The basilica was breathtaking, with staged lights giving it a golden glow. "St. Mark's Basilica," Rand murmured as I stared in awe at the rounded frescoes above each door, the recessed carvings, the beautiful marble pillars. It looked a bit like the Taj Mahal. "It's incredible," I told him, and gave him a giddy smile. "Is this what you wanted to show me?"

He nodded, as awestruck by the sight as I was. "I'd hoped it was still here, but I did not know." He pulled me against him and looped an arm around my shoulders, and for a moment, it felt like we were a couple. A shiver of desire raced through me.

"I'm glad it's still here," I told him. "For your sake. That the world hasn't changed quite so much in six hundred years."

"And I am glad you're here with me to see it," Rand murmured. He looked over at me and brushed a stray lock of hair from my face, and for a weird moment, I thought he'd kiss me. No teasing manipulation, no coyness, just a man wanting to kiss a woman. But then he gave me a crooked half smile and turned back to the basilica. "I cannot go inside, of course. Hallowed ground."

"Of course," I said, and didn't point out that even if it was open to the public, visiting hours were probably long over.

"But I like the sight of it nevertheless," he murmured, then gazed down at me again. "I like many sights in this time."

I felt my cheeks heat with a blush, and I bit my lip.

Rand held me against him again, and I pressed my cheek to his strangely silent chest. "We'll get her back," he told me in a gentle voice. "You have my word of honor."

"I trust you," I said. Weirdly enough, I did. It was as if seeing the piazza and the basilica had cemented in my mind the notion that history could meet with the present and still be beautiful.

Rand was ancient, but he was still a warrior. If anyone could save Gemma, he could.

Now the only thing that needed saving from him

were my girlish fancies. I blushed again as I pulled away from him, noticing that he touched my hair again as I did. "Think there's a place to get a bite to eat around here? I'm full but I could make room for something sweet."

"For you or for me?" he teased.

I batted his arm. "For me!"

THREE DAYS LATER

I parked my rental car on the side of the road, clutching the steering wheel as I gazed down into the valley ahead. A dark, ominous, deserted valley. "Is it too late to change my mind?"

"Much too late," Rand replied, unbuckling himself and opening his door. "We must do this."

"If we must," I said, getting out of the car, too. Despite my big talk of how we'd prevail, I was scared witless.

We'd received no other information from Guy. Instead, we'd quietly packed a few things from the Venice apartment and rented a car once we'd crossed the ferry. Rand had said that his "sensing" of the other vampire worked a bit like a compass (well, once we'd had a discussion about compasses), so we'd decided to try to head in the same direction at all times in order to disguise just how close we were. If Guy could only feel a vague direction, maybe he wouldn't realize we were coming after him. I drove, and Rand kept me on the path that only he could see.

And so we drove into the Alps in search of Guy.

I felt guilty as heck, but I'd had fun. Thoughts of Gemma niggled the back of my mind constantly, but I'd enjoyed traveling with Rand. Everything was new to him, and as we passed by scenery, he was fascinated by everything, from children on bicycles to the wildest sports cars that zoomed past us. He'd wanted to know more about how cars worked, so I'd pulled over at a rest stop in Switzerland and shown him a few driving points. He'd nearly torn the clutch off, and after that, I hadn't let him drive again. With Rand, though, somehow even the smallest things were fun. We'd stop to get a bite to eat, and I'd have to explain each item on the menu in depth to him, along with what ingredients were in it. A burger struck him as ingenious. And when we stopped during the daytime to sleep, we'd share a hotel room and cuddle while Rand regaled me with stories of when he was a crusader, or his days as a vampire. He'd told me he was a warlord, but it seemed that a lot of his time was spent on what sounded like even more crusades, except this time his leader was the Dragon and not the Lionheart. He kept away from stories full of violence, though I knew there were a great many of those. Instead, he'd tell me small vignettes about life in the field, like how William had once spent hours polishing a sword he'd won from an enemy, only to have it break the first time he used it in battle.

The stories made me realize that the Rand of then was not so different from the Rand of now. He was flirty, cocky, confident, and amused by the world despite the dark things he'd seen. And I was falling for him. Little by little, I began to imagine a life with him. I could do the nocturnal thing. I could handle the "inviting into rooms" and "avoiding holy symbols" thing. I could avoid garlic.

The blood thing, though. That was tricky, because no matter what I did, I'd never be enough for him. He'd always have to drink from someone else at some point, or risk killing me.

We didn't talk about it. Every day, in the early predawn hours of morning, just before we were about to settle in for "the night," Rand would leave me for a short time. He would return, skin flushed with warmth, and take a shower. I was pretty sure that all of the people he drank from weren't hookers, but he showered nevertheless.

It hurt me that he constantly had to seek out others. I couldn't feed him—we'd both decided that I needed to be full strength for our upcoming surprise attack, and even a hint of anemia on my part could work against us. So Rand drank from anonymous strangers.

And I tried not to let it get to me. I tried not to think about it at all.

Which meant, of course, that I thought about it constantly.

I wondered if they were all women. Were they pretty? Did the women swoon with an orgasm the moment he sank his fangs into them? Did he wipe their memories?

Did they taste as good as I did?

It was insane to think about these sorts of things.

Of course, nothing about our adventure seemed *sane*. It was all just . . . necessary. Like the fact that Rand had no identification, and the more we'd traveled and used public transport, the more it had been a requirement. At first, Rand had simply used his vampire wiles to make people ignore the fact that he'd had no passport or photo ID. But as the question had kept coming up, we'd looked up an office for the local American embassy and stopped there one night for an emergency passport renewal. I'd turned the other cheek while Rand had charmed and beguiled the girl working at one of the desks.

Two hours later, he'd had a drink and a temporary passport. He'd even gotten a photo ID with his name and a photo that sort of looked like him if you squinted hard. How he'd managed that, I wasn't sure.

I'd been sitting in the lobby, jealously fuming. But what else could I have done? He needed the IDs. So I'd ignored my hurt feelings, and I'd ignored the fact that he'd made it up to me by showering me with attention and compliments as we'd ridden the train.

I hated that I'd been so weak to fall for all the compliments, but they *had* improved my mood. And as we'd talked and chatted and journeyed across the Alps and up to Switzerland, I'd grown more and more attached to my vampire. Sure, it wasn't a ton of time, but it felt like we'd always been together. Rand had a wicked sense of humor and a flirty attitude that made his arrogance almost charming. As he and I grew closer, I felt more guilt over Gemma. It was my fault she was in danger, and I was starting to think that if it came down to a trade, I didn't know if I *could* give Rand up. It was more than just friendship. More than just a sense of obligation.

My life was starting to be defined as Before Rand and After Rand. And I couldn't imagine life without him. Without his awestruck smile as he saw a modern marvel that I took for granted. His chuckle as I told a corny joke. The way his hand played with my hair as we went to bed together. The cool touch of his fingers laced with mine.

We remained celibate, even though I knew we were both thinking about sex. It was on my mind every time Rand emerged from the shower, skin gleaming with damp, his body warm from stolen blood. I knew it was on Rand's mind when he'd watch my mouth as I spoke, or the hot caress of his gaze when he thought I wasn't paying attention.

But we couldn't. It wasn't just that Gemma was at risk, though that was a factor. It was that Rand would drink from me if we had sex. He'd made that extremely clear.

And while Gemma was in Guy's hands, we wouldn't touch each other.

But after?

I found myself unwilling to think of anything *but* after. There would be an after. We'd get my best friend back and then we'd see what happened next.

Rand came around the car to my side and squeezed my arms, the look on his face encouraging. "Are you ready to do this, Lindsey?"

Was I about to get the medieval version of the pre-game pep talk? "I think so."

"Do you have your stakes?"

I shifted my weight and felt the press of the wooden stakes I'd velcroed inside the pair of calf-high boots I'd bought specifically for this. We'd made the stakes from a pair of broken antique chairs in the Venice apartment. It had hurt my soul to see the wreckage, but at least it was going to good use. And it was fitting that if I had to stake someone, it would be with a chair the vampires had destroyed. "Got the stakes," I assured him.

He nodded. "Holy water?"

I patted the two flasks taped into my bra, between each boob and underarm. My sweater was loose-necked enough that I could reach through and pull one out, and I'd practiced the move repeatedly. I'd wanted to tuck them into the front of my sweater, but that had provided a quadra-boob effect that fooled no one. "Holy water ready."

"Garlic?"

I groaned. "God, I really hate this part."

Rand gave me a rueful smile. "It is as painful for me as it is for you." His hand caressed my cheek briefly, then he took a step back, waiting.

I sighed and reached into the backseat of the car. "This is the worst." In a bag, I had a plastic spoon and an extra large jar of minced garlic for cooking, plus a bottle of water and a tiny bottle of mouthwash. I glared at Rand, as if this was his fault. "I'm never eating garlic again when I get home."

"I would encourage that," Rand said, leaning up against the car and waiting for me to continue. His mouth tugged up in a teasing smile. "Be strong."

Strong. Sure. He wasn't the one that had to choke down minced raw garlic. I'd considered getting entire bulbs and just chugging the cloves, but that presented two problems—one, getting it in the car with Rand (who didn't seem to be affected by the jarred variety), and two, the fact that I'd have to chew all that garlic. At least the minced was chopped finely enough that I could mostly just swallow it down if I got it to the back of my throat.

Mostly.

I groaned as I unscrewed the lid on the jar. Normally I loved a bit of garlic in food, or garlic bread with my pasta. But this? This was just revolting.

I dug my spoon in, sucked in a deep breath, and shoved a mouthful in. *Think of Gemma*, I told myself as my gorge rose. I squinted, eyes streaming, and cough-gagged my way down.

"Keep going," Rand said.

"I'm going as fast as I can," I said, taking a swig of the water. "You try eating some raw garlic and see how fast you can go!"

"You know that wouldn't work at all," Rand said, and pointed at himself. "Vampire."

"Sarcasm," I retorted, then pointed at myself with the spoon. "Lindsey."

"Less complaining, more eating," he teased, keeping his distance. As I spooned another mouthful, I noticed he took another step back, his expression becoming less amused and more uncomfortable.

As much as I complained about the taste (because really, it was awful), this was all part of our strategy. If I happened to be found by a stray vampire, and if he was the bitey kind, he'd get more than he could handle. We were hoping it'd be enough, between the garlic and the stakes and the holy water. The garlic so far was the roughest part, because I couldn't slowly build up the amount in my body over a few days. It would have reeked out of my pores with the quantity I was currently chowing down on, and that would have been a dead giveaway.

As it was, all I needed to do was get through this jar and then freshen my breath with mouthwash. Lots and lots of freshening.

By the time I got a few more spoonfuls in, my

stomach was burning a protest, and my gag reflex was threatening to go off. "That has to be enough. I can't take any more," I told Rand, chugging the bottle of water before switching to the mouthwash. I rinsed and spat on the roadside a few times, then spritzed myself with a light, fresh perfume. I looked over at him. "Do you want to come smell me?"

He moved forward, expression wary, and gave me a quick sniff. "I smell that blue drink."

"That's mouthwash."

Rand sniffed me again, leaning so close his nose was practically in my hair. "You smell delectable, as always."

"I imagine that'll change once things digest and soak in," I told him ruefully.

"Then we shouldn't waste any time," he said. And before I could agree, Rand leaned in, grabbed me, and pressed his mouth to mine in a quick, firm kiss. "That is for luck," he said, then wove unsteadily on his feet.

"Eeep." I barely managed to grab him before he went down. "Maybe you don't kiss the girl that just tongued a bunch of garlic, huh?"

"I wanted to kiss you," he murmured, voice sleepy. He pushed me away gently, then braced himself against the car. "If this is to be my last memory, I wanted it to be a good one."

That was alarming. "Don't be so gloomy," I told him, keeping my voice cheerful. "We're going to get Gemma, and then we'll figure out what comes next."

He nodded, shaking off the effects of the kiss and straightening.

I looked down the road into the tiny, dark valley, where a small Swiss chalet was nestled amongst trees. That was Guy's hideout. "I guess I should start heading down."

"Stay safe," Rand told me, his gaze sober. "I mean that. I need you."

"Of course you do," I said blithely, capping the garlic and leaving it next to the tire. I didn't want it back in the car. "Who else will be your guide to the twenty-first century?"

"No. I need *you*, Lindsey."

Speechless, I gazed at him. At his handsome, sad, noble face. I wanted to say so much, but Gemma first. So I gave him a faint smile, then turned on my heel and began to race down the path toward the home of Guy. We needed to do this, and I wouldn't let Rand down. Or Gemma.

Determined, I kept walking. We'd found Guy's house and parked a mile or so away so we could have the element of surprise . . . well, such as it was. I had no doubt that Guy knew Rand was closing in. I just hoped that Rand's plan would work and any vampires in the vicinity would come after Rand and not me.

And I hoped Rand could handle them.

I paused and glanced back. The hills of the valley

were steep and green, but if I squinted hard, I could make out a shape darting through the trees at inhuman speed. Rand. *Stay safe*, I mentally sent to him. *If we get through this alive, you can totally use me as your personal juice box and I will love every moment of it*, I promised.

I headed down the deserted road, toward the tiny house. If I were a centuries-old vampire, I don't know that I would have chosen a remote little valley in Switzerland to set up shop, but everything about the place bespoke privacy. Maybe that was all Guy wanted after hundreds of years of servitude to the Dragon? Who knew how his mind worked? As I sprinted, I kept to the trees on the side of the road, trying to stay out of sight in case a car came down the way. The altitude was killing me, though, and I huffed and panted my way across the steep hillsides as I avoided the road.

I wished we'd done this in the daytime, when everyone was asleep. Maybe then I could have broken into the house, gotten Gemma out, and whisked her away before anyone could notice. Rand had been totally against the idea, though. What if Guy set traps? he'd asked me. He wouldn't be able to rescue me for hours on end, and at least this way, if things went south, I still had someone for backup. We'd purchased a burner phone for Rand, and even though he didn't really know how to operate it, he knew that if it rang, I was in trouble and he should come for me.

The Swiss house was an adorable sort of chalet set

off on one side of a steep, tree-covered hill. I imagined in the winter it would be nestled in snow, but for now it was just surrounded by wet green grass. My boots slipped as I scrambled up the hill, heading for the lit windows. After all, it wasn't as if I could go to the front door. The wooden chalet had a steep A-shaped roof and a balcony wrapping around the house. From where I was sneaking up, I could see a heavy stone fireplace, multiple windows, and what looked like a woodpile under the steps. The windows all had their shades drawn, which worried me a bit. Were we expected?

I circled the house, looking for the best way in. The front was a no-go, obviously. The windows were too high off the ground, and the balcony looked as if it was made of wood, and wood creaked. Since the chalet was set on a slope, though, the back of the house was closer to the ground, and I found a small window back there that looked as if it would open up into a room. Perfection. I snuck up on it, keeping my steps as quiet as possible. Rand had incredible hearing, so I wagered that Guy did, too, if he was home.

Please, please don't be home.

It felt like it took forever for me to cross to my chosen window. Once I was there, though, I put my fingertips carefully on the lip at the bottom and tried to pull it up.

No go.

I studied the window. It didn't look as if it was

locked. I tried again, then felt stupid when it gave *inward*. It was one of those windows you flipped *in* to open. Duh. European houses were different from American houses. I peered into the dark room. It looked like a bathroom.

Okay, I could deal with that. A bathroom could be a safe spot to enter the house. Heck, a bathroom wouldn't be used much by a vampire, so that could totally work. Carefully, I pushed the window in a bit more, judging the width. When it was big enough for me to slide in, I stuck my legs through, turned on my belly, and began to do a weird sort of shimmy into the house.

I misjudged the fall inside, though. My legs hung in the air, touching nothing no matter how much I pointed my toes. I wiggled a few more inches down than felt safe, trying to find a foothold—

—and my entire body crashed through to the other side. My head smacked against the lip of the porcelain tub, and I had to bite back a groan of pain as red shot through my vision. Dear God, that hurt. I lay on my back in the tub, panting, trying to fight back the pain, and hoping against hope that I hadn't made enough noise to bring anyone—

The door opened, light flooding into the small, dark bathroom. A man stood there, his hair inky black, skin pale. He had a neat, manicured goatee and pointed features. And he looked at me and tsked.

"Now that is just sad."

I struggled to sit up. This had to be Guy. "S-stay away from me."

"Right." His voice was smooth and lightly accented, and familiar. It was the voice from the phone. "Do me a favor and try not to break anything else with your head, will you? And shut that window. I don't want any birds flying in." When I didn't move, he sighed. "Come on, then. We both know you're not going to take me down with your superb fighting skills. You can't even sneak into a house." He gestured at the doorway, as if I'd been a guest. "You want to see your friend, right?"

Fifteen

Guy kept his hand on my elbow as he led me into his living room. "Would you like a cup of hot tea?"

Would I *what*? I stared at him as he ushered me forward. Offering me tea when he should have been ready to rip my throat out? "I—I don't think—"

"Lindsey!" Gemma's happy voice cut through my confused thoughts. "Oh my God, wow! It's so fucking good to see you!"

"Language," Guy warned.

"Sorry, of course," Gemma said in her sweetest voice. She was seated in a parlor chair near the fire. A bit of embroidery was in her lap, and she was wearing a long dress instead of the jeans she normally lived in. But she looked healthy, and she smiled at me when I entered. I wanted to weep with relief.

"Gemma," I breathed. "Oh my gosh, are you all right?"

"Of course I'm all right," she chirped. "And did you mention tea, sweetie? I'd love some, too."

Guy gestured that I should sit in the chair across

from Gemma, and I did, dazed. My cheek throbbed from my fall, and maybe it was affecting my brain, because all of this seemed really damn confusing to me. I watched as Guy headed to the far side of the living room and crossed into a nearby room, presumably the kitchen. Was he really going to make us tea?

The moment he left, Gemma grabbed my knee. I looked over at her in time to see her twirl a finger near her ear and mouth the word *crazy*. "Just go along with whatever he says," she whispered to me, then straightened in her chair and began to poke at her embroidery again.

Embroidery? Gemma? It looked like she was doing nothing more than doodling stick figures on the fabric, but I did have to admit that she looked perfectly ladylike. "What—"

She kicked me. Didn't even look up. Just kicked me and made a soft noise that said, *Talk later*.

I shut up. So much for ladylike.

Guy returned a moment later with two dainty china cups of tea. He handed me one, and Gemma the other. She thanked him with a sweet smile, then promptly put it to the side, shooting me a look. Right. Even I grasped that. Don't drink. I held the cup in my hands and watched as Guy pulled a stool up and sat near us.

"So tell me," Guy said. "To what do I owe the dubious honor of your presence?"

I blinked, trying to think of something clever yet

un-accusing to say. I had nothing. "I came to rescue Gemma," I said, deciding to go with the truth.

"Commendable," he said, smiling over at Gemma. She returned the smile, a little too brightly. Then he looked over at me again. "You do realize she was safe with me all this time, yes?"

"Because you want to exchange her for Rand?"

"That," he agreed with a slight inclination of his head, "and she is A positive."

I stared at him blankly. "Huh?"

"Blood type A positive," Gemma said helpfully. "Apparently it's not a favorite of vampires. Remember how Rand said I'd taste terrible? There you go!"

"Ah," I said. Because this was the weirdest conversation. I twisted my ID bracelet, knowing that it showed that I was actually Hh—Bombay blood— and super-rare. If he found out about my rare blood, it might make me even more attractive to the vampire.

"Gemma has been a true model of a prisoner," Guy said. "Once we gave her the appropriate clothing and coached her on her speaking, she's been a joy to have around." He gave Gemma a pleasant look, and she beamed at him, then stabbed her needle into her embroidery again. His gaze swiveled back to me, his eyes lighting with interest. "I do see why Rand has taken such interest in you, though."

I squeezed the teacup in my hands. "You do?"

"Mmm," he said, and leaned in toward me. I

scooted backward, but I could only go so far. Pinned between the chair and the vampire, I watched, horrified, as he took a long, languid sniff, so close that I could see his pores. Alarm pounded through me. Was he going to smell the garlic I'd ingested and take that as an attack against him? But he only smiled, his eyes thin slits of amusement. "AB negative?"

Oh. "My blood type?"

He nodded. "A rare and delicious vintage. You smell different, though. Sweeter."

My skin prickled. "I'm actually something called Hh. No antigens or something. It's called Bombay blood. Only sixty people in the world have it." God, why was I telling him this? He had to be using compulsion on me to make me confess. Now he'd want to taste me for sure.

"Ahhhh. Rarer than even the rarest of vintages. No wonder you smell so decadent." He smiled even broader, and I saw a hint of fangs. "It makes a man completely forget himself."

Oh dear. My teacup trembled a bit on its plate.

"Why don't you set that next to my drink?" Gemma offered, reaching over and taking it from my hands. I shot her a grateful look. "She's some weird rare blood, yes," Gemma told him. "But as for Rand, they don't get along. Why, just the other day—"

"Silence," Guy hissed, and Gemma's mouth snapped shut, her face going pale. He turned back to me. "Do I look stupid to you?"

Was this a trick question? I said nothing, my eyes wide.

He pointed downward, his finger digging into my thigh. "I know you are with Rand. I spoke to both of you less than a week ago. I am not a fool. No doubt he is even now distracting my guardsmen so you can come here and free your friend. I bet he did not expect you to be so incompetent, did he?"

No, he probably didn't. "W-what are you going to do with us?"

Guy leaned back, and for a moment, he wore the same sad expression that Rand often wore. "You assume the worst of me, do you not? Is your friend not safe after spending time in my company?" He gestured at Gemma. Frightened, embroidering Gemma.

"Perfectly safe," I whispered.

"I know Rand will come for you," Guy stated. He studied me thoughtfully. "If I had a blood vassal such as you, I would come for you as well. Not this one." He flicked a dismissive hand at Gemma. "A pretty face is easier to find than a pleasant taste."

Gemma's smile remained frozen.

I wanted to punch him. How dare he insult Gemma, who was sweet, outgoing, and kind, all because of her blood type? What a dick. "I don't let Rand drink from me," I told him.

"Then he's a fool."

"I guess he is, because I'm not his personal keg," I shot back.

"No, but you could be mine for the short time I have you," he murmured, and put a hand on my knee.

I pushed it away.

"We both know Rand is coming."

"You said that already."

Guy's smile was wry, lightly mocking. He sat straight and shrugged. "I can predict how this will all play out tonight. I knew he would not be able to wait the week. I knew he would never turn himself over to me." He gestured. "We are all puppets in a larger game. You. Me. Rand."

"Puppets?"

"Who do you truly think wants Rand dead, little girl?" Guy's look was sardonic. "Who else is intimately aware of his return after six hundred years of silence? Do you think I care whether or not my brother in arms has returned? Do you think I care so much that I will bring him to my home, my sanctuary, over one disposable human woman, all so I can wag a finger in his face before destroying him? After riding with him for two hundred years? Do you think it was my idea to kill William and Frederic?" His smile twisted into something ugly. "Do you think I have any control over any of this, at all?"

"It's the Dragon, isn't it?" I whispered. "The Dragon wants him dead." Because only the Dragon could give him release. Or death. Or a burrito. Or whatever Google Translate had come up with.

Guy gave a small nod, indicating I was correct. "The Dragon has decided that we are all expendable. Six hundred years ago, Rand showed stirrings of discontent, so the Dragon bade me get rid of him."

I bit back my gasp. Why was I surprised? I'd guessed as much myself, though I'd hoped that Guy was acting on his own and not at the behest of their mysterious overlord.

"And when Frederic and William showed their unhappiness, I took them out as well. It is not a task I have relished," he said, his face unspeakably sad again. "I am a coward. I've bought myself time with theirs. And I'd hoped that I could continue to live quietly, away from the Dragon's schemes. Perhaps, eventually, he would forget me. He has many vassals, after all. What is one more?" His smile twisted. "But Rand's return put us both on the Dragon's radar again. And do you know what he wants now?"

"He wants you to kill Rand? Again?"

Guy's eyes narrowed. Then he smiled brilliantly, which made my skin crawl just a little. "Flattering. You do not know that Rand was a genius on the battlefield, I suppose. There were none that could stand before his sword. Even Frederic, William, and I learned from him. Some men are born with innate talent, and Rand's is that of war. No, the Dragon has asked me to take care of Rand, but we both know that I will not survive if it comes down to a confrontation, as it must. The Dragon plays me as much as he plays Rand."

"You know you're going to die?"

"After so many years? I welcome it. I have out-lived or executed all of my friends. Even those I have surrounded myself with are mere sycophants. Even my thoughts are not my own, because they are pol-luted with the Dragon's touch. I am ready to die, to see what lies beyond all this." He gestured at his cozy living room, the fire flickering with warmth. "And Rand will be the one to do it. It's fitting, I suppose. And then we will all be wiped from this earth."

"Wait, what? What do you mean?"

Guy smiled, again his expression going sad. "You cannot guess? Rand will no longer wish to live under the control of the Dragon. He will destroy me, and then he will go after the Dragon, since it is he who instigated this. And either way, he is doomed."

"But you just said yourself that Rand is a great warrior. He might beat the Dragon," I protested. "He can win." I looked over at Gemma, and she had a pa-tient look on her face, as if to say, *See? Crazy.*

Guy shook his head. "He can win, yes, but you do realize the only thing that keeps Rand alive is his blood bond to the Dragon? If he kills me—and he will—all my vassals, my vampires alive by their bond to me, will become no more. I will no longer be there to sustain the link. What do you think will happen to Rand if he destroys the Dragon?"

My entire body felt cold with realization. "This is a suicide mission, then."

"It is," Guy agreed. "And Rand knows it. He's always known it, I imagine. He doesn't plan on coming out of this alive."

Sixteen

I hugged my arms as I sat in the chair, waiting. Nearby, Guy paced. Gemma kept picking at her embroidery. No one was speaking.

I'd called Rand's phone to give the "emergency" signal. Now we were all just waiting for him to appear so something—anything—would happen. I peeked over at Guy. He wasn't even trying to set up a war of any kind. There were no reinforcements, no bodyguards, nothing. Instead, he clasped his hands behind his back and walked slowly around his room, muttering to himself and gazing at the oil paintings on the walls. Maybe they were the old-fashioned version of a photo album and he was making his peace with his life. I pressed my ankle against one of the stakes in my boot. I wondered if I should attempt it, or if I should wait and let Rand handle things.

Did it even matter if I took Guy down or not? It wouldn't solve anything. Rand would still continue his mission to kill the Dragon.

And then he would die. Him and the Dragon both. Probably. Theoretically.

The thought made me sick.

I began to get worried about the late hour when there came a knock at the door. Well, less of a knock and more of a demanding thump.

My head shot up. I looked over at Guy, who had stiffened. Gemma kept sewing. I moved to the edge of my chair, anxious. What now?

I half expected Guy to force me to open the door. Or Gemma. Or to ignore it entirely. After all, a vampire couldn't cross a threshold without permission. Rand could not get to Guy as long as Guy was on this side of the door. But as I watched, Guy straightened his shoulders, rising to his full height, and approached the door. He threw it open.

Rand was on the other side. His shoulders were hunched, heaving. His hair was a sweaty, filthy mess atop his head. Blood and mud spattered his form, and there were gouges on one cheek. His sword was clenched in his hand. He truly looked like the warlord of the past that he was. I gasped at the sight of him.

"Well, well, well," Guy said, tilting his head. "Isn't this a pleasant surprise." His tone was flat, indicating it was anything but.

"Invite me in," Rand said gruffly. His gaze flicked to me, then back to Guy. "You have what is mine."

"So polite," Guy murmured. "After all these years. My, my. Just look at you. You don't look a day over six hundred." His mouth curved into a thin smile. "Never thought I'd see you again."

"Do not toy with me, Guy," Rand said. His fangs bared in a snarl. "I am in no mood, and you have no vassals left to guard you. I have made certain of that."

"They were weak," Guy said with an insouciant roll of his shoulders. "If they cannot beat you by sheer numbers, it is better I have none at all rather than a flock of incompetent fools at my beck and call."

Rand's gaze flicked to me again. His jaw clenched as he studied my face. "She is hurt."

"She is also an incompetent assassin," Guy said. "But she tastes oh-so-pleasant." He winked and licked his lips lasciviously, flashing a hint of fang at Rand.

I braced my hands on the arms of my chair, ready to spring forward.

Rand snarled, an inhuman sound, and made for the threshold. He bounced off it, as if repelled by an unseen force.

"Oh, are we sensitive about that?" Guy crossed his arms. "So we've found something Rand FitzWulf is willing to fight for? Now, that is interesting to me. Is it because of her blood, or something else?" He tilted his head, looking smug. "Perhaps what lies between her creamy thighs? I haven't yet had a chance to sample those, but there's time in the evening yet. Perhaps I shall even leave the door open so you may watch me claim her—"

"Invite. Me. In," Rand said through gritted teeth. He looked dangerous as hell. I was beginning to be a little frightened of him myself. How could Guy sit there and tease him when Rand looked as if he was about to go apeshit?

"So you can slit my throat?" Guy crossed his arms over his chest. "I don't see that happening. It's much more fun this way, don't you think?"

I stood up, careful to not make a sound as I did so. No sooner had I straightened than Guy said, "Do not even think about it, little one. I can rip out your throat with my teeth before you can bat an eye."

I froze in place. Looked at Rand. His eyes were gleaming with that odd vampire touch that told me he was inches away from losing all control.

I sat. Gemma reached over and grabbed my hand. I wasn't sure if it was to hold me in place, or for reassurance, but I squeezed her fingers back and remained seated. Whatever played out here would have to be without human help.

His hands on the door frame, Guy leaned forward, practically leaning outward. Now he was just taunting Rand with the fact that he couldn't get to him. Guy's back was to us, and I longed to put a stake through him. He was determined to harass Rand. "So, friend, did you like the whores I sent you all those years ago? You must have. You were so engrossed with fucking the one that you never noticed the other come around to stake you. That takes true . . . dedication to the cause." He chuckled.

"Do not needle me, Guy," Rand said in a deadly calm voice. "Not if you value your life. Now, let me in."

"My life is long ago forfeit," Guy sneered. "We are both the master's puppets—"

I gasped as something red and shiny sprouted from Guy's back. A sword point.

"If you will not let me come to you, then you shall come to me," Rand growled. He gave his sword another vicious shove forward, and Guy burbled something, blood spilling from his mouth. His limbs flailed, and the sword in his back grew longer.

Gemma's hand clenching mine threatened to cut off my circulation, but neither of us moved.

Rand lifted his sword, and Guy slid further down it. Then Rand stepped backward, and Guy, still spitted on his sword, went with him. Rand dropped Guy in the grass, and as I watched, he pulled his sword free.

Guy lifted an arm, a feeble protest at his treatment.

"Sleep well, brother," Rand said, and raised his sword again. In the next moment, Guy's head rolled away.

So . . . that just happened.

My stomach gave a nauseated gurgle. I ignored it, shook off Gemma's hand, and rose to my feet, approaching the doorway. "R-Rand?" Even though I was shocked at the brutality of things, I wasn't surprised. Deep inside, I'd known that either Guy or Rand wasn't coming out of tonight alive, and I was glad that Rand was the winner. In fact, I felt the absurd urge to fling my arms around him. Probably not the best call, considering he looked feral and was spattered with blood and God knew what else. I moved to the doorway, waiting to see what happened. Just like with the two vampires in Rome, a tense minute passed, and then Guy's body seemed to melt into the grass and flutter away as dust.

It was just like Rand said—a momentary pause for the body to catch up with the brain, then nothing.

Was that going to be Rand's fate? I felt ill at the thought.

Rand threw his sword onto the grass. He rubbed a hand over his face, staring down at the spot where the body of his friend had been. He staggered in place, then straightened, as if realizing he couldn't be weak. His gaze went to the doorway, to where I stood. His blue eyes were haunted with emotion. "It is done."

"It is," I said softly.

He took a weary step toward me, toward the door. "Invite me in, Lindsey."

Was this a test? To see if I truly trusted him?

Of course I trusted him. I knew Rand. I knew that no matter how savage and wild he looked right now, he was heartsick at having had to destroy his friend.

At being the only one of the four left. So I opened my arms. "Come and join us inside, Rand."

He went up the stairs slowly, with heavy steps. And as soon as he crossed the threshold, he threw himself into my arms, burying his head against my neck. I stiffened, anticipating a bite, but he was already warm with blood. And as his arms wrapped around me and held me tightly, I realized he simply wanted comfort.

My poor vampire.

I held him in my arms, and my hand went to his hair, stroking it off his face. "I'm sorry," I told him softly. "I'm sorry it came to this."

"I had such fear for you," he murmured against my skin. "I lost my wits when the phone went off. I feared he'd hurt you. That he'd drained you, unable to resist your delicious blood. That he'd deliberately done something to you to get at me . . ." His voice trailed off, his arms holding me tighter.

"Hush," I murmured. "I'm here, and I'm yours. No one has hurt me. All yours."

"Am I?" he asked, looking up at me. His face was brutal, all harsh planes and angles. There was nothing modern in this warlord. I'd just seen him run a man through and then behead him. His fangs peeped between his hard lips, and he was covered in blood and cuts from his battle.

"I totally want to kiss you right now," I breathed, dragging my fingers through his longish hair.

"Then do it," he murmured, his blue eyes locked to mine.

"I can't," I protested. "All that garlic—"

"I care not," he said. "You are mine." And then his mouth was on mine, his fangs scraping my lips.

I squeaked, surprised that he was kissing me despite the garlic bomb in my belly. But his mouth possessed mine, and I forgot everything but the feel of him against me. I moaned against his mouth, my arms going around his neck as he licked against my tongue, claiming me for his own.

"Mine," he murmured again hungrily, and his tongue thrust into my mouth, a blatant reminder of what he'd like to do to me. I whimpered and slid my own tongue along his, only to feel him take it into his mouth and suck lightly on it. A blast of pleasure swept through me, and my skin prickled, my nipples hardening in response. Oooh.

"Should I get you two a room?" Gemma called from off to the side.

Rand slowly pulled his mouth from mine. He brushed my hair back from my face, studying the bruise on my cheek. The look he gave me was tender and full of emotion, and I smiled at him. He smiled back . . . and sagged to the ground.

Damn garlic.

Seventeen

Should we do something about that?" Gemma asked, eyeing the dirty, sprawled vampire at my feet.

"Let's bring him inside to one of the rooms," I told her, getting his arms. "We'll stay here until the sun goes down."

"Do you think we'll be safe?" she asked.

"Completely safe. If Guy's dead, his vampires are, too, remember?"

Once Rand was safely stowed inside, we worked between the two of us to lift him onto one of the beds. When he was in bed, passed out in that weird vampire sleep, I turned to Gemma and put my arms around her. "Can I just say how glad I am to see you?"

She squeezed me close in a hug. "Not half as glad as I am to see you."

"What happened?" I asked her, sitting on the edge of the bed next to Rand's feet. "Tell me everything."

So she did, starting with the man who'd approached her in Venice, asking about the estate. She hadn't thought anything of it, because why would she? No one in their right mind would think another crew of vampires would be coming after Rand. Vampires weren't something people normally thought they had to be safe against, so Gemma hadn't paused to consider it. She'd just invited them in. Once inside the apartment, they'd held Gemma captive and started trashing the place. They'd looked for Rand, and when he wasn't to be found, they'd hauled her back to Guy.

"And Guy was crazy nuts. Like, the motherfucker didn't like me cussing or wearing pants. I'm guessing he's still a century or two behind the women's movement." She tilted her head. "Or . . . was."

I hugged her again. "I'm so glad you're safe. I was so worried he'd hurt you." The emotions of the last few days came crashing over me, and I felt tears prick my eyes. "When I saw the apartment wrecked, I thought the worst." I squeezed her tightly, not wanting to stop hugging her.

"I'm so sorry," she said, rubbing my arm. "I know you must have been devastated to see all that stuff broken."

"Gem, they're just things. They can be replaced. Well, maybe not those things, but you know what I mean. Vases aren't people. I can't replace a friend that's closer to me than a sister. You know that, right?"

"Aw, I know, baby girl. I love you, too. And I'm

fine." She gave me a squeeze. "He didn't hurt me. Didn't even drink from me. Lousy fuck, though."

I pulled back, staring her in the eye. *"What?"*

"Oh, don't judge me. I offered." She shrugged. "I figured as long as he was interested in getting some, I'd stay alive. I've fucked worse after a night at the club." She grimaced. "I've fucked way better, but I've fucked worse for sure."

"O-okay." I'd never get used to how casual Gemma was about something like that.

"Yeah, he was a pretty messed-up guy," she admitted. "Anxious as hell over stupid shit. Obsessed with Rand. And kept getting instructions from some other guy that was calling him constantly."

"The Dragon," I murmured.

Gemma nodded. "I'm thinking he's pulling the strings."

"I know he is," I told her. "He wants Rand. And I'm pretty sure he wants him dead."

"Poor Rand," Gemma said. "He's got a lot of damn enemies for a six-hundred-year old man."

"He does," I said, looking down at Rand's sleeping body. "He's going to want to go after the Dragon next. I know he will."

"And are you going to tag along?"

I nodded, swallowing the knot in my throat.

"Lindsey, I love you, but this guy is trouble. I don't know if this is safe. I worry he's going to get you in over your head." She gestured at the Swiss chalet.

"You know, like all this? Trashing the apartment? Kidnapping people? Beheadings?"

"I know," I said. "I know all that."

Her gaze sought mine. "I don't want you to get hurt. I know you care about Rand. I do, too. But he's in some deep shit, and I'm not sure you or I can hang with this."

"I know," I said again, then bit my lip. "Gemma, I'm going to help him. I feel responsible."

"Oh, sugar, don't do anything I wouldn't do."

I gave her a weak smile. "You slept with the enemy. That doesn't rule out a lot."

"I mean falling in love. Don't do that. Love 'em and leave 'em if you must, but don't get this"—she tapped on my chest over my heart—"involved."

Funny advice coming from Gemma, I thought with a smile. She fell in love with everyone. Of course, she also fell out of love just as quickly. "I'm afraid for him, Gemma."

"You should be afraid for us."

"I am. But Rand is out for vengeance." I clung to her arms. "He wants the Dragon dead, and if Rand kills him, the connection is severed . . . and Rand will die." The words choked in my mouth.

"Oh, sweetie." Gemma hugged me again, then gave me a gentle look. "I know you don't like the thought of it, but put yourself in his place. The Dragon can track him, right? He's got a mental connection to the man. Rand is never going to be free of him. He's also six hundred years out of his own time, and I'm not entirely sure he wants to be here. Maybe death would be kindest."

Tears blurred my eyes. "But I love him."

"If you love him, love him enough to respect whatever decision he makes," she told me in a soft voice. "And if he wants to let go, let him go."

I wasn't sure I could. But for now, I nodded.

Gemma and I secured Guy's chalet while Rand dozed. We locked down all the windows and barred the doors, and sprinkled a bit of my holy water on each windowsill and over the thresholds. Guy's vampires should be dead, but we figured you could never be too safe. I gave Gemma one of my stakes, and she went to sleep in one of the guest bedrooms.

I went back to Rand's room. I was tired, but I wanted to make my vampire comfortable first, just in case he woke up. So I got a warm washcloth, stripped his clothing from his sleeping form, and gently cleaned him, admiring his cool muscles and noble form. As I cleaned the blood from his face, I wondered.

If Rand chose death as the kindest option, could I stop him? Did I even want to? It would be hard to live with a vampire. I'd have to rearrange my entire life around his.

But it was something I was willing to do. For him. Because the alternative—a life with no Rand—didn't seem appealing any longer. If a life with Rand meant no garlic, no sunshine, and a life on the run, then it was the life I'd choose.

I leaned in and kissed his mouth, wishing he was awake. Then, worried about the future, I curled up next to his naked form and tried to sleep.

Eighteen

I woke up to a cool hand touching me, sweeping up my side, where my T-shirt had hitched up and revealed bare skin. Rand was kissing my neck, and my nipples reacted automatically. I whimpered and clung to him, shaking off the last of sleep.

"Good eve, sweet lady," he murmured against my throat.

"A-are you thirsty?" I asked breathlessly as his hand went to cup my breast. Oh, mercy. A newly awakened Rand was a naughty one. His fingers swept over my nipple, teasing it, and I arched against his hand. Oh, if he didn't stop touching me, I was going to shuck my panties and climb on top of him. My entire body ached and throbbed with awareness, and I wondered how long he'd been touching me before I'd woken up. The thought was a titillating one. I slid my hand down his front and felt the hard length of his naked erection. Oh, yeah. Someone was awake all over.

"Very thirsty," he said, lips tickling my throat.

"However, my thirst for all things Lindsey should perhaps wait until we speak with Gemma."

I blinked awake, remembering where we were. Guy's chalet. Right. Gemma was in the next room, and if I stilled, I could hear the sounds of someone tinkering in the kitchen. Crap. How long had she been awake? "I should get up," I murmured, even though I didn't move. His fingers were still caressing my nipple, and I wanted nothing more than to drag his head there.

Or lower. Lower was good, too.

"You should," he agreed, dashing my hopes. With one last tweak of my nipple, Rand gave me a sexy, heavy-lidded look that promised so many things that I wanted to forget all about my friend. But then he rolled out of bed and stood, his naked backside to me. "Have you seen my shirt?"

"It was destroyed," I told him. "We'll find you a new one." I got out of bed, too, my knees weak after our snuggle. I straightened my clothing, squeezed my own breasts in the hopes that it would make my nipples return to their normally un-prominent state, and left the room.

Gemma was in the kitchen, hovering over a skillet on the tiny stove. Her hair was pulled up in a messy knot, and she was wearing jeans and humming to herself as she cooked.

"Hey," I said softly.

"Hey!" She turned around and winked at me.

"Bacon and eggs okay? Guy didn't need to eat, but he kept the fridge stocked for me. All this food is going to go to waste if we don't eat it. And you will probably need your strength, since you're eating for two." Gemma gave me an embarrassingly exaggerated wink. "Right?"

Two? Oh Lord. Me and Rand. "Right. Need some help with that?"

"Nope, almost done," she said. "Do me a favor and set the table?"

I found dishes in one of the cabinets and set the table for us. It felt weird to be sitting down for a cozy breakfast in a dead vampire's chalet, but Gemma was right—there was no sense in fleeing when we needed to eat and regroup. And most of all, we needed to plan. So we sat down. Gemma shoved piles of scrambled eggs and bacon onto my plate, and I dutifully ate them, thinking about Rand and the fact that he needed to drink. I wondered if the garlic had gotten out of my system yet. I looked over at Gemma, wondering if Rand should drink from her.

Then I struck that idea down, because just thinking about it made me horribly jealous. Ugh. I crammed a piece of bacon in my mouth. Maybe I could kill any lingering taste of garlic with bacon. Bacon fixed everything.

Rand appeared a few moments later, sauntering into the room. His sword was strapped to its normal spot at his waist, and he'd found a T-shirt that looked to be two sizes too small for his brawny arms. It stretched over his muscles, which made my mouth water all over again. "Good eve, Gemma," he said, and sat down at the table. "I am glad to see you well."

"Right back at ya, sweetie." She flashed him a smile, then sipped her coffee. "So, what's our game plan?"

"The Dragon wants me dead," Rand said in a somber voice. "I must go after him." He looked over at me.

I said nothing. Just ate more bacon.

"Well, as fun as Switzerland has been," Gemma said sarcastically, "I need to head back to Venice and see what we can salvage. You guys rented a car, right?"

I nodded. "It's up the road. You can take it."

Rand's gaze was on me. "Will you go with her?"

I shook my head, not meeting his gaze. "I'm with you."

"You do not have to," Rand said. "It will be dangerous. The Dragon could have more vampires he'll send after me. They will be attracted to your scent. You will be vulnerable if we are parted."

"Then we won't part," I said simply.

"Being around me will be the most dangerous place of all." His expression was impassive, as if he didn't want to influence me.

"All the more reason for someone to watch your back," I said lightly. "Or, at the very least, provide a distraction of sorts."

Gemma snorted. "Just be careful, all right? You know I love you."

"I love you, too," I told her, "but this is something I need to do. I can't abandon Rand. Not now. Not when he needs someone the most."

"You will be safer in Venice," Rand said. "I want you there."

"No. Someone needs to be at your side. You need an ally." Now, more than ever.

"Just make sure you call me constantly and keep me updated," Gemma said, wagging a finger at me. "Or I'm going to worry."

"I will," I told her. "I promise."

We cleared the breakfast plates, packed Gemma's things, and walked her out to the rental car. I gave her the keys and Rand's burner phone. Then she hugged me tightly. "Please, please stay safe, Lindsey, okay?"

"You, too," I told her, an ache in my throat. "Don't invite anyone in. Not even me or Rand."

She nodded. "You be careful. Text me constantly to check in."

"I will."

Impulsively, she turned and hugged Rand. I noticed she whispered something in his ear, and he nodded. Then she released him, gave me a final bright smile, and jingled the car keys. "Well, my ass is off to Venice. You two kids have fun. And call me."

"I will," I said, and waved as she got in the car and slowly drove up the winding road.

Then it was just me and Rand. Feeling suddenly shy, I turned and started walking back up the road, toward Guy's chalet. We'd agreed that Rand and I would stay for another day or two to see if any other vampires arrived. If not, we'd continue on our hunt for the Dragon. I crossed my arms over my chest and headed down the path. After a moment, Rand joined me, coming to my side.

"So what did Gemma whisper to you just now?" I asked him.

"Nothing of importance," he said.

"Uh-huh."

"She did say you would ask."

She knew me well. "If it's not a big deal, then why not just spit it out?"

"Because it was for my ears alone." He slid an arm around my waist. "Are you sure you wish to stay with me? It will not be easy."

"I don't care if it isn't easy," I told him. "You need me with you."

"I am not used to needing people," he admitted. "But I am glad to have you at my side, regardless."

"You need to feed anyhow," I said, trying to keep my voice light. As if the thought of feeding him didn't make my entire body light up in response. "It's best I stick around for that."

"Lindsey." He stopped and pulled me with him, turning me to face him. "You cannot serve as my blood vassal in that capacity. Remember my warning? That if I fuck you, I would need to drink from you?"

I blinked. I hadn't expected him to protest. "Wait. Do you want to fuck everyone you drink from? Seriously?"

He gave me an exasperated look. "Of course not. Have we not discussed that you taste sweeter than most?"

Oh right. I had special, supertasty blood. Which didn't change things. "So . . . wait. Don't you want to fuck me?"

He groaned and pulled me close, his cool fingers brushing my jaw. He pressed his forehead to mine. "More than anything. Surely you must know this. Yet I would not force you to service me if it was not your wish."

"Two things," I told him, putting my hands on his chest. Oh boy, that shirt sure was stretched to the limits over his pectorals. "One. Let's not call it 'servicing,' okay? That implies bad things. And two, if I didn't want to be with you, I wouldn't be here." I looked up at him, feeling suddenly shy. It was hard for me to confess how I felt. "Rand . . . I care about what happens to you." I croaked the words out, then blushed. "I want to be your partner."

During my confession, I dropped my gaze. It was hard to keep eye contact when you were throwing your heart at someone. By the time I was done, I was staring at his chest, where my hand rested over his silent heart. He wasn't saying anything, and that made me nervous as heck.

After another moment of silence, I peeked up at him and gave his chest a pat. "Right about now, you should probably say something."

His jaw worked. "I am a man of action, Lindsey. Not good with words."

"Then action me something." *Don't just ignore me. Please.*

"You wish action?"

I wished anything at that point.

To my surprise, he leaned down and grabbed me behind my thighs. Before I knew what was going on, he flung me over his shoulder, my butt in the air. I gave a squeak of alarm as he began to walk decisively toward the chalet. "Um, Rand?"

"I am giving you action, Lindsey." His hand slapped my ass.

"What exactly are we doing?" I bounced and wobbled on his shoulder. My fists dug into his shirt as an anchor.

"I am taking you back to bed," Rand said, his voice matter-of-fact and determined. "And I am going to fuck you until dawn."

"I . . . oh." A hot flush of warmth crept through my body. "Okay." Yeah, that was pretty okay with me. More than okay. Heck, I was getting turned on just by him stating it. I squirmed on his shoulder.

A rumble moved through his chest. "I smell you getting aroused, Lindsey. Control yourself lest you want to be plowed in the grass here."

I gave another outraged squeak. Plowed in the grass? Control *myself*? I slapped at his back. "You're an arrogant prick."

He chuckled. "That is better."

Then he was setting me on the doorstep of the chalet. Without thinking, I went inside, pushing the door open. It took me a moment to realize that Rand wasn't following me. I turned around. "Rand?"

He stood at the doorway, his big frame swallowing up all the space. "Invite me in, Lindsey."

I drummed my fingers on my lips, suddenly titillated by the turn of events. "Oh, are you at my mercy now? Funny how these things happen."

Rand raised an eyebrow in my direction. "Do you invite me in or not?"

"Oh, I will soon enough. I just need . . . incentive." I studied him. "Maybe if you took your shirt off."

He tilted his head, confused. "Why would I do that?"

"Because I like looking at you."

He suddenly grinned. "Then why not ask me to take all of my clothing off?"

I fanned myself. "An even better idea."

His hands went to his belt and he began to unbuckle it. "Ask and I shall do as you please." He undid the buckle slowly, then pulled it free from his belt loops. "But be warned that I shall exact my revenge once you allow me inside."

"Naked revenge?" I asked, fluttering my lashes at him. "What does that entail?"

"Holding you down until you are as naked as I am, of course."

Why was it that I blushed at everything the man said? "We'll see about that." Actually, it sounded pretty awesome to me. My breathing was speeding up just thinking about it.

Rand pulled his shirt off, and I watched his pale six-pack flex as he did. I was entranced by the sight of those shoulders—good gravy, those shoulders—and his biceps as they moved. He tossed the fabric on the ground. "Shall I continue?"

"Oh, don't stop now," I murmured, unable to tear my gaze away from him.

His hands went to his zipper. Well, his button-fly, because he hadn't been a big fan of the zipper. Button by button, he tugged the denim loose until it hung loose from his hips. Then he gave the fabric a small hitch and it dropped to his knees, revealing a pair of gray boxer briefs that left nothing to the imagination.

Absolutely nothing.

My mouth watered at the sight. I'd seen Rand naked before, but seeing him aroused and naked was a mind-blowing experience. His cock jutted out from his hips, the underwear tented and taut across the front. The legs of the boxer briefs molded to his muscular thighs, and I felt weak at the sight. Even weaker when he stepped out of his pants and dropped them to the ground, the boxer briefs following.

Rand was naked on the porch. His cock gleamed in the moonlight, as pale as the rest of him. There was no flush of blood down there, but he was clearly erect. Magic, I supposed. Who knew how vampire physiology worked when there was no blood flow?

And why was I thinking about vampire physiology when he was naked and mouthwatering in front of me?

He leaned on the doorjamb. "Let me in, Lindsey." His voice was a soft, seductive purr. "I have done as you have asked, have I not? Are you not looking your fill?"

I licked my lips. There was still the hint of a predator to him, enough that I was getting little shivers of anticipation mixed with a bit of apprehension. Rand was a dangerous vampire who needed to feed. He was going to feed on me . . . right after he fucked me silly. Of course I was a little apprehensive. But there was also a layer of excitement racing through me that told me I liked his dangerous side. That aroused me as much as his masculine beauty did.

So I baited the tiger a bit longer. I twirled a finger, indicating he should spin. "Turn around."

"So we are to play more games? Very well." His chuckle was a deep rumble in his chest, but he threw his hands up and slowly turned, and I caught sight of a pair of magnificently taut buttocks. Oh yeah. He was just as nice from this side as the other. "Now, let me in."

"I think I want to hear what you're going to do to me," I said as he turned fully around, cock facing me once more. I kept staring at it, even though I was trying not to. It *was* rather eye-catching in its largeness.

"Do you wish details, then? Very well." He leaned against the door again and crossed his arms over his chest, the picture of relaxation. Only his eyes told me that the predator was still very much at the forefront. "I think I would start with peeling your clothes from your fine form. Then I would toss you down on the bed and kiss every inch of you. Your breasts are quite lovely, after all, and they deserve some attention."

"Mmm, keep going." This was nice talk, but I wasn't getting the good, dirty stuff yet.

"Then I would take your cunny with my mouth." His blue eyes gleamed. "And I would make you rub it against my lips, until you were shuddering against my tongue."

All right, definitely getting warmer. I shivered, wrapping my arms around my torso so he couldn't see how my nipples perked up at the thought of that.

"And once I have fucked your cunny with my tongue, I would push my cock so deep into you that you would scream for more." His voice had taken on a sultry edge. "And I would thrust into you over and over again, your ankles on my shoulders, my cock deep inside you. I would make you come a dozen times, and still not let you relax until I'm done with you."

My mouth was dry. "I s-see."

"Not yet, you do not," he said, voice soft. "Now, invite me in."

I licked my lips. Gosh, they were dry, too. I blinked repeatedly, heat pooling through my body. His words had put me in a daze. Then I gestured, not wanting to drag this out any longer. "Come to me, Rand."

He moved so fast he was a blur.

The next thing I knew, there was an arm locked behind my head, another behind my back, and my clothed front was pushed up against a very broad, very naked chest.

"But first," Rand murmured, "I will sip from your throat. Tell me you want that. That you want my fangs plunging deep into you the way you want my cock."

I pressed my fingertips to his chest. "I . . . I'm a little afraid of it. You won't drink too much, will you?"

"Not much at all," he assured me and leaned in to press small kisses against my jaw and throat. "Merely enough to whet the edge of my appetite. Enough to flush my skin so I am warm against you. Enough that my cock will not be cold as I stroke through your folds. Enough that I have the taste of you—all of you—in my mouth."

I shuddered at his erotic words. "Then taste me."

"I shall taste you in many places, Lindsey." His tongue licked at the hollow of my throat, and I moaned. "I intend on seeing if you taste the same in many places. Behind your ear, you are particularly sweet." His teeth caught my earlobe, and I shivered as he gave it a tiny nip, then licked the skin. "And your neck is soft like the finest silks. I wonder if the skin between your legs is equally as silky, or tastes as fine."

I trembled against him. Was he going to bite me there? "Taste me anywhere you want." My knees were weak at the thought.

"First, though . . ." he murmured, coming up to press a gentle kiss to my mouth before his gaze met mine, " . . . a promise is a promise."

Dazed, I wondered what he meant, then realized it when he grabbed a fistful of my shirt a moment later and ripped the front of it from me, exposing my bra.

Oh, boy.

He studied my bra with interest. "What is this garment?"

Had we never had the bra talk before? I thought he'd seen me naked, but maybe he'd never seen me in a bra. "It's to hold my breasts in place."

He fingered the join of fabric between my breasts, the small ribbon bow on it. "Where are they going?"

Where were they . . . I giggled, struck by the absurdity of the question. "No, it's to keep them from bouncing. From wobbling when I walk. People of this time wear them."

"Strange," he murmured, then ripped through the bra anyhow. My breasts popped free, spilling out. "I prefer you like this."

I made a noise of protest. That was the only bra I had with me. But as Rand's gaze devoured me, I found that I cared less and less with each passing second. I could go braless. Who cared as long as the man I was hot for gazed at me like that?

"Beautiful," he told me, and reached up to cup my now-loose breast with his fingers.

I moaned, closing my eyes and enjoying the sensation. His touch was gentle, if cold. His fingertips brushed over my nipple, teasing the peak into standing on end. "That feels good," I told him, wrapping my arms around his neck to hold myself steady. "I like it when you touch me."

"Then it is good for both of us that I plan on touching you quite a bit," he murmured, and his thumb slid over my nipple again, sending little sparks of desire through me. His hand went to my waist, and I felt him tug at the fabric of my jeans.

"Wait," I said, covering his hand with mine. "Don't rip those, okay? I'll take them off."

"Do it quickly, then," he said, voice thick.

I looked up at him and saw that his fangs had distended, rubbing against his lips. Oh. For some reason, that affected me as much as the sight of his naked cock, and I shivered with desire. Hasty, I fumbled with my jeans, undoing my zipper and tugging the thick fabric down, bringing my panties along with them. I wasn't exactly a blushing virgin, but there was something about Rand that made me feel shy and inexperienced. Maybe it was his centuries of expertise. I hoped he wouldn't find me lacking.

I avoided his gaze as I stepped out of my jeans and panties, then discarded the remnants of my shirt. When he still hadn't spoken, I peeked up at him. "All done."

A hint of a smile touched his face, and he made a twirling gesture with his fingers. "Turn for me."

"Dick," I exclaimed, laughing. He wanted to play that game? Fine. I put my hands on my hips and gave my sexiest, slowest, shimmying twirl, making sure to roll my hips as I moved.

He groaned. "Ah, Lindsey. Fate must have been smiling on me to wake me to one such as you." His hand reached out, stroked down the curve of my spine. "You are made beautifully."

"Thank you," I murmured, turning back to him. I put my arms around his neck again, and was pleased when his arms went back around me as well. "You look pretty hot yourself."

"No, I am not warm," he disagreed. "Not yet. Soon, though." And his eyes gleamed. "I shall sip from your body and warm myself with your flush. Only then will I claim you as mine."

Right. Cold fingers weren't a big concern of mine at the moment. I didn't care if he was Frosty the

Snowman as long as he touched me. So I dragged my fingers through his long, shaggy hair. "Kiss me now?"

He leaned in and gently pressed his mouth to mine. I felt his fangs against my lips, felt his tongue flick against the seam of my mouth oh so carefully. Kissing with fangs required a bit more attention to detail, and the kiss itself was sweet and full of soft, arousing strokes of Rand's tongue that made me wonder if he'd do the same slicking movements lower on my body.

I rather hoped that was a yes.

I whimpered against his mouth, my kisses becoming needy, more intense, until I was practically sucking on the man's tongue. When he pulled his mouth away from mine, I made a sound of protest.

"Shall I take the first of many sips, Lindsey?" He nipped at my lip, teasing me. "Or shall we keep going?"

Oh, no, I wanted him to drink. I wanted that orgasmic pierce of fangs. In response to his question, I brushed my hair off my shoulder and exposed my neck to him. My hand went to the back of his neck, and I drew him forward, against me. "Taste me, Rand. I'm all yours."

He dragged his tongue down my throat, licking the point where my pulse throbbed. "It will not hurt you, Lindsey. That I promise."

"I know," I breathed.

There was a tiny flash of pain, followed by the

shock of the penetration and the flick of his tongue against my skin. My throat felt hot as he drank from me, and even as he did, his hand reached to my breast and caressed it. I moaned and clung to him, full of intense pleasure as he teased my nipple and lapped at my throat. Too soon, he dragged his fangs free from my throat and licked the wound to seal it. "Delicious," he murmured. "You are sweeter than anything I have ever tasted. It humbles me that you are mine."

I clung to him, wanting more of everything. More bites. More breast teasing. More naked skin pressing to mine. "Rand," I murmured. "When I said I wanted to be your partner, I meant . . . in all ways. Bed included."

"I know." He swept me into his arms, leading me to the bed. A moment later, he laid me down on the blankets with infinite gentleness and gazed down at me. "You are a gift to me, you know that, Lindsey? I thought this new world I'd awakened in was full of nothing but cruelty, but I find that with you here, it has so much potential."

Tears burned my eyes at his sweet words. "Quit making me cry and kiss me," I told him, raising my arms.

He slid against me, and I felt his flesh warmer against mine. I loved the touch of him, and I stroked my hands up and down his strong back as he nuzzled his mouth against mine and kissed me once more. "Am I warm enough for you yet, Lindsey?"

I considered this, stroking a hand down his chest. "If I say no, will you drink from me again?"

He grinned. "Is that your wish?"

I bit my lip and nodded, wanting more from him. More of everything. So I hooked a leg around his thigh and pulled him against me, even as I cupped my breast and offered it to him.

Rand groaned and bent low to nuzzle my breast. "Such a sweet morsel for my tongue." He dragged the tip of it across my nipple, sending shivers through my body.

"Are you going to drink from me there?" I asked him, breathless with excitement.

He kissed the tip of my breast and looked up at me. "Do you want me to?"

I moved my fingers to his mouth and gently brushed them over his lips, feeling their soft texture. The tips of his fangs scraped against my skin, and on a whim, I dragged the pads of my fingers against them, curious to see how he'd react.

He shuddered, a low groan rising in his throat. As I watched, his fangs seemed to elongate even more. Oh, wow. That was surprising. "They get bigger?"

"The more I crave, the longer they get," he rasped. His head bent low, and his mouth went to my nipple again. "And right now, I crave very much."

A hot bolt of lust shot through me at his words, and I arched my back so he could nibble on my breast some more. To my surprise, he skipped the nibbling altogether and sank his teeth into the curve, avoiding the sensitive nipple. I gasped at the sensation, but he'd barely flicked his teeth into me before he pulled back, then licked the skin to heal it. My nipple ached, unloved and unattended.

"I dare not take much," Rand admitted. "You taste so sweet I could lose my head too easily."

I slid my fingers over his big, muscular shoulders. Mmmm, God he felt good against me.

"What happens if you lose your head?" I asked him lazily, swirling my fingers over his warming skin.

"I would tear out your throat."

Yipe. My eyes widened at that. "Have you ever lost control?"

"Never." His look became fierce. "I will never lose control with you, either. You mean too much to me. I will never forget my place in this bed, with you in my arms."

That sounded strange. Like he would always hold back? Hold back how much? I frowned at the thought. Then again, I didn't exactly want him chewing my head off, either. "Does that mean you won't come when I do?"

He tongued my nipple again, then buried his face between my breasts. "I will not."

Really? "Then . . . what?"

"I will leave the room and finish myself." His mouth licked lower. "But do not worry. I will ensure you will be well fucked at that point."

But he couldn't come normally? Couldn't orgasm? Or if he did, he was in danger of losing control if he was inside me? Sleeping with a vampire was new territory, and all this sounded dangerous. His words sent a shiver through me. There had to be something I could do to get him off, like he was planning on doing to me. Of course, I lost all sense of concentration when he licked down to my belly button, then continued to move lower. His mouth pressed against my skin, his fangs occasionally dragging against it as he moved downward, and then he was at my mound, where I was hot and slick and so darn ready for him to touch me.

I moaned and parted my legs wider for him, trembling. "Maybe instead of drinking, you can just . . . sip. Anywhere."

He chuckled. But instead of feeling the scrape of fangs against my labia, I felt tongue. I squirmed, surprised by the difference. I'd been bracing myself for hard, sharp delight and got a licking instead. As I wriggled, Rand's mouth moved over my sex, licking and stroking my folds with his tongue and lips. His fingers pressed against my core, and I felt him sink a finger in even as he tongued my clit.

I cried out at the sensation, gasping. "Oh wow, you're really good at that. You—" My words broke off in a whimper as he took my clit between his lips and sucked hard. My hips bucked, and then I was pressing my hips up against his face, over and over again, trying to ride his tongue as he worked my pussy over with his mouth. When I came, it was with a small scream, my knuckles pressed against my lips.

He kissed my pussy, over and over again, then moved his mouth to my inner thigh. I heard him inhale gently. "There's a large vein here, you know. It's irresistible to my kind."

"Then give it a shot," I offered, feeling drowsy and delicious from my intense orgasm.

His teeth nicked my skin and I felt him lap at my inner thigh, sending quivers through my body all over again, as if I hadn't just come moments ago. He groaned, his hand skimming down my leg. "Sweet, sweet Lindsey. I cannot wait to sink my cock deep inside you."

Oh, mercy, that sounded like a good idea to me. "Do we need condoms?"

He lifted his head, frowning at me. "What?"

"Condoms? Do you know what condoms are?" At the shake of his head, I rubbed my brows. "Oh, okay. So do you know where babies come from?"

Rand chuckled. "Don't be silly. Of course I do." He moved forward and kissed my belly button. "And do not be afraid. I will be gentle."

"Um, I'm not a virgin."

He lifted his head in surprise, then shrugged. "Many village girls were not. I am not bothered by this." He winked, then moved down to lick my inner thigh again. "The naughty ones are more fun."

Amen to that. "A condom is a sheath a man puts over his penis to prevent his semen from entering the woman's, uh, womb."

He looked thoughtful, then began to lick and nuzzle my inner thigh again, over that sensitive vein. It was making me squirm, but in a good, ticklish sort of way. "I admit that seems a silly method of preventing pregnancies, but I have heard stranger."

Well, now I was curious. "What have you heard?"

Rand shrugged. "I once fucked a woman that wanted to wear a weasel's testicles round her neck to prevent unwanted births."

I giggled in horror. "Really?"

"Truly," he agreed, then spread my pussy lips with his thumbs again and licked me long and hard, until I was shuddering.

His tongue flicked at the opening to my core. "You do not need to worry. My body produces no seed. A vampire can get an erection, but when I come, there is no spend." He tongued my opening again. "We must have you good and wet first."

I squirmed on his tongue. Oh, I was wet all right. "I . . . suppose . . . that's good . . ." I panted. "I'm pretty wet as it is."

"I want you soaked," he told me, and pushed a finger into my core.

I gave a soft cry as he began to stroke it in and out, and he slid up my body to kiss my mouth. I clung to him, my mouth frantic on his as his finger slipped in and out of my center. Over and over again, he stroked me with one finger, and then two, his mouth on mine. I rode his hand, panting with need and frustration. When my body began to make slick, wet sounds as he pumped his fingers inside me, he pulled them out, and I moaned a protest at the loss.

Rand kissed me again, and then I felt his weight settle on top of me, his cock resting against the cradle of my sex. Eager, I wrapped my legs around his hips, straining against him. But instead of pushing into me, he rubbed his cock up and down my folds, wetting it with my juices. The sensations only made me crazier.

I might have demanded that he fuck me immediately.

My vampire only laughed and continued to rub the head of his cock against my clit, which made me grab the pillow behind my head and scream in frustration. The man would not be rushed. Finally, after my panting, begging, pleading, he shifted, and I felt the head of him press against my opening. I lifted my hips to help things along, and moaned as his length stroked into me.

Yes.

This was what I needed so badly.

I clung to him as he began to stroke inside me. "That's my sweet girl," he rasped, even as he thrust deep. "Take all of me."

His body felt as if it fit perfectly with mine, his

muscles divine to the touch, his lips soft but firm against my own. The scent of Rand's musk was in my nostrils, the taste of him on my tongue, and the feel of him was deep inside me. In bliss, I felt another orgasm working its way through me, and as he rocked into me over and over again, he murmured encouraging words against my mouth until I was coming apart at the seams. When I came, my entire body shuddered with need, and I cried out his name, clinging to him.

Rand's fierce mouth pressed against mine as I came. Then he was kissing my neck, his fangs scraping against my skin, and I clung to him.

To my surprise, though, he immediately pulled away from me as if struck, and leapt off the bed. He began to pace as I struggled to sit upright.

"Um? Rand?"

He looked over at me, his eyes a wild, spooky green instead of the normal blue, his cock still wet with my juices. His fangs were longer than I'd ever seen them. "Do not touch me right now, Lindsey."

I nodded, sitting up on the bed and pulling my splayed legs together. I felt a little abandoned. I knew I was just being silly, though. Rand didn't want to hurt me. "Are you all right?"

He gave a brutal chuckle. "I am more than all right. I am shades away from losing myself in you. Never have I come so close." He turned his back to me. "I must feed."

"And not from me," I guessed.

"I need blood. In my mouth. To come." His words were sharp. Abrupt.

That made me a little sad. I wanted to see him come. "So all of this between us . . . was that just torture for you?"

He shot me a flashing grin. "The sweetest torture imaginable. One I would endure over and over again. I just did not know I would react so strongly to you." He turned away again and shook his head. "I wanted to give you more pleasure."

"I wanted to see you come," I admitted.

"I will not risk harming you."

"Is it tied to your orgasm?" I asked. "Can it be any blood? Like . . . can you bite yourself?"

"I can," he admitted, then looked at me with hooded eyes. "You would not think it shameful?"

"Are you kidding?" I leapt off the bed. "Not at all. I'd love to see that."

"I cannot be in you," he warned. "I do not trust myself not to sink my teeth into your throat if it's exposed to me."

"Can . . . can I touch you, then?" I asked, greatly daring and reaching out to stroke a hand along his arm. His erect cock called to me, to my mouth. I wondered if he'd let me lick him until he came.

The look on Rand's face was plainly wary. "What do you intend?"

I dropped to my knees in front of him, his cock at eye level. "I want to take you in my mouth," I said softly. "Lick you with my tongue, like you did to me."

He hissed, his fangs elongating. One hand went to his cock and began to stroke it. The other went to his mouth. As I watched, he bit the back of his wrist and sank his fangs deep.

But his gaze was entirely on me.

I licked my lips, leaning closer to the hand that stroked his cock. I wasn't quite touching him. I wasn't sure if he wanted me to. But it seemed he liked my words, liked the visual of me leaning in close. "I was thinking about taking the thick crown here," I said, gesturing at the head of his cock. "And running my tongue along it, feeling the velvety texture of you with my tongue. There's a vein on the underside, you see, and I imagine it feels big and hard against the rest of all that smooth skin."

He hissed again, his hand pumping his cock furiously. The other wrist remained glued to his mouth, and he gave a low, sexy growl.

"Then," I murmured, leaning in so he could feel my warm breath on his skin, "I thought maybe I'd take you in my mouth. Let your length skim my tongue until the head of your cock is pushing deep into my throat, so deep I can barely handle you—"

His entire body trembling, Rand gave a wrenching groan, and his hand shook. I watched as his cock seemed to flex, but nothing came out. I looked up at my vampire lover. Blood wetted his lips, and his wrist was still embedded with teeth. His eyes were closed, and a moment later, he sagged against the wall.

"Lindsey," he panted, his mouth red with stolen blood. He licked his lips, then dragged his tongue over his wrist. "Never have I come so hard."

I beamed up at him, feeling proud of doing my part. I would have preferred touching him as he came instead of just dirty talk. For now, though, I'd take what I could get. "I'm glad you enjoyed yourself."

He pushed himself off the wall and moved toward me. I took an involuntary step backward, startled, but he only pressed a kiss to my mouth, a kiss with no fang. I relaxed and leaned into the kiss, enjoying his touch. My pulse still pounded between my legs and I wanted him to touch me again, but I'd wait for him to call the shots.

"Come back to bed with me," he murmured against my mouth. "We shall rest momentarily, and then I intend on making you scream my name again."

I smiled up at him. "Deal."

Nineteen

Much later that night, after many bone-quaking orgasms for me, and two more wrist-drinking orgasms for Rand, we lay tangled in bed together. I was sweaty from the intense workout, and Rand's skin was warm and flushed from my blood. I was drowsy, but not ready to go to sleep just yet. Instead, my mind was full of worries.

I traced a scar on his abdomen. "What's this from?"

"Jerusalem."

"And this one?" I touched a half-circle shape under one rib.

"A torture weapon was used on me when I was a hostage."

"Are any of your scars from anything good, Rand?"

He chuckled, and his hand covered my tickling fingers. "War is never good, Lindsey, and my scars are because I am a warrior."

"I see." I dragged my hand out from under his and brushed my hand over his chest again. "At least it gave you good stamina, I suppose?"

"Verily," he said, his fingers pushing a sweaty strand of hair off my face. "Perhaps you should go to war yourself if you intend to keep to my pace, fair Lindsey."

I gave a small, tired chuckle. It was no secret between us that he'd tired me out. "Your pillow talk needs some work, buddy. This is the time where you're supposed to confess feelings to a girl to keep her on the hook." Another laugh escaped me, but it felt strained. Why was I leading the conversation down this path? I knew where it would go—nowhere. Yet I couldn't help myself. I wanted to know if Rand was starting to feel as . . . tied to me as I was to him.

"Lindsey." His voice was gentle. "If I were not what I am, I would cherish you eternally."

Sudden tears pricked my eyes. I tried to laugh them away. "If you weren't a vampire? Which is kind of funny, because if you were human, there'd be no 'eternally.' I'd settle for a good seventy more years or so, you know."

"I cannot change what I am."

"I wouldn't change you," I argued. Sure, he had his quirks, but I adored the man. But I was worried. Not just about my heart but about the upcoming confrontation as well. My fingers played with his long ones. "He'll know you're going to come after him, won't he?" I asked. "The Dragon?"

"He will."

"He'll know because Guy is dead," I guessed. "He'll feel that?"

"The Dragon is the original *upyri*," Rand told me. "I do not know if his immortality works the same as mine, but I imagine yes, he will know that Guy is dead and will guess that I will come after him. Even now, I feel his presence like a brand in the back of my mind." He shook his head against the pillow, his dark hair spilling on the pillowcase. "I would give anything to be free of him. You do not know what it is like to serve a man like him. The Dragon is not like me. Think of the powers I have . . . his have even more intensity. He can convince with a mere word. He can charm with a thought. And he is bloodthirsty like none other. If he finds me, I am done. I must find him first. Everything depends on it."

I shivered against Rand. "He'll try to kill you."

"I know. It has to be done."

I clung to his hand, miserable. "I don't want to lose you after I've just found you."

He pulled me against him and pressed a kiss to my head. "I don't want to lose you, either. But know that I am not truly free unless he is gone."

And I knew what that meant. Guy had hinted that if the Dragon was destroyed, Rand would be, too. I couldn't bear the thought of it. "Rand . . . Guy told me . . ."

"I know."

"You know?"

He nodded, gazing up at the ceiling. "Likely he tried to convince you that if I should pursue the Dragon, it would be my death."

"Is he right?"

He shrugged.

"That's not an answer, Rand." I poked his ribs.

"How can I possibly say? I have never killed the Dragon."

"Yes, but you've killed other vampires."

"Ah, but he is the first of his kind. Who is to say it is the same type of magic?"

"Who's to say that it's not?" I argued. "Rand, this could kill you!"

"And if it does?" He took my hand in his and kissed the back of it. "I do not belong in this time, Lindsey. Better that I take the Dragon's vengeance upon myself than wish it upon another man, a good man with a family and children. He has lost a vassal in Guy and is losing me. He will seek to make more unless I stop him. So . . . stop him I must. I am expendable. I have no one."

"You have me," I said softly, my heart aching.

He brushed his fingers over my cheek, his expression soft. "So I do."

We stayed in Guy's chalet for two more days, regaining our strength for the upcoming confrontation with the Dragon. I tried not to think about that, but it was constantly on my mind as we relaxed in the cabin.

There were things to do, of course. Guy had books and old chessboards and everything you could think of to entertain a jaded vampire. The rooms were cozy, and we were alone. We made love at least three times a day, each time better than the last. Rand drank from me every few hours, not enough to truly sate his hunger but just enough to not leave me exhausted. He said it was fine, but I worried.

I always worried.

I worried about Gemma, too, but the texts started rolling in the next night. She was back in Venice. The apartment was a clusterfuck. She'd found a few small things she could save. Were we okay? Did I fuck Rand?

Of course Gemma wanted to know. I kept my responses short, but the truth was, Gemma was a great distraction from the moody vampire at my side. Not that I didn't appreciate Rand in all his different moods, but when he went outside to practice with his sword during the night? I worried.

Rand had taken out Guy and all the other vampires without breaking a sweat. Did he really have to practice his swordfighting skills? Was the Dragon that fearsome?

Was poor Rand totally screwed?

I kept these worries to myself and packed bags for us out of Guy's things. I found extra clothing in Guy's guest rooms, but it made me a little nervous to think that he'd been expecting visitors. Or worse, that we'd find a bunch of dead people buried out behind the house. I reprepped my vampire kit, too. I was out of garlic, so I'd need to get some in town when we went back.

Eventually, when we could stall no longer, I' called and arranged for a rental car to come pick us up.

There was no putting off going after the Dragon. On day three of our chalet idyll, I ate a hearty breakfast of four eggs and four slices of bacon. Rand drank from my throat, which turned into a quick round of nookie. We showered, dressed, grabbed our bags, and headed out.

We crossed through to the nearest city, then opted to take a train over the Alps instead of driving. We snuggled in the train car, got a hotel before dawn, and continued our trek across Europe, heading eastward.

By the time the train disembarked on the second day and we made our way to our newest hotel, I realized two things: one, that my card was nearly maxed to the limit, and two, that Rand wasn't as healthy as he pretended to be.

"Rand?" I asked, pulling his cool hand into mine as we entered the hotel room. "Are you all right?"

"I will be," he said with a thin smile for me. "Shall we take to the bed?" He gave me a sultry look. "I've missed the taste of you on my tongue."

I went to the hotel window and double-checked

the curtains, then threw a blanket over them just to be on the safe side. "We don't have to have sex," I said, moving back toward him. I smoothed a lock of hair from his brow. He looked exhausted, strained. "You can just drink from me. I enjoy that as much as the sex."

He shook his head and pressed his forehead to my stomach. "I already drink too much from you. I should find someone else. You must stay here in this room."

I stiffened. "You are not going to drink from someone else while I'm here." The very thought of it made me sick.

"Lindsey," Rand murmured, getting to his feet. He tried to pull me into his embrace, but I slapped his hands away. With a sigh, he gave me an entreating look. "I am a vampire, sweet. You cannot possibly feed me as much as you think you can. You will need your strength."

"I have strength," I protested. "I've been eating like a fiend at every stop. I've put on five pounds with all the protein I've been downing. I take vitamins every day. I feel fine." I didn't understand this. It hurt. "You said you would drink from me."

"And I have, love. Sips here and there. You think I wish to sip from another?" He cupped my cheeks in his cool hands. "I want none but you. But I need to get my strength up if we are approaching the Dragon's territory. And you will need your strength, too."

"Will I really?" I bit out. "Does it matter if I'm

strong?" Tears flooded my eyes. "Because you seem to think you're going to die either way. You think this is a death mission, and you still insist on it." I dashed at my cheeks, hating that I was crying. "So tell me why it matters if you drink from me or not."

"Because it is a death sentence for me does not mean it has to be one for you," he said softly, kissing my brow, my cheek, my nose. He was so tender, so loving. It destroyed me that he was determined to confront the Dragon. "Because it matters to me that you live."

"We can be careful," I told him. "I know we can. And I want to be the only one for you right now, in the time we have left," I went on, clinging to his embrace. "I want to be the one you go to. If you drink from someone else, it's a betrayal to me."

"Ah, Lindsey," he murmured, but when I put my arms around him, he sank his fangs into my neck.

"Yes, Rand," I murmured, my entire body aching with delight as he licked and sucked at my throat. It didn't even matter that I felt woozy from the loss of blood afterward. I clung to Rand as he played with my hair and neither of us spoke. The future was rushing up far too soon for either one of us.

I thought I could handle this.

I thought I'd be okay with falling for Rand. That I'd appreciate the time we had together. That whatever I had with him was a gift and when it was done, I'd go on my way, sadder but wiser and full of memories. I was used to people not staying in my life, with the exception of Gemma. But as we approached the Dragon's home, I became more and more unhappy.

Why did Rand have to die? Why now? Couldn't we retreat to the far side of the world, like, say, Nebraska, and hide out from the Dragon there? Nebraska was a long way from Europe. After a few years, wouldn't the Dragon give up?

But Rand refused to hear any of it.

The Dragon must die, because he owed it to Frederic and William, and even Guy.

And what about Lindsey? I wanted to ask, but it seemed selfish to compare my feelings—only weeks old—to the brotherhood of men he'd fought with for two hundred years.

I'd simply have to adjust and steel myself for the worst. And it hurt more than I could possibly imagine.

Twenty

So where are we again?" I asked, stifling a yawn rising in my throat. If Rand saw me yawn, it'd worry him that he was taking too much blood, and that was the last thing I wanted. I lifted my menu and pretended to study it.

"In my time, this was called Wallachia, and this city Corona. It was fortified with walls. Great walls." Rand looked lost in thought, as if seeing the past instead of the bustling modern city around us. I was pretty sure it was called Brasov, but Corona sounded prettier.

"Mmm," I said, smiling at the waitress as she put a coffee in front of me. "And you think we'll find the Dragon here?"

Rand tapped his brow. "I feel him close by. He is very near."

I shivered. "Like . . . in this room near?"

He shook his head, his expression distracted, as if turned inward. "A few leagues from here but not close enough to worry yet. Before, he was like a small, dark stain in my mind. Now that we are closer, it feels as if my entire head threatens to be swallowed by his again."

"Again?" I asked. That didn't sound good.

Rand gave me a tiny, humorless smile. "It is not an easy life, that of *upyri*. Why do you think Guy hid away in the hills? Why do you think he did not live under his master's thumb? It is because it is not living at all. There were many dark times that my mind was not my own. That every thought that filtered through my head was his, and my limbs moved under his commands and not my own. I do not relish the thought of those times."

I swallowed hard, shocked. To think that Rand had been utterly controlled by someone else made me sick. I tried to imagine myself in his place, awake but unable to control my own actions. Now I started to understand why he didn't want the guy to live. "Is it safe for you to be here?"

He shrugged. "There is no safe in my world, Lindsey. Were we not attacked in Rome? Was Gemma not accosted despite being cities away from us? Better to confront the bear in his lair than to live a life of endless fear."

I wasn't sure I agreed with that. I made some sort of noncommittal response and sipped my coffee. Rand's fatalistic view of things hurt. It hurt to think that I might wake up one day and he could be gone.

I ached to think that Rand was choosing revenge

against the Dragon over a life with me. Tears pricked my eyes and I blinked them away. It seemed like I was constantly getting weepy lately. Maybe that was a side effect of all the vitamins I was chugging to feed Rand. Maybe it was the blood loss.

Maybe it was the cute messages Gemma kept sending to my phone, like LINDSEY + RAND = <3 <3 <3 4 EVA! I knew she was sending them to make me smile and to let me know she was okay, but every time my phone buzzed, my heart ached a little more.

Things weren't okay. I didn't know how to stop any of this, but helping my lover as he headed straight for death? Definitely not anywhere on my "okay" scale. But I wanted to be supportive, so I kept my hurt to myself and sipped my coffee and ate my Romanian breakfast of sausage and eggs, and some weird mush called *mamaliga*.

We paid the tab at the counter, and as we did, I noticed a stand of postcards. I idly turned the wheel as the girl swiped my nearly maxed credit card. Pictures of local castles, local graveyards, historical photos—

Rand grabbed one from the side. "It cannot be."

I smiled faintly. This was the first thing Rand had shown interest in—well, outside of me—in a few days. I nodded to the girl, indicating she should add it to our tab. "It's a postcard," I told Rand. "Photos are printed up on paper. Um, haven't you seen them?" He shrugged and so I went on. "They're uh, pictures. Paintings sort of. The image is captured in a lens and stamped on paper. Please tell me you know what paper is, because I'm running out of descriptive words here."

He simply stared at the card, tracing his fingers on it.

It was kind of cute, really. I took my credit card back from the cashier, looped an arm around Rand's waist, and dragged him toward the restaurant exit. "Okay, paper. Let me think. I guess I could google a definition, but it's a bunch of pressed fibers, right?"

"How is this possible?" Rand murmured. His finger stabbed at the surface of the card. "It is like he is here."

"Like who is here?" I asked, getting out my car keys. Rand would probably want to continue traveling, but I wasn't sure that we shouldn't go back to the hotel. His mention of the stain on his mind bothered me, and I wondered if we needed to prepare more. I'd bought more chopped garlic and still carried the stakes in my boots, but my holy water holster was packed in my bag, and . . .

"The Dragon."

That snapped me out of my thoughts. "The Dragon? Where?"

"Here," Rand said, and shook the card. "His face is here."

For the first time, I looked at the postcard he'd picked up. I took it from his hand and stared. There was a picture of a man on the postcard, a reprint of an old portrait. The man had a long, angular face bisected by an extra-long mustache. He had long, sweeping black curls and wore a weird jeweled hat. His clothes were red and old-fashioned, his brows heavy, his eyes prominent, nose long and pointed. Not a sexy dude. I flipped over the back of the card.

Vlad III, Draculea. Voivode of Wallachia. Also known as Vlad Tepes.

I shrieked.

"Lindsey?" Rand looked surprised at my outburst.

I shook the card at him. "Vlad Tepes? Vlad the Impaler? Dracula? We're chasing fucking *Dracula*?"

He looked surprised and took the postcard back from my trembling fingers. "Do you know of him?"

I moaned, pressing a hand to my forehead. "Oh, my God. This is not happening. This is not." I turned and looked at Rand. "I thought you said he was a Dragon!"

"That is his family name. Draculesti. His family is Dracul, his house Basarab," Rand's voice became thick, heavily accented as he pronounced the words. "He claimed to be the son of Vlad the Dracul, but that was simply another one of his warlords he turned and who then took command of his people. The Dragon is actually much older than that."

"Great," I said faintly. "I cannot believe we're going after Dracula. Why didn't you say something?"

Rand's eyes narrowed. "I told you he was the Dragon. *Dracul* is 'dragon' in the old languages."

I whimpered, feeling faint. I pressed a hand to my forehead and leaned against our car. "I need a moment to process this."

Rand's arms went around me. "Lindsey, are you well?"

I burrowed against him. What to say? *Oh, sure, I'm just dandy. Never mind that we just found out we're chasing a bad guy that happens to be legendary for being a nasty vampire. No big deal. Oh, and he's probably going to kill you.* I pressed my face against his throat. It felt cool, a sign he was probably thirsty. "I know you want to keep moving, Rand, but can we go back to the hotel? Please?"

He hesitated.

I pressed a kiss to his throat. "I just want to spend time with you tonight. What's one more evening?"

His hand stroked through my hair, and I felt his shudder of desire. "As you wish, sweet."

We went back to our hotel, and I made love to Rand in the shower. I noticed that he only sipped lightly from my neck, and I worried he wasn't keeping his strength up. That was my fault, too, because I was a jealous, horrible woman who didn't want him touching anyone else. It only made me feel worse.

As dawn approached, I lay in Rand's arms and pulled out my phone, doing searches of Vlad Tepes and Dracula so we could go over his legends together and pick apart fact from fiction. "They just found his tomb," I told Rand, flipping through news articles.

"Oh?"

"In Italy."

Rand snorted. "Not his, then. He despises Italy. Why do you think William and Frederic were there?"

Mmm, good point. "And you."

"I was staked in Brittany, though." He nuzzled my neck, teasing my ear. "Believe it or not, your warlord was once Norman."

"Oh, I believe it," I told him. "Not a lot of Romanians with a name like Rand FitzWulf," I teased.

He pressed a kiss to my jaw. "Tomb or no tomb, I know the Dragon is alive. I can feel him lurking at the edges of my mind. Waiting. Watching."

I shivered at the thought of that and picked up my phone again. I went to Wikipedia and looked up Vlad III. There was a lot about politics that didn't interest me. I wanted the creepy stuff. "Says here that he died in either 1476 or 1477. Possibly beheaded."

"Likely he had rumors spread that he was killed so he could come back again as a different incarnation. He had many names and many guises. Common men will not follow a man they believe to be hundreds of years old. This I know from experience."

I looked over at his handsome face. "Did you have many guises, then?"

"I did," he confirmed. "Though I do not remember most of them. Only that I would lead a group of men for a period, then be sent away to lead another army under a different name. The Dragon sent us to many different places."

"Why?"

He shrugged. "Why not? He was bored and liked to make war. I think he just liked human misery. He liked to stir things up, like stepping on a nest of ants to watch them panic. He was very old even when I met him. I imagine you get tired of life. You take it for granted."

Like Rand was doing now? I bit the thought back and turned to my phone again. "It says here that he impaled thousands of people."

"True."

I shivered. "Really?"

"He was sadistic. If he grew angry with a village or the lord of a village, all would suffer."

I felt sick. "But . . . impalement? Hundreds of people? It says here that there were forests of them—"

He put his fingers to my jaw and turned my face to his. "Lindsey," he murmured. "These are not things I wish to think about when I am in bed with you. Suffice it to say that my past is ugly, and my mind has not always been my own. But now do you understand why the Dragon must die, even if it will cost me my own life?"

I nodded and leaned in close to him, soaking in his scent, his touch.

For the first time, I got it. I really did. "I'm sorry," I

said, sliding my hands along his body. "I won't discuss it again."

"Just trust me when I say he must die."

"I trust you," I murmured, then pressed my mouth to his. I'd always trusted Rand. It was just that I didn't want him to die, too. Selfish or not, I still felt that way.

If only there was a way to imprison Dracula while not destroying him entirely . . .

Wait.

My fingers dug into Rand's shoulders as I was gripped by an exciting thought. When I'd found Rand, he'd been staked. Dormant. He hadn't aged. Hadn't breathed. Hell, he'd been in limbo for six hundred years. There had to be ways to stop a vampire. If staking made him dormant . . . I just needed to think of other ways. I wracked my brain for vampire lore, thinking of the kit Gemma had made me. "Hey, Rand, honey?"

"Hmm?" His hand slid down the curve of my waist. He was clearly gearing up for sex again. The man was insatiable.

"What does holy water do to a vampire?" I moved my hand to his cock, cupping it. "Is it a sleep agent, like garlic?"

He pulled back, eyeing me. "Why does this come up now?"

I shrugged, trying to remain casual. My hand stroked along his hard length, hopefully a distraction. *Because I'm trying to think of ways to save you?* "Because we were talking about vampires and impaling and stakes and I realized I never asked what holy water did."

"It is like poison." Rand studied me. "You would tell me if you drank some?"

"I haven't touched a drop." It was all still packed away in tiny flasks. I'd kept it, hoping it would have a use.

And now I could think of one. I pressed a kiss to the tip of Rand's nose and gave his cock a squeeze. Suddenly I was in a much better mood than before. If the Dragon thought he was going to get my man without a fight, he had another thing coming.

Twenty-one

The sun rose, but I was unable to sleep. I knew the exact moment it hit the horizon, though, because Rand drifted off mid-conversation and fell into his comatose vampiric slumber. I got up and checked the drapes on the windows, just to make sure not an inch of light got through to hurt my vampire. It was habit now, and it made me feel like I was doing my part to protect him, however small.

I had just crawled back into bed when a hand slid up my thigh, fingers dragging over my skin. I smiled even as I closed my eyes and snuggled against Rand. "Second wind?"

"I see you, blood vassal." Cold fingers dug into the flesh of my thigh, and Rand gave a long, hard sniff against my neck. "I can smell your blood from here." He inhaled deeply again, his face burrowing against my throat. "Like the sweetest taste of honey. Your charms are evident. It's clear why this disobedient slave likes you."

And his nails dug into the skin of my leg, drawing blood.

I yelped and jumped out of bed. That was *not* my lover.

He sat up in bed and swiveled his shoulders, as if testing his body. Then he looked over at me, where I cowered, naked, a few feet away from the bed. "Hello, lovely."

"Rand?"

A chuckle. An evil chuckle. "If you say so."

I noticed that his speech wasn't accented for the first time. My eyes widened. "Who are you?"

An evil grin stole across Rand's face. "Who do you think?"

I hated to even say the name aloud. "Vlad . . . Tepes? Dracula?"

"Very good," he purred, and a chill went up my spine. "I see you are bringing my vassal back so I can take care of him once and for all? You are too kind." His voice was sonorous, dripping with evil. It creeped me out to see it coming from Rand's familiar mouth.

"Get out of here," I said, covering my breasts with my hands. "Get out of Rand."

"I am never fully out of him, you know." The Dragon's smile was chilling. "I am always there. I know everything and see everything. You think our link goes one way? That he gets the benefit of my knowledge and my immortality and I get nothing in return? You think I am that kind and benevolent?"

"I think you're awful," I spat at him. "A monster. You're enslaving these men, forcing them to do your deeds—"

"And in exchange, I gave them eternity." He clapped his hands slowly, mockingly. "Truly, I am a monster."

"An eternity of being your lackey!" I shouted back.

He shrugged. "All gifts come with a price." His eyes narrowed, became shrewd. "I know how he feels about you, too." He tapped the side of his head. *Rand's* head. "It's all in here. His emotions, his thoughts. I see it all, feel it all. I know he's coming to kill me. He thinks he can defeat me. That I don't know every move he's going to make before he does it." His lip curled with amused disgust.

Fear rushed through me. If he knew every move Rand was going to make, then how could Rand possibly beat him? "Why?" I choked out. "Why do you want him dead? Why send Guy after him?"

"Because Rand is mine to control." He thumped his chest, bone-crushingly hard. "Mine to command. My vassal. He should *obey* me. Not incite rebellion amongst my men when he does not like my orders." He thumped his chest again. "I am in charge. And because he refutes me, he must die for it. I have other vassals, far more loyal than he. I need him no longer."

"Because he has a heart?" I taunted back. "Because he's not a mindless demon like you?"

"Because he is weak," the Dragon said. That eerie smile curled his mouth again. "But his efforts will not be totally in vain. He will bring me a tasty little morsel in yourself. It has been a long time since I've tasted one like you. AB negative, I believe Guy said?"

I remained silent. He was wrong, but I'd be damned if I corrected him.

"Delicious," he teased. "I'll enjoy enslaving you. Most of my playthings don't last for long, but they're usually quite glad to go. I can be quite . . . creative."

I shuddered, hugging my arms to my chest.

"And I might let Rand live for a bit longer to see that." He tilted his head. "Wouldn't that be vile? Letting the man that loves you watch while I destroy you? Forcing him to endure your screams as I drain you of your delicious blood? It would kill him, you know. It would hurt more than any wound I could inflict on him." He tapped his fingers over his chest. "You get him right here. He's confused. Never in his long life has he felt such emotions for another person. It frightens him that you're so vulnerable. His thoughts are full of the need to protect you, and of course, the need to fuck you. To own you. He is a vampire, after all."

I bit my lip, not wanting to respond to the taunting.

"Sometimes he thinks about abandoning you for your own good, you know." He put a finger to his temple again and gave it a swift tap. "That goes through this mind so many times a night. That he must protect Lindsey. That Lindsey's not safe with him. That sweet, sweet Lindsey is so vulnerable and it goes against everything in him to keep you with him." He tsked. "So noble."

"Go away," I hissed. "You're awful. I hate you!"

"What, do you not want to play any longer?" He gave me a cruel, thin-lipped smile. "Call me when you do. You know I'm listening."

With that, Rand's body collapsed back on the bed again.

Silence filled the room. I hunched down on the floor where I was, watching Rand's body, wary. When I was sure the Dragon was gone, I uncurled from my spot, my heart hammering.

The Dragon knew everything. Did I tell Rand when he woke up? Or should I keep it a secret? I stared down at my sleeping lover, unsure what to do. I sat on the edge of the bed and raked my hands through my hair, feeling alone and scared. Not just for me but for Rand as well. He didn't stand a chance against the Dragon, not if the man could predict every move, knew every thought.

And if I told Rand the Dragon had appeared, the Dragon would know that, too. Anything I discussed with Rand was suspect. A sob broke in my throat.

Just then, my phone chimed with a text message. I scrambled for it, using any excuse to get away from the bed.

Hey bb! Gemma sent. Just checking in on you. Everything ok?

I immediately dialed her. She picked up on the second ring. "I'm not okay, Gemma," I immediately blurted into the phone.

"What's wrong?"

"The Dragon," I sniffed, looking back at my lover in our bed. "He took over Rand and threatened us a moment ago."

"He what?"

"Took over Rand. Possessed him."

"Motherfucker!"

"He said he knows everything we're going to do, Gemma." A fresh sob caught in my throat. "And Rand just wants to plow straight in and attack him because he thinks the guy should die. Never mind that he thinks he'll die, too."

She made soothing noises on the other end of the phone. "What do you wanna do, honey? Wanna come home?"

"I can't leave him," I wailed. I wouldn't abandon Rand. I couldn't.

"I know! I know! I'm just . . . I'm worried about you, kiddo. This is some grim shit."

"I don't know what to do," I told her, curling up in a chair with the phone. From my vantage point, I could see the bed and Rand peacefully sleeping in it. He had no idea of what had just happened.

"So what's the plan right now?"

I pressed the heel of my hand between my eyes, feeling a headache coming on. "Our plan or the Dragon's?"

"Both?"

"It sounds like our plan is that we find the Dragon, and maybe I provide a distraction and Rand attacks him. Then we hope for the best."

Silence on the other end. After a moment, Gemma added, "That's all you've got?"

"I *know*," I cried, ready to burst into fresh tears. "We've got nothing! I mean, I know Rand is a great fighter. But it just feels like there should be more to it. More that I can help with. I've got holy water and garlic and a pair of stakes, but Rand doesn't want to stake him." I lowered my voice in case "Rand" was listening despite being asleep. "He wants to behead him to make sure he's dead."

"But won't beheading him also take out Rand? Doesn't it cut the link? The whole vampirism pyramid scheme thing where everyone feeds off the top?"

"Yeah," I said, nodding miserably. "I mean, no one's ever taken down the top dog before, but I don't see how that'll change anything, right?"

"Fuck, I don't know. I've never killed a vampire before."

That made two of us. "I'm worried that if we just stake the Dragon, it won't work or someone else will wake him up and we'll be back to the drawing board."

"Ah," said Gemma. "And the Dragon's plan?"

"Well, considering he can read all of Rand's thoughts and feelings? My guess is that it's 'wait for Rand and kill him.'"

"Yeah, that plan sucks," she agreed. "New plan."

"What's that?"

"Abandon ship."

I stiffened. "I'm not leaving him alone, Gemma."

"Okay, well, I'm superworried for you, girl. Because what is the Dragon going to do with Rand's partner in crime if Rand bites it?"

I said nothing. I already knew from our creepy conversation earlier. A long, slow death involving lots of bleeding and bloodsucking. And possibly torturing Rand.

"See, silence is *not* good right now. That tells me shit is not good. I am *worried* about you! Please, please come home. I don't want to lose my best friend!" Now Gemma sounded sniffly. "Come on, Linds. Just admit that you're in over your head and come back to Venice."

"I'm in way over my head," I admitted shakily. "But I won't abandon Rand. I can't."

"Then you need to work around him," Gemma said. "Have a plan B and don't let him in on it. Because if you do, the Dragon is going to know about it. Right now, the only thing we have going for us is the fact that he doesn't know what *you're* thinking."

She had a point. "Should I tell Rand that the Dragon possessed him while he slept?" I asked, unsure. The loyal part of me said that of course I should tell Rand. After all, it was his body and his enemy.

Gemma hummed for a minute, thinking. "Actually, no, you shouldn't tell him at all. I mean, what's the benefit there? Freaking him out more than he already might be? Letting the Dragon know he's onto things? I think you keep a lid on it. It'll make the Dragon curious what you're up to. Let him wonder."

I nodded, feeling a little more in control. "Good idea."

"Now, give me your address so I can come up there."

"You . . . what? Really?"

"Yes, really! Puttering around in Venice while you're having a life-or-death struggle with vampires? I'm not going to sit here with my thumb up my ass while you do this shit! I'm going to come help you out."

Fresh tears started. "Oh, Gemma, you're the best friend a girl could ever have."

"I know, right? I'm pretty fucking awesome. Now give me details, and whatever you do, *don't tell Rand*."

And between the two of us, we hatched a plan.

Twenty-two

Rand and I walked the streets of Brasov that evening, trying to get a feel for where Rand was "sensing" the Dragon. Because we were so close, he told me his normal blood sense was blurred, and he wasn't entirely sure of the location. Just that when we found him, he'd know.

So we walked. I had my holy water vials tucked in their holsters under my arms and the garlic vial stuffed into a bra I'd bought at a quick boutique stop earlier. The stakes were in my boots. My fingers were clasped in Rand's cold ones, and I tried not to worry.

Or at least, I tried not to show Rand that I worried.

I watched him carefully, looking for signs that he was not himself. But Rand was ever affectionate, full of kisses and caresses. He hadn't drank from me that evening. I'd offered, but he'd declined, saying he wanted me to keep my strength up. The chill of his skin against mine told me he wasn't drinking from anyone else, either. So there was another thing for me to worry about. He was starving.

As we walked the night streets, Rand suddenly stopped. "There."

I turned to see where he was facing. There was a castle up on a hill, complete with turrets and surrounded by trees. It loomed over the rest of the city. "Really?"

"Yes," Rand said. His hand squeezed mine tightly. "That is where he is waiting for me."

I got goose bumps. He'd spoken with an accent, so I was pretty sure it was still Rand. Nevertheless, I wanted to test it. "What about his tomb in Italy?"

Rand's brows drew together, and he looked over at me. "I told you, he hates Italy." He shook his head and pointed up at the castle. "I can feel him there, lurking. Like a vulture waiting for the battlefield to be cleared."

It was my Rand, all right, though what he was saying wasn't making me very happy. The idea of the Dragon waiting for Rand was a creepy one, especially now that I knew the Dragon was aware of both of us. I shuddered, remembering this morning.

"Come," Rand said, giving my hand another squeeze. "Let us go."

"Wait," I said, panicking. "Go where?"

He looked at me in surprise. "To meet the Dragon. To get this over with."

I stared, wide-eyed. Now? But Gemma was still on her way, probably catching a million trains between here and Venice. I needed her at my side. We had a plan. Then this would be it. Once Gemma got here, it would be the last time I saw Rand . . . if this mission was the death sentence I truly thought it was. It would be the last time I held him. Kissed him. Saw his smile. Felt his touch, his caresses, his sweet affection.

I burst into tears. I was afraid I was falling in love with the guy and he was doomed.

"Hush, love," Rand said quietly. He pulled me against him as I sobbed. "This day must come at some point." He cupped my face, pressed gentle kisses to it. "You know I would do anything I could to prevent this."

"Then let's stake him," I sobbed. "And you can come home with me." *Suck on that, Dragon.*

"I do not know that staking him will work," Rand told me, his thumbs wiping away my tears. "And what do we do with him once he is staked? Where does one hide a body like that?"

"A secret room?" I asked hopefully. "You did fine in one for six hundred years."

"And so he may continue his reign of terror in a few years when someone finds him once more?" Rand gave me a soft, sad smile and shook his head. "Better to end it once and for all than let him put another through what he has done to me, to Guy, to the others."

It was noble. Noble, and utterly pigheaded. I cried against his chest for a little bit longer, then began to press frantic kisses to his face. I needed time to enact my plan. Time for Gemma to arrive. So I stalled. "Please, Rand," I said between kisses. "Give me tonight."

"We had last night," he said gently.

"Give me this night so I can say my proper goodbyes to you," I told him. My lips moved over his. "Let me make love to you one last time. I want to share all of myself with you, and I want all of you with me. No holding back. Give me a memory to take with me. Then we'll come after him. I promise."

Rand hesitated, and I could see the indecision on his face. He was torn between pleasing me and doing what he felt was his duty. I took his hand in mine and lifted it to my mouth, pressing tiny kisses to his knuckles as he thought. Then, because I had no ammo but sex, I took the tip of one of his fingers into my mouth and nipped it with my teeth.

His eyes flashed with lust. *There we go.*

"Tonight," he murmured. "Then we must face our fates."

"Tonight," I agreed, and wrapped my arms around him, pulling him close.

Tonight, I'd put my plan in action and save Rand.

We went back to our hotel room, me with a mixture of grief and wariness clogging my throat. Tonight,

I would be betraying my lover. I hoped that Rand would understand and forgive me.

And if he didn't, then I would just live with the fact that he hated me. As long as he breathed and flourished, I would be fine. As long as he existed, I could deal with his hate. I just wanted him to *live*.

I kept these stewing thoughts to myself, though, my hand clasped tightly in his as we headed up the stairs back to our room on the second floor. The innkeeper was surprised to see us return so soon and made clucking noises as she talked up a storm in Romanian. But eventually we were able to escape her, and then I was back inside our room.

"Invite me in?" Rand asked, voice husky as he gazed at me from the other side of the door.

"Come in," I told him, and extended my hand to him.

He took it and brought it to his mouth, pressing kisses to my palm, my fingertips, my wrist. He continued to kiss up my arm, loving me with such aching tenderness that it made fresh tears spring. God, I loved this man. I hated that we'd have to do this. I hated that what I was going to do was probably going to hurt him. But I didn't want him to go on without knowing how I felt, no matter what happened.

"I love you," I told him softly, feeling tears brim in my eyes. "I love you so much, Rand."

"In a thousand years, I will never find another

woman as wonderful as you," Rand told me in a gentle, loving voice. He cupped my chin, tilted my head back, and pressed a light, loving kiss to my mouth. "I adore you."

I smiled faintly at him, then shut the door to the room and locked it. "Why don't you get in bed while I run and freshen up in the bathroom?" I widened my eyes, hoping I looked innocent.

He grinned and pressed another kiss to my mouth. "As long as you do not come out with weasel's testicles strung along your neck, freshen all you like."

I chuckled and headed to the restroom, stripping off my clothing. I pulled my phone, now set to vibrate, out of my pocket.

Status check? I sent her. Rand wanted to go after Dragon tonight. I'm stalling!

Stall, woman, stall! Gemma sent back. I'm waiting on the last train to Brasov. Be there in a few hours! Hold him off! I'm coming prepared!

K, I sent back. Hurry!

Putting my phone away, I looked in the mirror, inhaled deeply, and set about Operation: Vampire Seduction. I pulled out a tiny needle and pricked my finger, just enough to draw a tiny bead of blood. I dabbed the blood behind each ear, then rubbed it on my wrists, as sure an aphrodisiac as any I had when it came to Rand. I undressed, removing my stakes, my holy water, my garlic.

The garlic, I ate. Well, I didn't eat it inasmuch as I

held my nose and choked it down. Minced or not, the stuff was vile. Once I'd managed to gag it all down, I brushed my teeth and then, because Rand might suspect mouthwash, ate a few bites of peppermint candy that I'd cooed over earlier as we'd walked. Hopefully that'd be enough to disguise things. After all, Rand would never suspect that I'd deceive him. I was the only person he trusted.

The thought was like a knife in the gut. I blinked back tears, fluffed my hair, slipped out of my bra and panties, and went to meet my vampire.

He was facing the bed, pulling his clothing off, and I watched in a moment of pure, unadulterated pleasure as he tugged his shirt over his head, muscles rippling as he did. He was so incredibly beautiful. My heart ached to think I'd never see this again. I moved forward and put my arms around him, pressing kisses to the back of his shoulder as I did.

Rand leaned back against me, his pose one of pure relaxation, pure satisfaction. He gave me a sleepy smile. "I love your mouth, Lindsey. Love it when you press your lips against my skin."

I kissed his muscles again, just because I could. "I love you, Rand," I murmured, sliding my hands around to the front of his jeans, where I began to undo his buttons. He groaned and relaxed against me as I tended to him. The jeans grew loose a moment later, and I let them fall to the floor, then dragged his underwear down. "Thank you for giving me tonight."

"I'd give you every night if I could," he said quietly. "You know this."

"I do." If he wasn't going to give them to me, I'd take them. I just wouldn't leave the decision to him. So I kissed his shoulder again, then moved around to his front, kissing his skin. I made sure to avoid his mouth, because I knew a kiss from me would put him right to sleep.

He was naked, and he was all mine. Rand groaned, nuzzling my ear. "You smell so good tonight," he murmured, his fangs scraping along my skin.

"Hungry?" I asked, relieved he couldn't smell the garlic over the perfume of my blood.

"Ravenous," he murmured, and licked at the cords of my throat.

Oh God, that felt good. I shuddered from the sensation but forced myself to pull away. "Ah ah," I teased. "Don't get too eager." I gave him a coy smile and sat on the edge of the bed, then crooked a finger at him. "I wonder how long you can hold out for."

He grinned down at me, all sexy vampire self. "You think I cannot control myself?"

I shrugged, pretending to debate it, even though our plan hinged on Rand biting me. I'd just have to make myself irresistible to him. Mmm. Not hard to do. I loved touching the man, and loved him touching me. So I smiled. "I know you can't. You love a taste of all this too much." I gestured at my naked body.

Rand grabbed my ankle and tugged my leg into

the air. He kissed my calf muscle, then began to work his way toward my knee. "Perhaps I do," he said softly. "Perhaps I don't want to control myself. I might be too eager to lose myself in your charms."

I giggled at his description. "My charms, eh?"

He looked surprised. "Are you not charming?"

I laughed again, and the laugh turned into a sob. How I loved this man. "I suppose that I am." And then I began to cry.

"Shh, love," he murmured, moving over me until his weight pressed mine into the mattress. "Don't weep."

"I can't help it," I said, my throat knotted with unhappiness. "I love you and I'm losing you."

"I am thankful for the time we had together," he said, pressing a kiss to my nose, my mouth, my chin. "Every moment, I have cherished. Every hour with you, I have felt alive. Free. Happy. You do not know what a gift that is."

I smiled tremulously at him, brushing my fingers over his mouth. "And tonight will be your last gift to me."

A roguish look entered his eyes. "Then I suppose I had best make it an impressive one, yes?" He gave me a lascivious wink and began to kiss downward, moving over my neck, then down to my breasts. "Christ have mercy, but your scent is enticing tonight," he said with a groan. "I long to sink my fangs into you."

"Not yet," I said lightly. "Make it last, Rand." That was the selfish part of me wanting to extend my time with him. I wanted my last hours with Rand. And if I only had a few of them left, they were going to be utterly delicious and so worth it. I bit my lip and watched him kiss his way up my thigh, heading straight for my pussy. The man did it like he was going for the gold.

At the last moment, though, he switched directions and gave me a thoughtful look. "On your stomach, love."

Oooh, something new? I rolled onto my stomach and glanced at him over my shoulder. "Are you going to take me from behind?"

He'd leaned in to kiss my buttocks, and as I said it, he straightened, a shocked look on his face. "I . . ." He looked around, then leaned in. "Do people do that?"

I stifled a giggle behind my hand. "All the time."

"Like animals?"

"Like animals," I agreed. "It's called 'doggy style.'"

"And . . . the Church sanctions it?"

I had no idea if they did or not. "I don't know if anyone bothered to ask," I admitted with a smile as his hand rubbed my buttocks. "Wanna take a chance?"

"Well, now I do," he said with a groan. "You won't think it immoral?"

"Absolutely not," I said, giving a wiggle of my bottom. "Have you never had sex like that? What about sitting up? Or against a wall?"

He looked utterly awestruck. "I thought what we did with your mouth on my cock . . . I thought that was sinful. An intimacy you bore simply because of my vampire state."

"Baby, there are lots of things you have yet to learn. This is a very enlightened time."

"It sounds it." His expression looked sad. "I wish I would be here to explore things with you."

Oh, I did, too. The tears threatened again, so I turned away and pushed my butt into the air, giving it a little shake to entice him. "You can do whatever you want to me, Rand. You know that, right? There's nothing wrong between us. Nothing weird or profane."

His hand skimmed down my back. "I . . . want to put my mouth between your legs. With you like this."

I relaxed and spread my thighs a little wider. "Then do it."

Rand placed both hands on my buttocks, his gaze moving over my body as if I was an incredible sight. "The view of you like this nearly makes me undone, love. Would you let me drink from you? Like this?"

My eyes widened. "Um, where would you bite me?"

"Anywhere you'd let me."

I looked back at him and saw that his eyes were hooded with lust. Just like that, I became intensely wet, and a moan rose in my throat. I had to force myself to say no, because that wasn't part of the plan.

"Not tonight, I think. Tonight I want you to hold out for me," I told him. "Can we do that?"

"Of course." He leaned in and pressed a kiss to my butt, and his mouth felt cool on my flushed skin. "We shall do whatever pleases you. Always."

"Everything you do pleases me," I told him, arching my back to thrust my ass out a bit more. "I love you. I love your touch. I love everything about you."

His mouth went to my buttocks and he kissed each one, making me squirm.

His touches made me anticipate what was next, so I wasn't entirely surprised when he spread my thighs wider and put his mouth on my pussy from behind.

I moaned as he began to lick me, encouraging me with his tongue. It speared my core, and I whimpered, rocking back against it. I was so close already.

Even as he licked me from behind, one hand moved to my front and gripped my breast. I moaned as he pinched the peak, rubbing it as he tongued my core. The sensations were overwhelming, and moments later, I was crying out, wracked with my first orgasm. I pressed my cheek to the mattress, dreamy. "God, that was good."

He chuckled, giving me one final lick that made me shudder, then straightened. His fingers continued to play with my pussy as he teased the tip of one in and out of my core. As he pushed a second finger into me, I began to back against it, rocking against his hand.

"You are a beautiful sight to see, Lindsey," he murmured. "Your eagerness and your beauty send me reeling. To have these days with you, I feel as if I am the luckiest man alive."

The finality of that statement made my heart hurt, but he began to pump his fingers in and out, and my sorrow turned to arousal just as quickly again.

"I want you, Rand," I told him, panting as I pushed against his fingers. "Please. I want you inside me. Now." Screw the "let's make it last all night" concept. "I need you."

"Whatever happened to patience, sweet Lindsey?" he asked with a sexy chuckle, stroking those teasing, tormenting fingers in and out of me, mimicking what my body needed. "What happened to teasing each other until we were mad with pleasure?"

"Already there," I told him, whimpering as he stroked in again. "I want you so badly I can hardly stand it. Please, Rand."

"I love it when you say my name," he murmured, and his hand slid free from my pussy and I felt his cock nudge against me. "How can I resist when you ask so sweetly?"

"Don't resist," I encouraged, my hands fisting in the blankets. "Don't . . . oooh." I moaned as he sank into me from behind. He was hard, his skin cool to the touch, so it felt a bit like being penetrated by a popsicle. Which was startling at first, but then felt incredible. "Oh God, Rand. Yes, that's it."

He gripped my hips, and I felt him give a slow, teasing stroke. "I think I like this position. It feels deviant."

I giggled at that. If he thought this was deviant, I'd have to show him some other stuff later. Once we'd taken care of the Dragon.

If there even was a later.

I shook my head to clear it of the dark thoughts. I didn't want them in my mind while Rand was making love to me. "Keep going, my deviant warlord," I teased, and moaned anew when he pumped into me again, rougher this time.

"You like me deviant?" he murmured, fucking me with stronger, more powerful strokes. "Does it please you, Lindsey?"

"Everything," I cried out. "Everything you do pleases me."

He groaned, thrusting harder into me. "I can feel you tightening. You are about to come, aren't you?"

"Yes," I cried, my entire body quivering. Another orgasm was building. I couldn't last long with this man, not the way he touched me. Everything about him aroused me beyond belief. "Don't stop!"

"Never," he gritted out, and began to thrust harder, his movements so forceful they nearly shoved me across the blankets. I braced my knees and arms, pushing back against him to add to the friction. Then I was coming again, and I grabbed a pillow and bit down so it'd muffle my screams. Oh God, he was so good at that. "Rand," I cried out into the pillow. "Rand. Rand. Rand."

"I feel you clamping around me," he hissed, and I could tell from the thickness of his accent that his teeth were emerging, his fangs elongating. That made my pussy quiver anew, and I whimpered as the orgasm continued. "Want . . . to . . . bite you. Drink from you."

I stiffened under him. For a split second, I didn't want him to. I wanted us to keep playing all night long. To make love for hours more.

But that would ruin the plan. The moment Gemma got here, we needed to race to find the Dragon. I'd only have one chance to get this right. The moment Rand found out I'd drugged him, he wouldn't trust me again.

I couldn't let that happen. So, fighting the pain in my heart, I gave my ass another wiggle. "Bite me, then, love. Do it."

His cock slid from me, and I experienced a moment of loss so great I mewed aloud. *Please, God, don't let that be the last time I feel him*, I thought as he pulled me upright until I was on my knees. He clamped my body against his, cock pressed against my back. His arm went around me, his hand to my neck, and he nuzzled at my throat from behind.

I tilted my head, closed my eyes, and waited for him to drink.

He sank his fangs, and I sucked in a breath at the

sensation, holding extremely still. Then I felt him begin to suck, felt a bit of blood spill down my neck. He moaned, and I felt his entire body jerk behind me, coming with the force of his own orgasm. "So sweet," he rasped, licking at my blood again.

I twined my fingers in his shaggy hair, holding his head there. "Take a bit more," I encouraged. "You're thirsty. I know you are. I can handle it."

I expected him to protest, to pull away, but instead, he took another long, hard pull from my throat. And another. Then he reluctantly licked the wound, sealing it, and held me against him, his body warming.

I leaned against him, wrapped in his arms, his scent, his love . . . and felt content. "I love you, Rand," I told him. "So much."

I felt the moment it hit him. He shifted against me, then staggered. I moved forward, darting across the bed, then turned to look at him.

He put a hand to his forehead, blinking, his expression woozy. "I . . . something is wrong."

"I love you," I said again. "I'm so sorry."

Recognition flared in his eyes even as he slumped forward. I caught him and laid him on his back.

"Why?" he asked as I tucked a pillow behind his head.

"Because I love you," I said, leaning in and kissing his slack mouth. "And I'm going to save you."

"Lindsey," he breathed, reaching for my hair. His fingers touched it, and then his hand fell back.

For one horrible, frightening moment I thought I'd killed him. I knelt on the mattress and stared at his body, watching. I worried that he was wrong. That garlic wasn't a soporific but a poison, and I'd just killed my lover.

But when he didn't turn to dust, I breathed a little easier. I fixed him up on the bed, pulling the covers up to his chin and dragging his legs onto the mattress, making him comfortable. Stupid, but it helped ease the guilt raging through me. And I kissed his sweet face over and over again. "I'm sorry. I'm so sorry. Please forgive me."

Then I got dressed, sucked in a deep breath to calm myself, and leaned over him once more.

"Vlad," I called. "Are you there?"

Rand's eyes flicked open, but the rest of his body didn't move.

"I think we need to talk."

"I am listening." The hollow, creepy voice was back.

"I want an exchange," I said. "Me for Rand."

"Why would I want you?"

I made my voice a sultry purr. "Because I taste *divine*. You trade me Rand's freedom, and I'll come to you."

Twenty-three

Two hours later, I waited at the train station, desperately trying to hold my shit together. Rand was asleep in our hotel room in the middle of the night, when he should have been conscious. He was completely and utterly vulnerable. It bothered me like crazy that I had to leave him. He was safe, I told myself, as long as he was in the room. No vampires could be invited in. I ignored the thought of a vampire charming a hotel employee and then coercing them to invite him in the room, because if I let myself go down that path, I'd go mad.

Rand was as safe as I could make him.

The train I was waiting on pulled in, and I breathed a sigh of relief when I saw a familiar face step off.

"Lindsey!" Gemma waved frantically and rushed forward, her large purse tucked under her arm. "Thank goodness. I was starting to think I'd never get here."

It didn't help that I'd felt the same. I gave her a

wavering smile. "Hey. Ready to kick some vampire ass?"

She patted her bag. "I've got some gear here. Let's get someplace private so we can talk and prep, okay?"

I nodded and followed her lead.

"Someplace private" ended up being the train station family-designated bathroom. We went inside, and Gemma locked the door.

She turned and studied me the moment we were alone. "You okay to do this?"

I sat down on the toilet and nodded weakly. I felt like crying, but it was too late for tears. "I'm good."

"Is our boy tranquilized?"

"Yeah, he should be out for a while," I told her. "I have the place the Dragon is staying, too." I pulled a piece of paper out of my pocket with the hastily scribbled address on it. "I'm going to meet him at this place at two in the morning."

"Okay, cool. Let me show you what I brought." She set her bag down on the sink and began to pull all kinds of things out. A jar of minced garlic. Bottles of holy water. Crosses. Knives. More stakes. Then she pulled out a few things that caught my interest. A package of needles. Two T-shirts in green. And a brown wig that looked suspiciously like the color and length of my hair.

I gave her an odd look. "I can guess some of that, but I'm blank on some others."

"So we know where you're meeting him, right?"

I nodded. "I looked it up on Google Maps. It's an old graveyard."

"Creepy."

I drummed my fingers on my mouth. "He thinks I'm heading over there to give myself up in exchange for Rand."

Gemma shuddered, then composed herself. "Okay. So here's what I'm thinking. You want to stake him and not just kill him outright, right?" At my nod, she continued. "I dress up like you. We wear the same shirts. Same hair. We smell different, so we'll need to prick you and rub me with your blood. Gross, I know, but that's what he's going to notice, so we'll disguise it. Then, while he's occupied with me, you sneak up and stake him!"

I nodded slowly. "It could work. Are you sure you want to do this? It'll put you in danger."

"The best weapon we have is our blood," she said, and pulled out two flasks of holy water. She handed me one, then passed me the jar of garlic. "Drink up, eat up, and let's get this shit on the road."

I wrinkled my nose. "We're in a bathroom."

"No time to be picky. Just wash your hands before you eat, and touch nothing." She tapped her holy water flask to mine. "Now, bottoms up."

An hour later, I hunched behind a gravestone. We'd found the old graveyard, and the place the Dragon had picked out couldn't have been creepier if it tried.

Trees, bushes, and other greenery surrounded the graveyard, which wasn't all that surprising. It was on the edge of Brasov, after all. But what I found unnerving was the sheer number of graves. Back in the US, it seemed like our graveyards were perfectly spacious. Here, headstones were crammed over what felt like every freaking inch of the place, and if there wasn't a headstone, there was a stone cherub with soulless eyes staring off into the distance. I hid behind an enormous cross topped *with* a cherub.

Like I said, creepy.

The center of the graveyard had a small cobblestone path and a fountain with a bench. I guess it was for people who wanted to spend their afternoons hanging out amongst the dead or something. It was there that Gemma sat, holding my purse and playing with my phone. She wore the wig and had her head bent, presumably so she could hide the fact that she wasn't me.

Me? I got to sit and squat in the back of the graveyard, stake in hand, waiting for my moment. My stomach roiled from a mixture of too much holy water and even more garlic, and the bottles tucked into my bra jabbed my armpits. The ground underneath my feet was muddy, and it was fricking cold at two in the morning.

On top of all that? The stupid vampire was a no-show. I shielded the screen of Gemma's phone and peeked at the time: 2:06 a.m. He was supposed to be here at two in the morning, and every minute that ticked past made me that much more anxious. I thought of Rand, completely alone in our room. What if this was all a ploy to get him alone, and I'd fallen for it?

No, I had to be positive. The Dragon didn't know what we were thinking. He didn't know Gemma was helping me. He thought I would be here alone. Why wouldn't he?

The phone in my hand vibrated with an incoming text.

Bogey at six o'clock.

I peeped up, gazing around the old graveyard. Gemma sat in a circle of moonlight, but in the distance, I saw a form moving underneath a tree and sneaking up behind her. It was a man with long, flowing dark curls.

At her seat, Gemma glanced around the graveyard, then returned to typing on her phone, her face lit up from the backlight. She knew he was there but was pretending otherwise.

This was my chance. I palmed a stake, gripping it in my sweaty hand. I could do this. As the vampire moved through the shadows toward Gemma, I crept a few steps behind him, stake in hand. His long hair fluttered as he walked, his hands unnaturally pale in the moonlight. He wore a dark shirt and dark pants but otherwise was nondescript. I hadn't gotten a good look at his face, but it had to be Vlad. Who else would be here late at night, making a beeline for Gemma? Who else would have that long, freaky hair and such pale hands?

I bit my lip and continued to move quietly behind him, readying myself. The moment he bent to touch Gemma, I'd stake his ass.

As I crept up behind him, I heard him inhale deeply. He touched Gemma's shoulder. "I see it is you, little one."

There was no mistaking that creepster voice, the flat, hollow sound of it, the lack of accent. With an adrenaline rush, I surged forward and plunged my stake into the monster's back. It went in like butter, tearing through clothing and flesh as if they were nothing.

An unholy shriek arose from the creature. He stiffened and staggered a few steps away, even as Gemma leapt off the bench, eyes wide.

The vampire fell to the ground on his stomach. The stake jutted out of his back, slightly off to the side.

"Did you get his heart?" Gemma panted, clutching her chest.

"I don't know!" He wasn't moving, but it didn't exactly look like I'd hit his heart, either. I grabbed another stake out of my boot and rolled the vampire onto his back. His eyes were staring sightlessly up at the sky, his mouth slightly parted. I had a horrible feeling for one moment that I'd staked a normal guy. *Please, please let this be a vampire.* I reached out to touch him.

Ice-cold. Relief shot through me.

His gaze darted to my face, and then he grabbed my hand.

With a yelp, I stuck my second stake into his front, this time through his heart. Gemma smothered her scream behind her hands.

He groaned, shuddered, and lay still.

I looked over at Gemma. "Did we do it?"

"How the fuck should I know?" She threw her hands up. "What's supposed to happen now?"

Something gurgled. I glanced down at the vampire at my feet. Nothing.

"What—"

I held out a hand. "Wait for it."

We waited. Nothing happened.

I frowned, then remembered. Staking didn't kill anyone. It was the beheading. "I think we need to cut his head off," I told her, reaching down to grab his hair.

It came off in my hand.

What the heck . . .

I stared down at the limp corpse of the vampire at my feet. His hair underneath the wig was . . . blond?

Hands slowly clapped from behind us. "Bravo," said a cold, humorless voice. It was familiar, but it wasn't hollow like it was when it normally came out of Rand's mouth. My skin pricking with fear, I turned and faced the newcomer.

This man had short hair. And a goatee. His mustache was thin, his nose long and pointed. He had a massive underbite and prominent eyes. Dark, slashing eyebrows.

And he looked mean as hell. His eyes gleamed that weird vampire green that Rand's sometimes changed to.

And he clapped. Slowly. Mockingly.

I stared down at the vampire at my feet. That wasn't the Dragon. I'd heard his voice, seen the hair, and thought him fooled. But he'd fooled me. He'd sent another vampire in his place. Another vampire wearing a wig, and he'd talked through his mouth.

This was bad.

"Gemma." I licked dry lips. Clutched the stake in my hand.

"Y-yes?" She stood next to me, utterly frozen.

"Run," I breathed.

"Oh shit," Gemma said. She turned and ran—

The vampire moved, a blur of motion in the darkness. Before I could even comprehend what I was seeing, he grabbed Gemma. Her body arced backward, and she flew through the air. Her back smacked into a tombstone in the distance and she lay still, unmoving.

I stared in horror, unable to move. Not that it mattered. A mere second later—*how was the Dragon so fast?*—a cold hand wrapped around my neck. Fingernails dug into my skin. A hard body pressed up against my back, and I gasped as the hand dragged my head backward, extending my throat.

"Do you think me stupid, little one?" Vlad hissed into my ear.

I said nothing. I was too afraid. Fear coursed through me, turning my blood to ice. My heart slammed so loudly that it felt like it would break my ribs.

"I am thousands of years old," he said, voice turning silky. "Do you think I have not seen every trick in the book? That I cannot predict what you will do?" His fingernails dragged down my throat, leaving welts in their wake. "Do you think I cannot smell an imposter?"

"I had to try something," I whispered. I was utterly terrified. Was Gemma dead? What had happened to her? Dear God, what was going to happen to me?

He clucked in my ear. "Poor, sweet fool. I imagine you did, didn't you?" Something hard and bony prodded my cheek. His nose. "I can see why Rand is so besotted. Such a pretty package. Sweet, tasty, nubile."

I shuddered. His voice made my skin prickle.

"And so very determined to keep him safe." He sniffed me again. "However misguided your actions are, I find them very amusing. And so few things amuse me as of late. I must say, I'm intrigued by you. By all of this."

I licked my lips, terrified. "Let me go."

"Since you asked nicely?" he mocked. "But mere moments ago, you were trying to kill me. Would I not be a fool to do as you ask?"

"Please," I whispered.

"Please what?"

"Please let me go."

To my surprise, he released me so quickly that I stumbled forward. I caught myself, straightened, and turned to look at him warily.

He gestured at me. "You are released, delicious one. What will you do now?" His eyes gleamed, and I felt suspiciously like a mouse cornered by a cat.

Was he truly letting me go, or was this another trick? What could I do? I couldn't run, that was for sure. He was faster than me, stronger than me, and running wouldn't solve anything.

One of my stakes lay on the ground nearby, and I snatched it up, then held it like a sword.

Vlad took one look at me, then threw his head back and laughed. "Oh, you *are* fun."

"You're an asshole," I told him. "You should leave Rand alone. Why are you hunting him? What's he done to you?"

"He is a disloyal soldier," Vlad said, taking a stalking step toward me.

I instinctively moved backward, nearly tripping over a gravestone. I skittered around it, still brandishing the stake. It didn't feel like nearly enough. Why had I thought that I could take down someone like Vlad the freaking Impaler?

"I once had four loyal knights. He's told you this, yes?" Vlad waved a gesture, dismissing this. "Of course he did. He tells you everything, does he not? I am sure he told you about all the times that he rode at my side, slaughtering innocents and burning towns in my name? The warriors he killed by the dozens? The men he impaled on spikes at the gates of their castles as a warning to others?"

I swallowed hard, clutching my too-small stake. "He told me that you controlled his mind! That you sit there like a spider in the back of his head and take over everything."

Vlad shrugged, the movement fluid as he continued to move toward me. "There is always some sacrifice with immortality, sweet one. They did not ask what my price was. They simply agreed to it."

"Because they were dying!"

"One might argue that death is not always the worst that can happen to a man, as your Rand might attest." Vlad's strange mouth curved into a cruel smile as he continued to stalk forward, heading directly for me.

I clutched the stake tighter. I could do this. I could. He just needed to move closer, and then—

The vampire moved forward, motions so quick that I could barely process them. In a flash, he'd batted the stake from my hand and grabbed me by the forearm. He wrenched me forward, eliciting a cry as I felt the bones in my arm crack.

Then he had me by the throat again, tucking my body against his.

"Four loyal knights," he hissed into my ear, so

close that I could feel his lips move against my skin.

I shuddered.

"And one by one, he turned those knights against me with his sad tales. That a life of rampage and war for all eternity was somehow wrong. That what they did was evil."

"It was evil!"

"Of course it was, you fool." His hand tightened on my throat, nearly choking me. I wheezed and gasped for breath as he continued. "The others were my vassals because they could not think for themselves. Only Rand was not content. Only Rand would not stop asking questions. He had to be removed."

"So you had Guy take him out," I whispered.

"But his poison had already filled their minds," Vlad mused. "It was too late, and one by one, I have had to dispose of my most skilled soldiers. I like this time period and its luxuries, but it breeds rotten warlords. No one wishes to make war anymore. They want to stay in their safe homes and stare at computer screens and politick. They are worthless." His fingers glided down my throat. "But occasionally, they also breed lovely creatures such as yourself. Spirited. Loyal. Heedless." He licked my neck. "And so very delicious. I don't think I've ever tasted your like." He sniffed my throat. "No wonder Rand prizes you so. Lovely *and* delicious. It is no surprise he was afraid to bring you to me."

And here I'd disabled him and run straight into

Vlad's arms. I squeezed my eyes shut. God, I was stupid. "Are you going to kill me?"

"Eventually," he said, stroking my throat again. "I imagine feedings will eventually destroy you. But deprive myself of your taste before then? No. Yours will be a long and torturous death, I'm afraid, my lovely little one. I'll drain you dry and suck on your corpse before I'll give you up to death."

That sounded nightmarish.

"But first," he said, fingers gliding over my throat, "we're going to use you to lure your misguided lover out of his lair."

I stilled. I'd drugged Rand and left him alone in the hotel room. Did the Dragon realize that? "He's unavailable right now."

"Is that so? Because you seem to forget I have a mental connection to him," Vlad said, and leaned in against my throat.

For a brief, shining moment, I thought he was going to bite me. *Yes!* I thought *Bite away! Drink all my polluted, holy-water-and-garlic blood!*

But he only scraped his teeth over my skin, making me shudder with disgust. "He is awake, he is angry at you, and he is on his way here to confront me and save you." Vlad tsked.

He was awake? Oh God. He must not have drank enough of my blood. I wanted to ask questions, but then that would let on to Vlad that I'd done something to myself . . .

And there was still a chance he might drink from me.

I needed to hint about it. So I pulled away from his grip, turning my head. In the process, I exposed my neck to him, something that never failed to turn Rand on. "Don't drink from me. I don't want you to put your fangs on me."

My heart thudded with excitement and hope as Vlad scraped his teeth over my skin again. "I never mix pleasure with business, sweet. You'll simply have to wait."

Crap! I didn't want to wait. I struggled in his arms for real this time. "Wait for what?"

"Why, for Rand to come and plunge headlong to his fate. The poor, misguided fool is heading straight for his death. I suppose I should thank you for luring him in. I know he was hesitant before because he did not want to leave your side. Now I shall kill two birds with one stone, as you would say. Rand is an accomplished warlord, but he will not dare attack me while I hold you captive, for fear of harming you."

I closed my eyes, hating myself for screwing this up. I'd just made things worse. Now, Gemma was probably dead, Rand was heading here so Vlad the Impaler could kill him, and I was going to be a vampire sippy cup for the rest of my life. And worst of all? I'd spiked my blood with all kinds of vampire-harming things and Vlad wasn't even going to take a taste.

I'd made such a mess of things.

Twenty-four

Minutes ticked past like hours, the chill of the night making my teeth chatter as we waited. Tears streaked my face, despite my stubborn determination not to cry. I sat on the ground, my jeans damp from the soil beneath me. The Dragon sat on the park bench next to me, one long-fingered hand carefully curled around my throat. A pile of dust sat at our feet, the remnants of the Dragon's failed soldier. He had no need for weaklings in his army, he'd told me, and beheaded the man even as he slept on, unaware.

Cold bastard. I supposed I should have been relieved that it was one less vampire in the world, but all I could think of was Rand, waiting in his coffin for six hundred years.

Tonight? Waiting felt like an eternity.

There was no sign of Gemma. Vlad had tossed her to the far reaches of the graveyard. I didn't know if she was dead or alive and simply unconscious, but my heart cried out in misery at the thought of her being hurt or dead. She'd been such an incredible friend, risking her own life to help me and Rand. She deserved better than this, and I'd destroyed her.

It seemed I destroyed everyone I came into contact with, and that sent another wave of misery through me.

"He comes," Vlad intoned, his hand tightening on my aching throat. "Even now, he rushes through the streets, hell-bent on finding me and rescuing you. Such loyalty. Such love. It would warm my heart . . . but it stopped beating many, many years ago." The vampire chuckled. "Even now, his mind is full of terrible images, picturing all the things I could do to you. I'd love to humor him, but I find I'm getting selfish in my old age. I want to savor your taste, not waste your life on petty revenge."

Well, that was a small blessing, I supposed. I swallowed hard, trying to think. The other vampire's ashes were long gone, blown into the cool night wind. My stakes were scattered somewhere amongst the tombstones, lost to me. The holy water flasks still dug into my bra, but if they were poison, I didn't know that they'd do any good if I flung them on Vlad. You had to drink poison, right? I didn't want to alert him to the fact that I had holy water on me, either. I needed to get Vlad to drink from me without trying to be obvious about it. The moment I even suggested something as innocent as *Hey, are you thirsty,* his hackles would go up and he'd suspect something. He wasn't stupid, and I'd already underestimated him once. I had to think of a new tactic.

And I needed to think of something fast, because if Rand got here first, it'd be too late for him.

Rand, I thought, fresh pain coursing through me. *I'm so sorry I fucked this up. I wanted to save you. Please forgive me. Don't die thinking I betrayed you.*

"Close now," Vlad said softly. "Can't you taste him on the breeze?"

For a second, I imagined that I could. That his spicy, intoxicating vampire scent filled my nostrils. I closed my eyes and willed it to go away. *Run, Rand. Run and never look back.*

Footsteps.

I held my breath, waiting.

Then there he was at the gates of the graveyard. So beautiful and masculine that it hurt me to look at him. His stance was one of total ease, his posture that of a man confident in his territory. His sword was out, reflecting the low light of the moon. He looked ready for battle. Only his eyes betrayed his turmoil—they were narrow slits that scanned the area looking for something.

Looking for me.

"Call him," Vlad murmured, hand tightening on my neck. It wasn't a request but a command.

A knot formed in my throat. I wet my lips and

tried to say his name, but all that came out was a soft whimper.

Rand's gaze immediately turned to me.

Our eyes locked.

Maybe he saw the begging, the pleading, the love and fear in mine. The regret. Whatever it was he saw there, he seemed to understand it. He gave me a brief nod, then his gaze flicked to the man holding me captive.

"Let her go." Rand's voice was quiet. Direct. "She has no quarrel with you."

"On the contrary," Vlad said, rising to his feet. He didn't let go of my neck, which meant I had to awkwardly follow, or else my head would be pulled off. When I stood, he yanked me against him, an unwilling shield. "She came here with her little friend and botched an assassination attempt. Now she is going to be mine to play with as I choose."

Rand's gaze flicked to me again.

"I wanted to save you," I said.

"Isn't she sweet," Vlad purred. "So giving. I'm going to take that giving spirit to new heights, you know. I haven't tasted one like her before. I'm looking forward to it." He slid his tongue over my neck, and I shuddered.

Rand's nostrils flared and he stepped forward.

Vlad held up a finger. "Ah ah," he warned. "Do that and I'll rip this pretty little thing's head right off, tasty or no."

A whimper escaped me. I couldn't help it.

Rand stopped. A tortured look crossed his face. "Do not harm her. Your fight is with me."

"No, there is no fight," Vlad said. "You have simply forgotten that you belong to me." His smooth voice turned vicious, the hand holding my throat tighter. "I am your master. I own you. Shall I possess your body again and show you?"

Rand blanched, and I knew that one hit home. He hated the Dragon being in his head. Hated it. A reminder that he'd been possessed had to hurt.

My gaze focused on Rand, and I tried to communicate with him somehow. Maybe I could provide a distraction of some kind. When Rand's eyes fixed on me, I gave him a meaningful look, flicking a glance back at his sword then at his face again.

Vlad laughed, the sound brittle and wheezy. "Even now you both think to surprise me? I can hear every thought in your head before it even surfaces, Rand. I am intimately attuned to you. And you will *not* win."

A growl erupted from Rand, and he charged forward.

Things became a blur. I heard the snap of bone, the slap of flesh meeting flesh. A wet snarl. The Dragon had left my side before I'd had time to blink, and he and Rand fought in a flurry of limbs and movements so fast my eyes couldn't focus. Rand was good, his motions smooth as he parried, but the Dragon was so inhumanly fast that it was a losing battle. I watched as a blur of black shoved Rand backward, and then the sword went arcing through the air and clattered to the cobblestones a short distance away.

Rand was disarmed. Just like that. Vlad was so fast that it had taken less time than it took for me to draw a breath. As I watched in horror, Vlad slammed an arm across Rand's back, knocking him forward to his knees. One of my warlord's arms hung at a weird angle, broken.

He'd lost.

A sob broke from my throat. "Rand," I cried out, moving forward to him. I wanted to touch him, to hold him one last time.

Just like a flash of lightning, Vlad was back at my side, gripping my throat and pulling me close once more. "No no, little betrayer. I trust you even less than I trust him. At least I can read his thoughts." Vlad's smile was toothy and evil. "I always wonder what's going on in that silly little human mind of yours. Like what could possibly make you think you could take me on? What did you expect to do with me?"

I looked at Rand, then back at Vlad. This might be my only chance to explain to Rand what I was doing. That I wasn't betraying him. "I wanted to stake you," I told Vlad baldly. "Stake you and put you in hibernation so Rand wouldn't have to kill himself to destroy you."

The Dragon's eyebrows rose and Vlad gave another cruel, mocking laugh. "So he could stay with you? That is charming." His thumb ran over the vein in my neck, digging into my skin. "You were trying to have your cake and eat it, too, weren't you? And look what it's gotten you." He glanced back at Rand, his arm cradled to his chest. "Your lover, beaten before you. All hope gone. Even now, he watches me to see if I'm going to take a bite out of you."

Rand's nostrils flared with anger.

I stilled. "No," I breathed.

YES. YES! my head shouted. *DO IT.*

Vlad's mouth curled. His thumb dug harder into the side of my neck, and I whimpered as it broke the skin, blood trickling.

Rand made an incomprehensible sound of anger.

Vlad's eyes just lit with cruel pleasure. "Smell that. How utterly wonderful the scent of you is." He leaned in and sniffed. "Like the purest honey. No wonder he cannot resist." He dragged my face toward his, forced me to look into his eyes. "Imagine how he'll suffer to watch me drink from you."

"No," I said again, struggling against the hands that held me. "Don't you fucking touch me!" *Touch me! Drink from me!*

"Leave her alone," Rand gritted. "She's human. Vulnerable. Weak."

"Delicious," Vlad pointed out, licking his lips.

"I'll do anything you ask," Rand said in a defeated voice. "Just don't hurt her."

Oh, my sweet Rand. How I loved the man. I blinked back more tears.

"Fool," Vlad said cruelly. "You know you have no control here."

And he leaned in and licked at the blood spilling down my neck.

I froze in place, barely daring to breathe. At the feel of his gross tongue on my throat, though, I pushed at him, struggling. I had to make it look good, after all.

"No," Rand cried, even as Vlad's arms went around me and he sank his teeth fully into my neck.

YES!

My glee at tricking him faded away in a blink. His bite hurt. Even as his teeth burrowed into my throat, he began to suck great mouthfuls from me. I struggled feebly against him, but I couldn't budge him at all. How much blood would it take to poison the original vampire? How long would it take?

And as he continued to suck at my throat and my head grew foggy, I wondered if I'd even be alive to see it. I pushed at the vampire again, hoping against hope he'd stop drinking before he took too much.

At my throat, Vlad made a coughing, choking noise. I felt his fangs pull away, and he shoved me backward, wiping at his bloody mouth.

I slammed into a gravestone and clung to it for strength.

"What . . ." Vlad touched his fingers to his mouth, then gagged. "What is this?"

"That's a big 'fuck you' from me to you," I said. Blood dribbled steadily from my neck, the wound unsealed. My shirt was sticking to my skin with it, and I knew I was losing too much. It didn't matter. Nothing mattered anymore other than delivering this last final screw-over. I was a bit gleeful when I added, "It's holy water and all the garlic I could pound back."

His eyes widened and he hissed at me, full of anger. Behind him, I watched Rand slowly reach for his sword.

I forced a smile to my face, even though I felt weak and unsteady. "Gotcha, Vlad."

With an inhuman growl, Vlad lashed out, back-handing me. That, combined with the blood my throat was now leaking all over the place, made me go down this time. My head smacked into the dirt, and I lay there on the grass, stunned and nearly passed out.

A few feet away, Vlad staggered, his fingers curled, and he clawed at his own throat, as if trying to pull my tainted blood back out of his body. *That's what you get for being a greedy jerk*, I thought foggily. I watched as Rand raised his sword behind him.

He was going to behead him.

"No," I breathed, just as the sword whistled through the air. He couldn't do that! Not while Vlad was disabled and we could stake him and have our lives together. "Wait—"

"This is for Lindsey," Rand bellowed as he swung his sword. Vlad's head went flying.

Losing blood, utterly broken, I blacked out.

Twenty-five

The world was black.

Every bone in my body ached, but my head hurt the worst. I tossed and turned in the narrow, uncomfortable bed, unable to adjust myself in a way that would make my throbbing head and neck stop hurting so much.

"Poor Linds," a familiar voice murmured. "You want some ice chips?"

My eyes fluttered open, and I looked into a wonderful, sweet face. "Gemma?"

She smiled at me, one eye black and puffy. "Hey. How you feeling?"

I looked around. I was in a white room. Completely unfamiliar. The surroundings were bland, neutral, and there was a shower curtain on one side of the bed, which threw me off. I squinted at it. Huh. How did I feel? "Like I was stomped on," I said, struggling to sit up.

She put a gentle hand on my shoulder. "Stay

down. You're not well. As for being stomped on . . . you probably were. Both of us were."

We were? My brain was full of fog, my mind throbbing. "I can't think straight."

"I know, Linds. You're still missing a lot of blood. The hospital tried to give you a transfusion and almost killed you. I had to make them understand about your blood type. That was a fun conversation. Thank God for your bracelet, or you'd be toast." She wrinkled her nose. "Luckily you're on the mend, but you're still weak and tired. You can't get up yet."

Blood loss? I vaguely remembered a graveyard, and Gemma flying across the air. My eyes widened, and I looked at her. "You're not dead?"

She picked up a paper cup on the side of the bed. It had a plastic spoon in it. She dug a few ice chips out, then offered them to me, and I realized how utterly dry my mouth was. I accepted the ice chips without a word of protest. "I'm all right," Gemma said, her voice cheery. "A cracked rib and a shitty black eye, but otherwise I'm dandy. You, however," she said with a shake of her head, "had a concussion and a class two hemorrhage. You nearly went into shock. So it's been a slow road for you, girl, but I'm glad you're finally awake." Her smile was weak, wobbly. "I thought I'd lost you for a bit there."

I reached out and clutched her hand, surprised at how weak I was. "Oh, Gemma," I breathed. "You're not dead. I'm so glad." Tears, again with the tears, rolled down my cheeks. "I thought he'd killed you. I really did."

"Does it make me a chickenshit if I admit I played dead? Because I did. As soon as I smacked the gravestone, I went unconscious from the pain, but when I woke up, I pretended I was still gone. I didn't want him to find me and start chomping on me like he did you."

I touched my neck. It was swathed in bandages and hurt like the dickens. "I'm still fuzzy on things." I felt like I was missing a big piece of the puzzle. Like something vitally important was gone, and I couldn't think of what it was. It hovered on the edges of my mind, on the tip of my tongue, but I had nothing. My head hurt really freaking bad, though. I rubbed my forehead, wincing. "Can I have more ice chips?"

"Of course," Gemma said. She spoon-fed me a bit more, then frowned down at the cup when it was empty. "Lemme go get you some more. Stay here."

I gave her a wobbly smile. Like I was going anywhere? I couldn't even freaking lift my head without being exhausted. "I'll be here."

She got up and sashayed behind the curtain. As she did, I got a glimpse of the ties in the back of her hospital gown. Her back was exposed, the wrappings there visible. I smiled at the sight of it. Only Gemma would wander around like that. Rand would freak if he saw her—

Rand.

Oh, God.

The missing part of the puzzle clicked into place.

My mind played back the last few scenes I remembered, over and over again.

Rand's sword swinging through the air.

Vlad's head doing a somersault before crashing to the ground.

Blackness.

Rand had killed the Dragon.

In doing so, he'd killed himself. He was now nothing more than ash and a memory. *Only the Dragon can give you death's release.*

A harsh sob caught in my throat, and agony rocked through me.

Rand was utterly gone.

I closed my eyes, mourning. He hadn't staked the Dragon. He'd wanted to make the world a safer place for everyone. For the Frederics and the Guys of the world. Heck, even me. He couldn't allow the vampire to live a moment longer if it put someone else in danger.

I thought of the hurt in his eyes as he'd knelt before the Dragon, utterly defeated, broken arm cradled against his chest. Another sob tore through me, and then I was weeping openly, like a child. Did he realize I'd tried to do everything for him? Because I loved him so much that the thought of losing him was driving me mad with grief? Or had he gone to his end thinking that I'd betrayed him as surely as Guy had? That made me sob even harder.

I buried my face in my hands and wept.

All my hopes and dreams, my love for him, utterly crushed. He'd only been in my life for such a short, brief time, but he'd changed it. He'd made me realize I didn't have to be afraid to love. That I could jump right into life with both arms outstretched and experience something so wonderful it left me breathless. That another person could be so protective but generous. So loving. So utterly perfect.

So very gone.

I cried and cried until I was exhausted. The sobs died away to weeping, and I hiccupped for what felt like hours, staring at the wall. Gemma hadn't come back, and it was just as well. I didn't want her to see me totally break down.

Over and over again, I mentally replayed how the scene must have gone. Rand standing over the Dragon's dead body. Chopping off the head. The minute ticking past.

Then . . . dust.

Nothing but dust.

The visual of Rand as a cloud of dust made me weep even harder. I blamed myself for everything. If only I hadn't decided to try to outsmart Vlad. If only I'd gotten him to drink from me sooner.

If only I'd left Rand in the coffin for another six

hundred years. After all, if he was in limbo, staked, at least there was a chance at a second life. Now there was no shot at all.

Sobbing bitterly once more, I curled up in the bed, utterly broken and depressed. The thought of going on without Rand hurt like a knife wound in the gut. Even now, as I looked around the room, everything made me think of him. The box of Kleenex, because I pictured his derisive laugh at such an object. The beeping machines, because he'd be filled with wonder at the sight of them. The chair at the side of my bed, because it was empty and he should've been in it. The sunlight that spilled through the blinds of my room's lone window.

He'd been such a mixture of boyish innocence and ruthless arrogance. To think I'd chided him for calling me wench. Now I'd give anything to hear him say that again.

For a moment, I even wanted Vlad back. Just so I could have a few more minutes with Rand.

I pictured his handsome face and doubled over, grief hitting me anew. My poor, poor vampire.

Some time later, Gemma wandered back in with a new paper cup, dressed in jeans and a T-shirt. "Sorry, Linds. Some nurse saw me wandering the halls and insisted I put some clothes on and . . . what's wrong?" She dropped into the chair next to my bed. Her hand went to my forehead. "Are you okay?"

I sniffed, then felt my face crumple as I began

to cry again. "Rand," I blubbered. I couldn't speak around the knot in my throat. No other words would come out. It felt too raw, too fresh.

"Oh, honey, you're making yourself sick. Your eyes are all swollen and you sound all snotty." She patted my arm. "Listen, about Rand . . ."

I sobbed harder.

"You know what? Actually, I'll be right back." Gemma left the paper cup beside the bed and disappeared from the room.

A nurse came in a moment later, cheerily saying something to me in Romanian. I just continued crying, and she got a concerned look on her face, switched my IV drip, and noted something on my chart. She leaned down. "You pain? Yes?"

Heart pain, yes. Physical pain didn't matter. But maybe if I said yes, she'd give me some good drugs and I could forget what had happened for a few more hours. "Yes," I said, weeping.

She gave me two pills and a cup of water, and stood there while I took them. Then she patted my leg and gestured at the Call button if I should need anything else. I lay back against my pillows and stared at the ceiling, waiting to go under.

"Heeeeere we go," Gemma called cheerfully. "One primo hot seat coming right up."

I looked over, wiping my eyes. My friend had rolled one of the hospital wheelchairs into my room.

As I watched, she patted the back of it. "Come sit."

I shook my head and pulled the blankets over my head. "I don't want to." I didn't want to do anything. Anything except mourn Rand, maybe.

"Don't be like that. Just come on. Please? I think you'll like what I'm going to show you." When I started to cry again, she shook her head and grabbed my IV. "I'm going to force you to come with me. Now, come on."

Even though I protested, Gemma made me walk the three steps to the wheelchair, and from there, she swaddled me in my blanket, pushed me from the room, then began to wheel me down the hall. I clung to my IV, feeling woozy from the drugs the nurse had given me. "Is this going to take long?" I asked Gemma, struggling to keep my eyes open.

"You're going to want to see this," she repeated. "Just down the next hall."

I doubted it, but I was too tired to fight, so I leaned heavily on one side of the chair and waited as she wheeled me in front of a glass window and then parked me. My thoughts were far away, my mind on Rand. Was he in heaven? Where did vampires go after they died? Where—

I was so focused on Rand that when I saw his face through the glass, it didn't register at first. There was a man sleeping in a bed, hooked up to several IV units and monitors. His face was turned away from the glass, so he hadn't noticed me, but the shaggy brown hair was familiar. Two doctors stood nearby, arguing.

It was Rand.

My Rand.

He was *alive.*

"Oh my God," I burst out as I realized it really was him. "Rand!"

I stood up . . . and immediately collapsed on the floor, my legs going out from under me. My IV crashed on top of me a moment later with a massive clatter.

"Lindsey," a familiar voice bellowed from the other side of the glass, and Rand bolted up from the bed. I sat up with Gemma's help and watched as he ripped IVs from his arms and bellowed my name, paper gown flapping as he flung himself toward me. He slapped a hand against the glass. "Lindsey!"

The doctors scurried into action, going after Rand.

He squatted near the floor, his worried face searching mine.

"Rand?" I whispered, my fingers brushing the hospital glass as if I could touch him. I couldn't believe it. "You're alive. How . . ."

He flashed a brilliant smile at me, relief on his handsome face.

I laughed and sobbed all at once.

The doctors hauled him backward, ignoring the way he fought, and put him back in his bed. It took four orderlies to hold him down, and the more they tried to hold him back, the more he fought.

"Oh," I said, trying to get to my feet. "Oh, they're going to hurt him—"

"Calm him down," Gemma said. "Tell him to calm down. He won't listen to anyone."

"Rand," I said through the glass, and noticed that he stilled. I made a "calm down" motion and he nodded, easing. The doctors began to replace his IVs, muttering to each other. He gave me another alarmed look, but I only gave him a smile and blew him a kiss. "How . . ." I murmured. "How is this possible?"

"Fuck if I know," Gemma said. "Remember the translation?"

"You said it was death's release!" I cried, clenching my hands together under my chin, unable to stop staring at Rand's wonderful, gorgeous, *human* face.

"So the translation was wrong! It also mentioned a burrito! That should have clued us in!"

I sagged against Gemma, feeling a hundred pounds lighter. Not death, then. Just a release from being a vampire.

Gemma rubbed my arm. "You know we kept thinking that whatever was holding the vampire pyramid scheme would collapse if the big guy went away? I don't think it was a release of death, but just a regular ol' release from the curse."

"That's amazing," I breathed. It hadn't occurred to me. I'd thought for sure it was instant death for Rand if we killed the Dragon.

"The police found all three of us in the graveyard sometime after sunrise. Rand had a broken arm, a fever, and was babbling in a language no one could understand. You were bleeding out, so that was everyone's first concern. Now that we're back at the hospital, they think Rand has 'amnesia' or a 'stroke.'" She made finger quotes around the words. "I tried telling them he was a time traveler, but they thought I was just being a shit and sent me away. He kept asking for you, which is why I brought you here." She gave a happy sigh and clasped her hands. "Twu wuv."

"He has a fever?" I asked, scarcely able to believe it. I couldn't take my eyes off him in the hospital bed. Even there, he radiated strength. He looked as if he'd been a lord deigning to give his subjects a few moments of his time instead of a man bound to a hospital room. As my worried gaze skimmed over him, I noticed the beige cast on his one arm for the first time.

"Yeah, they were saying some other stuff, but I don't speak Romanian, so I don't know what it is. He seems to be fine, though, other than the fact that he doesn't speak a word of any language anyone recognizes, and the only word he knows is your name. He keeps screaming for you."

I pressed my fingertips to my mouth, smiling. "That's not such a terrible thing."

"I thought it was kind of cute, myself."

Rand saw my smile, and from the other side of the glass, he raised a hand in greeting, a hint of a smile touching his mouth.

"When can I see him?" I asked, stifling a yawn. Oh, no. My meds were kicking in. Stupid, stupid. "Can I see him now?"

"Let me go ask," Gemma said. "Wait here."

Like I was going to wheel myself somewhere else? I nodded, my gaze on Rand's wonderful, gorgeous face as I waited. New tears—this time, tears of joy—flowed down my face. How was this possible?

I didn't know. All I knew was that I was so utterly thankful, so happy. "*I love you,*" I mouthed to him.

But by the time Gemma returned with a doctor, I was passed out from my medication, sound asleep.

Twenty-six

I woke up several hours later from my drug-induced sleep. My room was empty, the faint moonlight wafting in through the blinds showing that it was dark outside.

Rand.

I panicked, looking around. I was back in my hospital room. Where was my vampire? I needed him. I never wanted to leave him again.

There was a note left on my bedside, and I calmed a bit at the sight of it.

You're totally konked at the moment, Linds, so I'm back at the hotel. They said you can check out in the morning once they're sure your vitals are ok. I took over your hotel room and am watching your stuff. Call me if you want, otherwise will be there in the AM. XOXO your BFF.

PS Rand's room number is 403.

And that was why my best friend was awesome. I quietly unhooked my IV, glanced around to see if any nurses came running, and slipped my legs over the side of the bed.

Now to find room 403.

I tied the laces of my hospital gown shut, but it still gaped open in the back. One hand clutching it shut, I padded down the hall, looking for room numbers. I couldn't remember the way Gemma had taken me earlier, so it took me a few moments to find his room.

The blinds in Rand's room were drawn, and I couldn't see through the glass walls to tell if the lights were on or if anyone was home. For a horrible moment, I thought they'd discharged him. I pushed the door open, peeking in.

A familiar shaggy head rested on the pillow.

His eyes opened, and he immediately sat up at the sight of me. "Lindsey!"

I motioned for him to be quiet, then I shut the door behind me and tiptoed to his bed. I could hold back no longer and flung myself into his arms. "Rand," I whispered, over and over again. "Oh, Rand. You're alive!"

His hand stroked my hair, and he said something in a language I didn't recognize.

I pressed happy kisses to his face, his cheeks, his hair, and he kissed me back, just as frantic. His hand cupped my chin and he kept talking in that weird, fluid language I didn't understand.

He didn't know English anymore. His connection

to the Dragon was gone. I laughed, utterly giddy, and showered him with new kisses. "You can't understand a thing I'm saying, can you?"

"Lindsey," he murmured. "Lindsey, Lindsey."

"I'm here," I told him between kisses. "I'm here and you're warm. You're warm to the touch. It's incredible." I skimmed my fingers over his face, feeling the delicious flush of his skin. To my delight, I could even feel beard stubble coming in on his chin. He'd never had stubble before. Fascinating. It was like all the processes in his body had stopped the moment the Dragon had instated his connection, and now that it was free, so was Rand. "Can you see sunlight?" I asked him, suddenly curious.

He cocked his head and looked at me, then gave it a small shake. He didn't understand.

I looked around. His windows went out to the rest of the hospital. No windows outside. I guess we'd have to save that question for another day, because I didn't know how to communicate "sunlight" with our language barrier.

Rand said something else, and his good arm went around my waist. "Something something something, Lindsey," he told me.

"Is that Old English?" I asked, curious. "French? Spanish? Um, Prussian?" I tried to think of all the places he said he'd been.

He just gave me a quizzical look and tugged me into bed with him.

I went because God, I never wanted to be separated from him again. I slipped my legs under the thin
hospital blanket and snuggled up against his side. My
hand smoothed down his chest as I tucked my head
into the crook of his shoulder. His cast-covered arm
lay atop his lap, and I touched it gently. "Does your
arm hurt?"

"Hurt?" he repeated.

"Arm," I said, patting his arm, and then mine.
"Arm."

"Arm," he agreed, accent thicker than I'd ever
heard it. Then he grabbed my hand and kissed my
palm. "Lindsey, arm."

I giggled. "Lindsey's hand," I corrected.

"Hannnnd." He nipped my palm with his teeth—
normal teeth.

"That is adorable," I told him. "We're going to
have to teach you English all over again. And can I be
the one to say I don't mind in the slightest? Because
I'd rather have you unable to talk to me than have
you with that horrible vampire in your thoughts."

His eyes narrowed, and he gave me a helpless
shrug. His arm locked tight around me, and he pulled
me against him, then kissed the top of my head, hugging me close.

Tears pricked my eyes. Yeah, I knew just how he
felt. "Me, too, love. Me, too." My hand continued to
smooth up and down his chest, the ability to touch
him incredibly soothing. Just having him here again,

with me? It was worth everything in the world. I pressed my hand to his chest and wept again to hear his heart beating strongly in his chest.

It was incredible. We were so lucky.

Whatever dark "thing" had given the Dragon his immortality had been removed when he'd been destroyed. We'd thought Rand would be ash, but by destroying his maker, he'd become utterly free once more.

His hand pressed over mine.

I smiled and tilted my face up to his, just so I could look up at his masculine beauty.

Rand leaned in and kissed me, his tongue grazing my lips. I was a little surprised, because he tasted different. It wasn't the spicy, heady taste that drugged the senses like before. Now, he tasted like man, and he smelled like soap.

I decided I liked the changes. I kissed him back, flicking my tongue against his.

He groaned and pulled me tighter against him. "Lindsey," he breathed.

"I know," I murmured. His lips were flushed and deliciously full, and I nipped at his lower one, then sucked on it, which elicited another groan from him. "I liked you as *upyri*, but I like you even better as human."

"*Upyri?*" he asked huskily, recognizing the word.

"Human," I repeated, and patted his chest again, in the thump of a heartbeat.

"Human," he agreed.

I got a naughty idea and slid my hand under the blankets, to his erection. He was rigid under the hospital gown, and it made for easy access. So I took him in hand, loving how scorchingly hot his skin was. "Human," I said again.

He sucked in a breath, and that tiny sound reminded me that he was, in fact, breathing. I was filled with another rush of love and decided right then and there I was not leaving this room until I made love to him.

"Wait right there," I murmured, and gave him another light kiss on the mouth. He didn't want to let me go, but I slid out of his grip, went to the door, and moved a chair in front of it. I checked all the blinds to make sure they were drawn, and scanned the room for cameras. Nothing.

Perfect. He was all mine.

A month ago, I might have turned my nose up at having sex in a hospital bed, with no privacy except that of an unlocked door barely blocked with a chair, the windows only covered by blinds. But a month ago, I hadn't been to Venice.

A month ago, I hadn't pulled the stake out of a vampire's heart and woken him from a six-hundred-year slumber.

A month ago, I hadn't been attacked in the streets, visited night graveyards, killed vampires, and chugged more garlic than any human possibly wanted to.

A month ago, I hadn't fallen in love.

Hours ago, I thought I'd lost the man I loved. The grief had been so horrific, so wrenching, that I still felt hollow inside. And I vowed that nothing was going to come between us and our happiness ever again.

And if I wanted to have sex with the man in his hospital room, by golly, I would.

As I approached the bed, I slipped my hospital gown off. I wore nothing underneath, and I strolled toward him, nude and proud. When I reached him, my hand went back under the blankets and found him again.

Hard as a rock. I sighed with pleasure.

"Lindsey," he groaned. An entire stream of words followed that, and I had no clue what he was saying. His good arm went around my shoulders, and he tugged me closer to him, until my breasts pressed against his hospital gown.

I sat up and tugged at the fabric. "Let's get this stupid thing off you, hmm?"

Despite our communication barrier, he understood exactly what I was asking. Between his good hand and both of mine, we managed to pull it off him. I tossed it to the side and gave a sigh of pleasure as I slipped back under the covers and laid down against his warm skin. Rand as a vampire was sexy, but Rand as a flesh-and-warm-blooded man? Utterly divine. I couldn't keep my hands off him. I trailed my fingers down his chest, feeling the hints of old scars. I pressed my lips to his shoulder, then kissed his collarbone, his neck, his jaw. All the while, my hand on his stomach slid lower and lower, until it returned to the curls at his groin, and then, his cock.

I gasped to feel something wet and pulled the sheets back. Pre-cum dotted the head of his cock, and my eyes went wide with surprise. That was new.

Rand dragged my fingers to his cock, trailed them over the pre-cum. "Human," he told me in a thick voice.

Oh God, was he ever. "Human," I agreed. "My human." I lifted my hand and tasted him from my fingers. He was salty, musky. Delicious. "Rand."

He reached for me, then winced, his bad arm falling back to his side.

I put a hand to his chest. "Let me," I told him. "I'll take care of our pleasure. You just sit back and relax."

"Lindsey," he murmured again, and I pulled the blankets back over his hips . . . and went under them.

My hand went to his cock again, curling around the base. My mouth followed, and I licked up the pre-cum dotting the crown of his cock, sighing with pleasure as his taste touched my tongue. The more I licked, the more appeared. I took the head of him into my mouth and sucked gently, then lapped him like I would a treat.

His hips jerked, and I felt his good hand twine in my hair. "Lindsey," he murmured again, followed by another stream of soft syllables. I could imagine what he was saying. More, more, more. As I sucked, I began to take him deeper, pumping him with my mouth.

Rand began to rise to meet my mouth, his hand holding my hair in place until he was fucking my face, his movements rapid. I kept pace with him as best I could, excited that I could turn him on so much with just my mouth. I felt him shudder, expecting him to come.

Instead, he pulled his hand from my hair and brushed his fingers over my shoulder, trying to get my attention. "Lindsey."

I popped my head up from the sheets. "Hm?"

He tugged me toward him and dragged his mouth over mine, his kiss hungry and devouring. "Mmm," I sighed, and put my hands on his neck, leaning against his bare chest and pressing my breasts against him. I slid up and down against him, letting my nipples rub against his skin, growing more and more aroused as his mouth possessed mine.

Rand's hand went between my legs, pressing to my sex. I heard his soft exhale as he found me wet for him, and I rocked against his hand, encouraging his touches. I loved his touch. Adored it. Wanted it everywhere. "Touch me all you want," I told him, breathless. "I'm all yours."

As if he could understand my soft commands, his fingers pressed deeper, seeking my clit. I moaned as he found it and began to rub back and forth, teasing the sensitive hood. My mouth became frantic on his, my hips moving on his hand as he continued to finger me, making me mad with desire. I ached for him. "I want you inside me," I told him.

"Lindsey?" he asked, a question on his breath.

I thought about condoms, then decided to skip it. If we made a baby this night, I'd take it and be glad. I wanted anything and everything that came my way, from now until forever. So, kissing my love, I straddled his hips and settled over him. And as I kissed him, I reached between us and guided his length to my entrance.

He pulled back a little, gazing into my eyes. He said something, then tapped my breast, a grin lighting his beautiful face.

And I laughed because I knew what that meant. Weasel balls. Was I going to wear them for birth control? I shook my head and kissed him again, then guided his hand to my stomach to let him know that we were going to take things as they came . . . literally.

Rand nodded, his smile widening.

Guiding him deep, I pushed down on his cock and moaned as he palmed my breast, then teased the nipple. I was so wet that it didn't take much to seat myself entirely on his length. Then, I put my hands on his shoulders and began to ride him, my hips moving in gentle rolling motions.

He reached down and pressed his fingertips to my sex, then began to rub my clit as I rode him, which made me crazy. Gasping, I clung to him and began to ride him harder and faster. His hips began to jerk under mine, until we were shaking the hospital bed with the force of our exertions.

I came, crying out his name, and as I did, he ground me against him, slamming me down on him until he came moments later. I felt the heat of his spend inside me and reveled in the difference.

My Rand. No longer a vampire. Still all mine.

Leaning in, I kissed his face over and over again. I wanted to collapse on top of him and go to sleep, but, first, hospital gowns. With a small smile, I asked, "Is it okay if I stay here tonight?"

He only tilted his head at me, then rattled off another stream of words I didn't understand.

I yawned. "I'm going to take that as a yes, babe." I leaned in and gave him a peck on the mouth, then slid off the side of the hospital bed.

He grabbed my hand as I did and shook his head, a silent entreaty for me to stay.

"I'm not leaving," I told him, smiling. I pointed at the discarded hospital gown a short distance away. He let go of my hand reluctantly and was pleased when I redressed and joined him in bed again. Rand pulled the covers over me and tucked me against his side, and I snuggled against him to catch a few hours of sleep before the hospital orderlies could chase me away.

I was never leaving Rand's side again.

THE NEXT MORNING

It turned out the hospital was keeping Rand isolated because they'd thought he had a mysterious illness that had caused memory loss. His language barrier was also stumping them, except for the fact that he'd managed to learn a few words overnight. They were baffled, because other than his now-gone fever and his hurt arm, there was nothing wrong with Rand.

He made it very clear, though: he wanted to go home with me.

Since he had the fake ID with the Venice address, there was no reason to suspect more than a freak medical occurrence. And since the hospital couldn't come up with a good reason to keep him, they let him go, with a promise to send his bill in the mail. I was also declared healthy enough to check out, though they did ask me if I'd be interested in donating blood in a week or two so they could study my rare blood type.

I declined. I'd given out enough blood in the last month.

Gemma picked us up and our little party caught the next train back to Venice. To the place that was starting to feel like home, oddly enough. Strange how

Venice had seemed so odd to me a month ago, and now all the little canals gave me a happy feeling of relief.

When we got to the old apartment, it was a joy to not have to invite Rand in. Instead, he grabbed me and swung me under his good arm, then carried me over the threshold like a sack of potatoes. I squealed with laughter the entire time.

"You guys are fucking weird," Gemma said, but she grinned. "Try to control yourselves for a bit, will you?"

"No promises," I said, kissing Rand.

"No promises," he echoed, though I wasn't entirely sure he understood what he was saying. He just knew it made me smile.

Gemma rolled her eyes.

Rand gave me a smacking kiss and set me down a few feet inside the apartment. "Lindsey home," he said, showing off his new English.

"That's right," I said with a pat to his big, brawny chest. I'd been trying to teach Rand a few words so he could communicate, because I knew he was frustrated. Right now his vocabulary was worse than a caveman's, but it was a start, and he was a fast learner. "Apartment in Venice," I told him.

"Lindsey apartment in Venice," he agreed, moving inside. His hand found mine and we twined our fingers. I loved the feel of his warm touch and let him take the lead.

In the few days Gemma had been in the apartment while I'd been traveling in Eastern Europe with Rand, she'd done a lot of cleaning. Gone was the utter carnage of boxes. The floors were swept clean of debris, and most of the furniture was gone. Two small, lonely boxes waited by the door to be shipped back home to Nebraska. To see the place so empty made me ache a little. Before, this apartment had been crammed full of life and memories. Now it was just barren, waiting to be filled again. I gave Rand's hand a little squeeze, thinking of how lucky we'd been to come out of this unscathed. I mean, my credit cards were maxed, but what was a little debt when I was holding the hand of the man I loved?

"There's a few things left here and there," Gemma said, bustling past us into the near-empty apartment. "I guess the good thing was that those jerks came in and destroyed everything, because after that, it made cleanup a lot easier. I paid the lady downstairs, and she came and helped me toss most everything into the trash."

"You did great, Gemma," I told her. "Really great."

She gave me a proud look over her shoulder and headed up the narrow stairs. "I'm going to check on a few things up here. Why don't you two peek into the kitchen and see what you can find for the bottomless pit there?"

I chuckled. "Will do."

As if on cue, Rand's stomach rumbled. He rubbed it ruefully and looked over at me. "Lindsey, eat yes?"

"Absolutely," I told him, and led him into the tiny kitchen. Ever since becoming human again, Rand's appetite was voracious. Gemma and I liked to joke that he was stockpiling to make up for all the years in which he'd only drank blood, because the man could definitely put away a plate, or two, or three. Not that I minded. Every little signal that he was human now just gave me even more pleasure. "I'm pretty sure we have some bacon in the fridge that probably hasn't gone bad yet. Maybe some eggs."

The kitchen itself was mostly clean, too, with only a chipped plate and cup in the sink. The cabinets were bare, so I cleaned the dishes off and dried them with a scrap of a towel so Rand would have something to eat off of. I was pleased to see that the silverware was intact. I guess there was only so much destruction rampaging vampires could do. I made a mental note to pack it up and ship it home to sell. I found a skillet and set it on the stove as Rand hopped up on a counter to sit.

"Cross your fingers that there's something good in here, babe," I told him as I opened the fridge to get the food. I peeked in to see the contents—

And stopped.

Blinked.

And screamed, "GEMMA!"

"Lindsey?" Rand asked.

"It's okay," I told him, trembling. "I think." And then I began to laugh hysterically.

Gemma came thundering down the stairs a minute later, her eyes wide. "What, what is it?"

I showed her the jars of pasta I'd pulled out of the fridge. They weren't pasta jars at all but delicately made Chinese ginger jars of the palest white. If I rubbed my fingers on the porcelain, I could feel the designs etched into them that would only be visible with the right lighting.

The gorgeous anhua jars that I thought were completely lost?

Two of them were currently holding what looked like fettuccine. "How is this possible?" I asked her, holding the jar with shaking hands. "How?"

Gemma blanched and bit her fingernail, looking sheepish. "So, like, you were gone, right? And I ordered pasta from that place we like, and they sent a double. And I thought it'd be silly to throw it all away when we had a perfectly good fridge, but I couldn't find a good container with a lid. And then I remembered the jars in the basement and thought, well, she'll never know, right? So I might have snagged two of them." She held her hands up and moved forward. "But don't worry! I kept those little pieces of paper that were stuck inside them."

"Little pieces of paper?" I asked blankly, still in shock. I'd thought all of the priceless porcelain down in the secret room had been completely and utterly destroyed. Smashed to bits. Gone forever.

"The bill of lading or whatever it was that got you so excited," she said, moving past me to open the fridge. She plucked something from the shelf, and sure enough, there were the original receipts with the dates. The crucial papers that proved the jars had provenance.

I felt faint. "Fettuccine, Gemma? Really?"

She looked abashed. "I really thought you'd never know. And then the vampires showed up, and well . . ." She shrugged. "I guess they didn't look in the fridge."

"I'm not mad," I told her, gently setting the jar down on the counter. Oh God, she'd kept the receipts and the lids and everything. Once the jar was safe on the counter, I turned to Gemma and hugged her. "You are the bestest friend ever and I love you."

She giggled and hugged me back. "I finally did something right, huh?"

"You are amazing," I told her, awed. "I'd be lost without you, and I mean it. Those jars are going to pay for everything this trip has cost us, and more."

She brightened. "So we're not broke?"

"Not by a long shot!"

"Good?" Rand said, interrupting our celebration.

I turned to him, beaming. "Very, very good!"

Epilogue

Y ou're sure it's here?" I asked Rand, consulting the road map I'd bought at the last gas station.

"Yes, here," Rand said, getting out of the passenger side of the car. Even five months after living in the "modern" world, there were things about cars that still confounded my lover. Coming to England and finding out that the steering wheel was on the wrong side of the car? He'd nearly lost his mind. "It is not right," he'd told me, over and over again, all while I'd laughed and laughed.

Nearby people had looked at me like I was crazy, but I was getting used to that.

I pocketed the keys and got out of the parked car, following Rand up the grassy hill.

Automatically he waited, turning and offering his hand to me.

I took it with a smile and squeezed his hand. "Excited?"

"Not sure," he told me. "Feels . . . strange. This place . . . I have not come in long, long time."

I knew that feeling. "We can leave if you want to."

"No, I want . . ." He struggled to find the right word. "Here."

"Okay, babe," I told him, and put a hand to my belly, where I carried our child. I'd gotten pregnant that night at the hospital. I'd figured it out a month or two later when we'd gotten settled back in Nebraska and I'd gotten sick every morning and had had massive cravings for peanut butter. Turned out that one time without a condom was enough after all.

We'd gotten married right away, and Rand had spent the next few months helping me expand the business (now called Gemma and Lindsey's Favorite Finds). We'd sold the anhua jars at Sotheby's for an amount that still made my head spin. Gemma and I had split the money from the precious jars into thirds—one-third for her, one-third for me, and one-third for the business. With my money, I'd bought a condo for myself and Rand, and we'd started a fund for the baby.

I knew the fact that Rand wasn't bringing money into our small family was bothering him. We'd been discussing things he could do for a living once he learned the language and became accustomed to modern society. He'd started taking jiujitsu and karate lessons at the local dojo and was utterly fascinated by all the combat forms. If nothing else, maybe he could learn enough to teach. I knew he enjoyed it.

Life was pretty perfect, overall. I was happier than

I'd ever been. But I knew there was one thing in particular that still bugged Rand sometimes. So when my warlord had suggested we go look for his old stash in England, I'd agreed.

Why not?

It turned out that several place names had changed over time, as they were wont to do. So while we'd looked for a particular hill and what was left of a castle Rand remembered, he'd scoured guidebooks and pictures of scenery and Google Maps until he'd found the location that he'd sworn was the correct one. So we'd asked about it and gotten directions from locals. Half a day later, we'd found the place.

As we crested the hill, Rand was silent. I figured he was lost in memory, comparing this place to whatever it had been in his past. Not much of the settlement remained from six hundred years ago. A few rocky tumbles were all that was left to suggest the place had been something other than a sheep pasture. The place, according to the postcard, had suffered from a fire in 1450, and recurrences of plague and strife had emptied the village. The keep had never been rebuilt, the lands deeded to the king and then parceled away to random nobles over the years. Rand had wanted to claim it, but he'd backed down once I'd made him realize that no one was going to honor a six-hundred-year-old claim from someone who was the current age of about thirty. He'd understood, but he wasn't happy.

I think he wanted a legacy to pass to our baby. Legacies didn't matter to me, though; a happy family did. It was something that I'd never had growing up. No mother, no father, just the state home and Gemma, who was beside herself with excitement at the thought of a baby. She was even trying to wean herself off cussing as much so she could be a better influence.

"There," Rand said, pointing in the distance. "The wall."

I followed where he pointed, and sure enough, there was a bit of stone left between a few old trees. "You think that's the place?"

"I know it," he said, and squeezed my hand. "Come."

We got shovels out of the back of the rental car and crossed the hill. I kept an eye out for observers, because I didn't want to explain we were treasure hunting on someone else's property. That wouldn't go over well. Once we got to the wall, Rand closed his eyes and gestured. "There was a . . . how say . . . top?" He gestured. "Long? Tall?"

"A tower?" I asked.

"Yes, a tower," he agreed, grinning and giving me another smacking kiss for filling in the word for him. "Treasure is three tens steps south of tower."

Okay, thirty steps. I nodded and took the shovel from him as he moved to where he assumed the tower had been, then watched as he counted off steps. I might have gotten a little distracted, looking at his broad shoulders in the flannel henley he was wearing, which fit tight over his gorgeous body. Ever since getting pregnant, my already charged libido had been through the roof. Definitely needed to tackle me some of that when we got back to the hotel.

He counted off in his old language, then stopped near the center of the crumbling wall. Then, he turned and took two big steps outward. "Is here."

It looked like nothing more than a patch of grass. "You're sure?"

He shrugged. "We dig and find out, yes?"

"All righty," I said, and handed him his shovel. When I tried to help out, though, he protested and insisted I sit on the wall and watch him. He pressed a kiss to my slightly rounded belly, grinned at me, and returned to digging. I took a few photos of him on my cell phone and texted them to Gemma.

Me: Treasure hunting with Rand.

Gemma: Tell him I call dibs on any bling!

Me: Not sure he knows the word bling yet.

Gemma: Dammit thwarted again! Srsly tho, good luck you two!

I smiled and was just about to text her a message back when I heard Rand's shovel *clang* as it hit something metallic. I looked up just in time to see a huge grin cross his face.

"Is here!" he called out, kneeling down to the hole he'd dug. "God be pray!"

"Praised, baby. God be praised," I corrected, and hopped off the wall to see what we'd found.

There was an old iron-covered box in the hole, and Rand had to spend several minutes clearing away more of the dirt to pull it free. Then he hefted it out of the hole with a grimace. "Heavier than I memory."

I didn't even correct his English. I was too fascinated by the box itself. Part of me had thought we wouldn't truly find anything after six hundred years. Logic said it was a long shot.

Then again, when had logic ever played a part in our relationship?

Rand hopped out of the hole and sank to the ground next to the box. "Rusted," he pronounced, and pulled out the knife he carried at his belt (a habit I couldn't break him of except in airports). He took the hilt and hammered at the crusted lock on the front until it broke away.

Then he pried the lid open.

"Holy crap," I said, spotting the items inside.

The box was full. At first it looked like a bunch of moldy junk. It was clear that Medieval-Rand had tossed a bolt of silk into things, and it had rotted a while back. But under the scraps of fabric, there were small flasks, jeweled crosses, and a necklace with stones as big as chicken nuggets.

"My war spoils," he told me, pulling out a flask. "This expensive . . . pepper? Red? I do not know word."

"Spice?" I asked him, taking it from his fingers. The cork stopper was rotted, and I wrinkled my nose. "Probably didn't last the storage."

He looked disappointed. "Cloth is gone. So is book." He nudged something in the corner that looked like sludge.

"But look at this other stuff," I exclaimed, leaning in. "Is that a cup of some kind?"

"For drinking," he agreed, picking it up. It was tarnished, but I could see gems sticking out of the sides. In the bowl of the cup there were coins, all crusted together, and what looked like a few brooches. Holy jeez. Medieval coins. Gold. Jewels. "Is it good?"

I shook my head, scarcely believing it. When we'd sold the anhua jars for six figures, I'd been stunned. This stuff was worth so much more. "Baby, this is better than good. This is amazing."

"It is for our family," he told me. "You, me, and baby Frederic."

I laughed. "We need to talk about names."

He got to his feet and pulled me in his arms. "It is great honor to name a child after a man."

I patted his chest. "I love you, but I am not calling my child Freddy."

His brows drew together. "Frederic. Not Freddy."

"Nickname," I said, then giggled. "Oh my God, why are we arguing over baby names when we're rich?"

"Rich is good," he said thoughtfully. "I want to make good life for you and baby Frederic."

I put my hands to his cheeks, feeling the slight beard he'd grown out. He loved having facial hair again, and I loved his rough cheeks. "Rand, every day with you is a good life. I love you. What we have is utter perfection."

"Perfection plus one," he said, putting a hand on my stomach.

And what could I do but agree?